best of me

LK FARLOW

DEDICATION

Dedication: To my Phoobs. Somehow, you always manage to bring out the best of me.

Dedication part 2: Renee, dude, thank you! Without you, shudders I don't even want to think about it.

PROLOGUE

DUKE

The first time I ever laid eyes on Valorie Parsons, I could've sworn I was looking at an angel. I remember it as if it were yesterday…

It was the first day of tenth grade, and I was posted up at my usual table in the cafeteria with some guys from the team, shooting the shit and talking about our first game later that week. And then she walked in. Swear to God, the air crackled with her presence. She was only a freshman, but she waltzed into the room like she owned that school. Her long blonde hair was done up in those messy waves that immediately makes guys think of sex, her skin sun-kissed like she'd spent the entire summer lounging at the beach, and her lips…her glossy, perfectly kissable lips had my heart—and my shorts— feeling more than a little tight.

As crazy as it sounds, I knew right then and there that she was it for me. Right hand to my heart, I leaned over, nudged my buddy's arm and said, "I'm gonna marry that girl." Laughing, he replied, "You don't even know her." I shot him a grin and hopped up from my seat. "Not yet, but I'm about to."

The rest, as they say, was history. From that day on,

Valorie Parsons was my girl. The two of us were damn near inseparable, spending all of our free time wrapped up in each other. And now, eleven years later, I'm hoping like hell that when I drop down to one knee and offer her my all, that she agrees.

"Rook, are you even hearing me?" my partner, Cal, asks as he hangs a sharp right onto the four-lane highway.

I jolt in the passenger seat. "Huh? What? I've been riding shotgun with you for the better part of four years, asshole; I ain't no rookie."

Cal laughs, a deep gruff sound. "You're damn sure acting like one, sitting over there looking like a possum on the side of a busy street. You got something on your mind?"

I shrug, not quite sure how to verbalize exactly what I'm feeling; hell, I'm not even sure I'd want to, even if I could.

"Listen up, Kincaid. We may not be blood, but we're family. We talk. We break bread. We work through our shit so we can stand in the sun together, you feel me? We don't keep secrets. So, I'm gonna ask you again, what's got you so out of it?"

I glance over toward my partner, the man who's had my back for the last four years, who eyes me warily. He's fucking right. If there's anyone I can tell my deepest fears to, it's Cal. "I got plans to ask my girl to marry me tonight."

"That's good, man, real good." He quirks a brow. "Y'all are still pretty young though, huh?"

I heave out a deep sigh. He's not saying anything I haven't heard before. But I've been thinking about asking Val to marry me since she agreed to that first date all those years ago. What she and I have is special—it's that once in a life-time, knock-you-on-your-ass kind of love.

I wanted to marry her the day she graduated high school. Hell, I even went as far as dropping down to one knee outside of our favorite summertime ice cream spot with nothing but a waffle cone of rocky road to accompany my proposal. But she always said she didn't want us to be two dumb kids who stumbled down the aisle in a fit of lust and bad decisions. She wanted to finish college first so we could have a solid foundation to build our future on, and who was I to argue with that logic?

But now, I'd say we're well on our way.

Last month, Valorie donned her cap and gown and collected her diploma. I was proud as punch when my girl told me she wanted to study law. In my mind, we'd be like superheroes, working to keep our small town safe. I could just see the headline in the local paper: *Local cop and his prosecutor wife working together to fight crime by day and make babies by night.*

Then she dropped the bomb that she wanted to be a defense attorney, and my dream shattered. Us being on opposing sides of the law was a fissure in the armor of our relationship, but I knew our love was enough to mend the crack.

Last week, she accepted a position with a hotshot law firm over the bridge in the city. Some Ivy League asshole with a reputation for fucking his female employees and representing the worst of the worst runs it, and even though it burns my gut, I know Val getting hired there before she's even passed her bar exam is a big deal.

"Yeah, Cal, we're young. But...I think we've got what it takes to make it for the long haul."

My partner eyes me knowingly. "You sure you're not just rushing to put a ring on her finger before she starts working for that greasy little shit?"

My heart clenches in my chest. I've asked myself that same question. And, yeah, maybe I want him to know she's one hundred percent off limits to the likes of him, but I also trust her all the way down to my soul. Eleven years we've been together—I know she's faithfully mine, just as I'm hers. I have loved the girl as long as I've known her, and I'm more than ready for us to take this step. The thought of seeing her walking down the aisle toward me in a white gown...her belly swollen with our first child...our first Christmas as a family...those are things I dream about at night.

We've worked hard to build up our foundation, and now I'm ready to frame up some fucking walls—I'm ready for her to wear my ring and to take my name and for us to officially start the rest of our forever together.

So even though there's a sliver of doubt niggling around in the back of my mind, I decisively nod my head and snap, "That's not it. I'm just ready for her to be my wife. She's... she's everything to me, plain and simple as that."

Cal holds one hand up in surrender. "Okay, Kincaid. No need to get your panties in a wad; I was just askin'."

"You ready to head in?" I ask, nodding toward the clock. Our patrol shift only has twenty minutes left, and by the time we drive our loop and make it back, it'll be time to punch the clock.

"Yeah, man. Let's roll."

The closer we get to the station, the more my anxiety gives way to pure, unadulterated excitement. By the end of the night, I'll be the luckiest man on the damn planet, and I have big plans to celebrate, starting with reminding my girl just how good we are together.

With only ten minutes left on our shift, the radio crackles with a call from dispatch. "Report of a motor vehicle accident, injuries unknown, just past mile marker fifteen on ninety-eight. Available units, please respond."

We're less than two miles away. "Shit, let's go," I say, a sick feeling settling in my stomach.

As much as I love being a cop, car wrecks are the worst for me. My parents were in a horrible accident when I was in middle school; my dad got behind the wheel drunk and wrapped his car around a telephone pole. Of course, that jackass walked away with barely a scratch, but my mom wasn't so lucky. It was the passenger side of the vehicle that had wrapped around the telephone pole, leaving her with a shattered pelvis, a punctured lung, and a bleed in her brain. In the end, her injuries were too great for her to recover, and she died a day later.

"10-4," Cal calls back, and with a flip of a switch, the sirens are screaming and we're on our way.

The accident scene comes into view, and I see a mid-size, blue vehicle in the tree line with parts and pieces scattered about. As we draw closer, the details come into focus with startling clarity. Time stops and that sick feeling from earlier turns to pure fucking panic. Policy and procedure be damned —I'm out of the car and hauling ass toward the scene before Cal even has the squad car in park.

"No, no, no! It's not her. It *can't* be." My throat constricts and my chest heaves as I draw closer. "Jettas are common— It could be anyone..." I try and reassure myself, but it's in vain.

I stop in my tracks when I see her hot pink monogram decal on the trunk, my heart dropping to my feet. "Fuck. *Fuck!* Val, baby? Valorie?" I yell her name, taking off at a sprint. Cal lands a hand on my bicep, trying to stop me, but I shake him off. There's nothing on this earth that will stop me from getting to my girl. Not even the pleading, frantic shouts of my partner.

I draw up short when the front end of the car comes fully into view. It's mangled to the point of being unrecognizable, but even still, I'm holding on to hope that Val's fine. I'm desperately clinging to the notion that she's going to walk away with nothing more than a few bumps and bruises—no worse for wear. But it's utterly destroyed, and there, in the grass, is the woman I planned to make my wife.

She's covered in glass and blood, broken and bent in the most unnatural angle, completely still. I squeeze my eyes shut, sucking in ragged breaths, praying like hell that when I lift my eyelids, this will all have been a nightmare—that Val will be sitting up, awake and fine.

However, when my eyes open, the scene is wholly unchanged, except now the tinny smell of blood—*her blood*—fills my nostrils, along with various fluids leaking from the engine.

A guttural scream tears past my lips as I drop to my knees and pull her into my arms. My brain switches to autopilot, and I check for a pulse, "Please, baby, please." My voice grows hoarse as I beg her to open her eyes…flinch…*anything* to let me know she's still with me.

Shards of glass from the shattered windshield dig into my knees, but I don't feel anything but a staggering sense of loss and despair. I know I shouldn't be touching her, moving her, and there will be consequences to my actions, but none of that matters as I cling to her, sobbing, blood seeping through the fabric of my once-pristine white shirt.

"Kincaid!" Cal shouts, his hand coming down hard on my shoulder. "The ambulance is here. You…you gotta let the medics get her." His voice cracks on his last words. He knows what we've just rolled up on. We've all known a fellow brother in blue that's responded to a scene where he knew the victim. But this time it's different.

This time, it's me.

It's my accident scene.

It's my loved one.

It's my life—my fucking future—that's vanishing before my very eyes.

He drops to his knees beside me, wrapping an arm around my shoulders in support. "Please, you gotta let the guys take her. We'll follow them to the hospital."

I glance over my shoulder at my partner, seeing my own grief reflected back at me, before looking back down at the woman I'd been planning to spend the rest of my life with. Shaking my head, I pray to God for him to bring her back; I plead with Him to take me instead. But it's useless…He's not fucking listening.

With her head cradled in my blood-streaked hands, I lean down and press my lips to her skin one last time. Even in death, she's still the single most beautiful person to ever walk this earth. The first time I ever laid eyes on Valorie Parsons, I could've sworn I was looking at an angel.

And now…she is one.

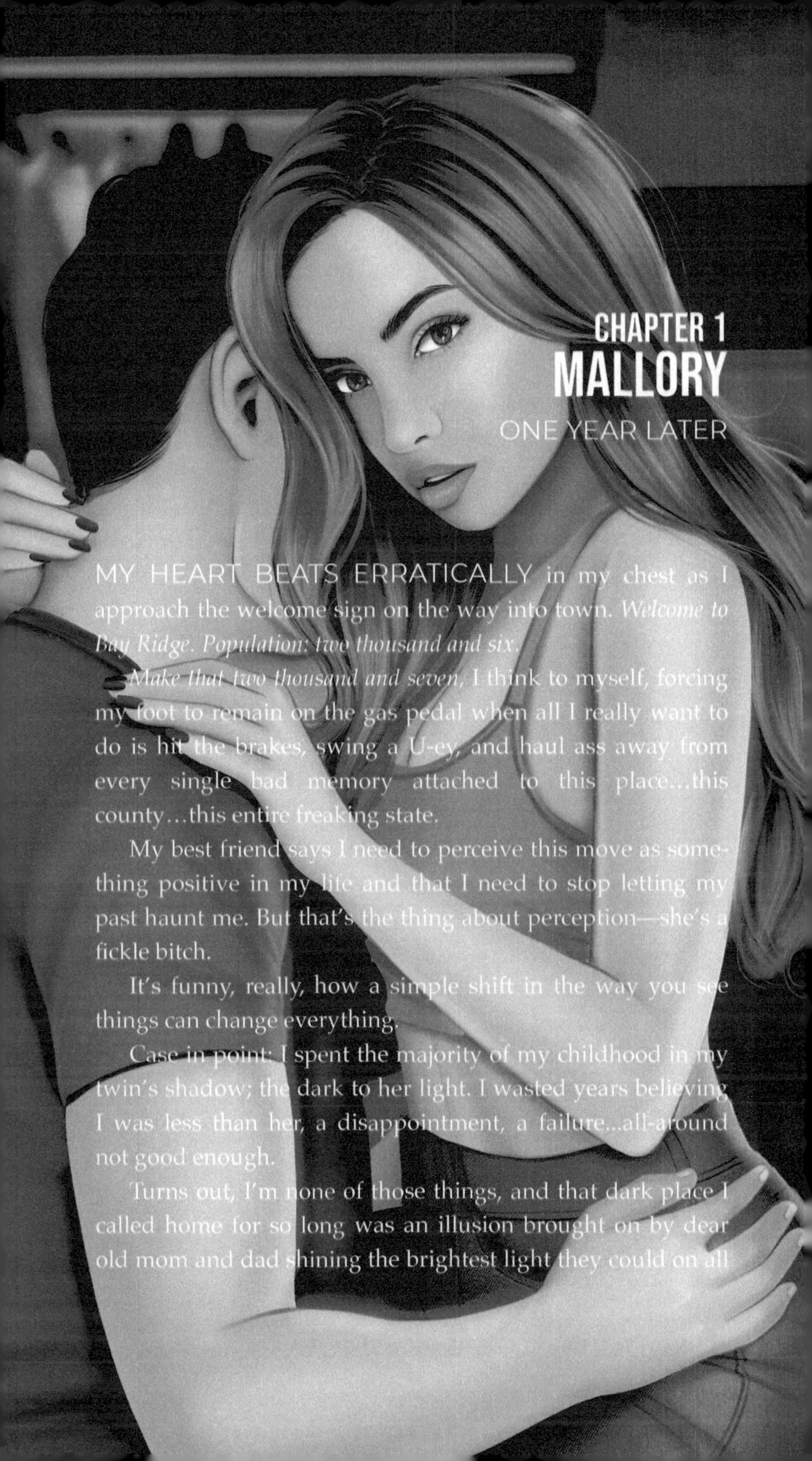

CHAPTER 1
MALLORY

ONE YEAR LATER

MY HEART BEATS ERRATICALLY in my chest as I approach the welcome sign on the way into town. *Welcome to Bay Ridge. Population: two thousand and six.*

Make that two thousand and seven, I think to myself, forcing my foot to remain on the gas pedal when all I really want to do is hit the brakes, swing a U-ey, and haul ass away from every single bad memory attached to this place…this county…this entire freaking state.

My best friend says I need to perceive this move as something positive in my life and that I need to stop letting my past haunt me. But that's the thing about perception—she's a fickle bitch.

It's funny, really, how a simple shift in the way you see things can change everything.

Case in point: I spent the majority of my childhood in my twin's shadow; the dark to her light. I wasted years believing I was less than her, a disappointment, a failure…all-around not good enough.

Turns out, I'm none of those things, and that dark place I called home for so long was an illusion brought on by dear old mom and dad shining the brightest light they could on all of Valorie's achievements, thus casting all of my *perceived* shortcomings into her shadow.

When I think back on everything, it's blatantly obvious. I'm not stupid, or selfish, or ugly, or unlovable. I simply had the misfortune of being born to shitty parents who never wanted me to start with.

The worst of it though is the way I let their actions poison my relationship with Valorie. Through their ceaseless cutdowns and comparisons, I began to resent my sister.

More fucked up than any of that is that it took Valorie dying to change my perception. I spent so much of my adolescent years wishing she would just disappear so our parents would love me the way they did her. I thought maybe if she was gone, all of my shortcomings wouldn't be so noticeable.

Now, Valorie's gone, and me...I'm still not good enough for them.

The sound of my phone ringing through my car's speakers pulls me from my inner turmoil. I don't bother to see who's calling—my best friend Ashley is the only person who would bother. "Is it too late to change my mind?"

"Mally, you're gonna be fine. Everything's gonna be fine." The sound of her voice soothes my frayed nerves.

"Easy for you to say," I groan, flicking on my blinker as my GPS bings, signaling me to turn.

"I know it's hard being so close to home—"

"Not my freaking home," I grumble over her, but she presses on.

"But you're a boss, Mally. You've got this. Plus, you're not actually in your hometown, just...near it."

"I'm still too close. Anywhere in this godforsaken state is too close. Swear on all that's holy, it's like the universe is messing with me with this job. Out of everywhere I applied, the only place to offer me a job is located fifteen minutes outside of my own personal hell."

"Orrrrrrr," she starts, drawing out the word, "maybe the universe knows that you need closure. But, being the stubborn bitch you are, the powers that be decided to intervene and are forcing you to face your skeletons."

I scoff as I turn into the quaint little drive for the bed-and-breakfast I'll be calling home until I find a rental. "Right. Because it's just that easy. Move back to Hell, face the Devil, and then everything will be all happy-happy-joy-joy."

"I never said it was gonna be easy. Real talk, Mally, it's probably going to hurt like a bitch. From what I know of your...family...there may even be some bloodshed. I know it's hard and that you'd rather be anywhere else. But I truly think, that in the long run, this will be good for you. Who knows, Bay Ridge may even be where you belong." Ashley is a big believer in fate—and all of that other woo-woo crap.

It's on the tip of my tongue to rebuke her, but I bite back the words—not because I agree with her, but because she's the one person on this earth who's on my side, and the thought of fighting with my only friend isn't particularly appealing.

A long-suffering sigh escapes my lips, and Ashley changes the subject—hallelujah for small mercies. "Have you found anywhere to rent yet?"

"Not yet, but I'm sure it won't take long."

"Just make sure it's safe."

I snort out a little laugh. "Ash. This place is Cottonwood on steroids. Bay Ridge is so quaint, the freaking trashcans in town are housed in flower planters. Let that sink in...the trashcans have flowers."

She snorts out a little laugh. "Still. Flower-domed receptacles doesn't necessarily equal no crime."

"Will it make you feel better if we video chat when I check them out?"

"Immensely."

"As you wish," I mutter, quoting our favorite movie. "I'm gonna go get checked in, I'll text you later." After we say our goodbyes, I press the power button on the dash, killing the engine. Outside, I stretch—it may have only been a three-hour drive, but when everything you own is crammed into your small, two-door hatchback with you, three hours may as well be an eternity.

The Wilde Bed and Breakfast, named after Irish poet and playwright Oscar Wilde, is a soft pink, turn of the century Queen Anne Victorian-style house with pristine white trim, and a large, welcoming front porch that faces a tree-lined street. Like the rest of the town, it simply oozes charm.

The check-in process goes smoothly, and due to a last-minute cancellation, the owner upgraded me to their king suite, which has an old clawfoot soaker tub. The thought of a long, hot bath honestly sounds better than sex. Sadly, it's been about the same length of time—*way too long*—since I've had either. My apartment in Cottonwood only had a small shower stall, and my ex-boyfriend was far more concerned with sexing up his side pieces than he ever was with me.

My room is tastefully decorated with neutral-colored walls trimmed with ornate molding. The flooring looks to be original to the house, but most of it in here is covered with a beautiful oriental rug. The bed is high off the floor and made up with a thick comforter and more throw pillows than I've ever seen in one place. A quick peek into the en suite shows me that, aside from the glorious tub, it's nothing fancy; but with that beauty of that bathtub, who the heck cares?

I quickly unpack, tossing my casual clothes into the little four-drawer dresser in the corner before hanging my work clothes in the armoire—hopefully they didn't get too wrinkled, because let's just say ironing is not my thing. I set my laptop up at the small writing desk, plug my phone charger in next to the nightstand, and fish my Kindle out of my bag and toss it onto the bed. *Home sweet home,* until I find a real home…it's not much, but it'll definitely do.

THE WEEKEND PASSES IN A BLUR, and before I know it, Monday morning is dawning. Normally, Mondays are the worst, but I have a meeting scheduled with the principal of Bay Ridge Elementary today, so I'm up with the sun, excitement and anxiety both swirling inside my gut. As much as being this close to my hometown sets me on edge, I know how blessed I am to have been offered this teaching position. While I applied to pretty much every school within a hundred miles, Bay Ridge pays their teachers above and beyond any of the other schools I applied to, and they have great benefits.

I've spoken to Mr. Simms several times over the phone, and we've corresponded countless times by email, but this will be our first time meeting face-to-face; needless to say, I want to make a stellar first impression. I take my sweet time getting ready, soaking in the tub with a mask on my face and a conditioning treatment in my hair.

Two hours later, my long locks are styled in loose waves, and I'm dressed in a polka-dotted, navy-blue blouse tucked into a pair of high-waisted toffee-colored linen pants, with cork wedges on my feet. Professional yet quirky, this is my go-to interview outfit. It might be a little loud to some, but it's so *totally* me, which is something I value. After trying to be someone else for so long, my identity isn't something I'm willing to compromise on—*ever*—for anything or anyone.

In my car, I check the time and see I still have a solid hour before I have to be at the school, so with time to kill, I head out in search of caffeine. Driving toward the center of town, I take note of the shops and restaurants I'd like to check out in the coming days. As I roll through the stoplight where the two main streets meet, I notice an empty parking spot, and lucky me, it's right in front of a little coffee shop called Oh, Sugar.

From the white-washed bricks to the sunny yellow door with a striped awning hanging over it, Oh, Sugar is as cute and charming as the rest of Bay Ridge. At the counter, I order my usual—an iced Americano with a splash of heavy cream —before shuffling to the side to wait. A corkboard hanging on the wall catches my eye, and I venture over for a closer look. It's covered in all of the usual stuff: flyers advertising dog walkers, babysitters, and lawn care companies galore. But it's the small paper in the bottom corner with FOR RENT stamped across it in bold that catches my eye.

The barista calls my name, and I snap a quick picture of the flyer with my phone with the intention of texting the number listed later today. But first, coffee.

My meeting with Mr. Simms ends up being a breeze, and my classroom is better than I could have ever imagined, with its spacious layout, wall of windows, and a smartboard. I honestly don't think I've ever been so excited about the start of the school year before. Back in my car, I program my GPS to take me to the nearest Target before dialing Ashley.

"Yo! How goes it, fair maiden?"

"You are so freaking weird," I murmur through my snort of laughter.

"Damn straight!" Pride colors her tone. "Now, answer my question; how's everything going?"

My knee-jerk response is to lament about how much I hate

it here without her and how proximity to my family alone is already draining my life-force, but I know that won't fly with Ash. She's a ride-or-die-no-bullshit kind of friend. Talking with her is like gazing into a mirror at my most honest reflection—she won't ever let me hide, even when my truth hurts.

"Honestly, I'm kind of…excited." I go on to tell her about meeting my principal and seeing my classroom. "I'm actually pulling into Target right now to hit up the dollar spot."

"You know it's not called that anymore, right? It's Bullseye's Playground now. First, everything was a dollar. Then it was the one, three, and five-dollar spot. And then—" I suck in my lips, knowing better than to interrupt her tirade; it's one I've heard countless times before, and I know she won't be able to focus on anything else until she gets it all out. "Hello? Mally? You still there?"

A small laugh escapes my lips. "Yeah, I'm here. I just didn't wanna interrupt your rant."

"Yeah, whatever. For real though, I know it's only been a few days, but I'm really proud of you."

"I haven't done anything to be proud of," I mumble, laying my head against my steering wheel.

"Mallory Parsons. Yes, you have. You had a shit home life, and instead of letting it beat you down, you got out and made something of yourself. You went to a top-notch university and graduated with a three-point-five GPA. You didn't let your shitbag ex drag you down. You weren't scared to leave a good job for a *great* one. And now, here you are, facing your fears like the boss-ass bitch you are. You've taken your adversity and conquered it. You're a freaking warrior, Mally!"

Even though I'm in my car alone, I can feel the blush staining my cheeks crimson. After a lifetime of only ever having insults hurled my way, I'm still learning how to accept a compliment. "Oh! Guess what else?" I ask, desperate for a subject change.

"What?"

"I saw a flyer for a rental house. I haven't seen it or even contacted them, but...I don't know, something about the ad stood out to me."

"Text them. Right *meow*!"

"Okay. Stay on the phone with me while I do?"

"You know it."

With my bestie's strength at my back, I grab my phone and fire off a text to the number from the flyer.

ME

Hi. I saw your flyer this morning at Oh, Sugar. If the house is still available, I'd love more info and to maybe come and see it.

"Okay, I did. Gah. It's probably not even available anymore. And if it is, I doubt they'd even want to rent—"

Ashley cuts me off. "Mallory, you're spiraling. Chill. If it's not available, it wasn't meant to be. As for renting to you, they have no reason not to. You can cover the deposits, you have a good history, can pass a background check, and—if I do say so myself—have the most kickass personal reference there ever was."

"You're right." She doesn't say anything, but I swear I can *hear* the *I-told-you-so-smirk* she's undoubtedly wearing. "Okay. I'm gonna do my Target run. I'll let you know what happens."

"Good. Love you big."

"Love you bigger," I reply and end our call, my heart feeling a little bit lighter.

———

Two hours and three hundred dollars later, I'm walking out of Target with a buggy full of classroom essentials, along with some snacks, a new coffee pot, two pairs of pajamas, a robe, and a pair of fuzzy slippers. Once I have the trunk loaded down and the air conditioner cranked to high, I grab my phone from my purse, intending to snap a picture of my receipt to email to the school secretary, only a text notification catches my eye before I can.

Oh, holy guacamole! It's the number from the flyer! My nerves take flight, ricocheting around in my belly like a pinball. I force myself to take a deep, calming breath as I release my swipe-down screen, tap open my camera app and finish the task at hand. With my email sent and my belly only fluttering a little, I return to the text thread.

UNKNOWN

The house is still available. What days are you free to come check it out?

We chat back and forth for a few messages, and when all's said and done, we agree on tomorrow afternoon for me to come see the house. I know it may be a little premature, but I head back to the B-and-B feeling optimistic—like maybe it's meant to be.

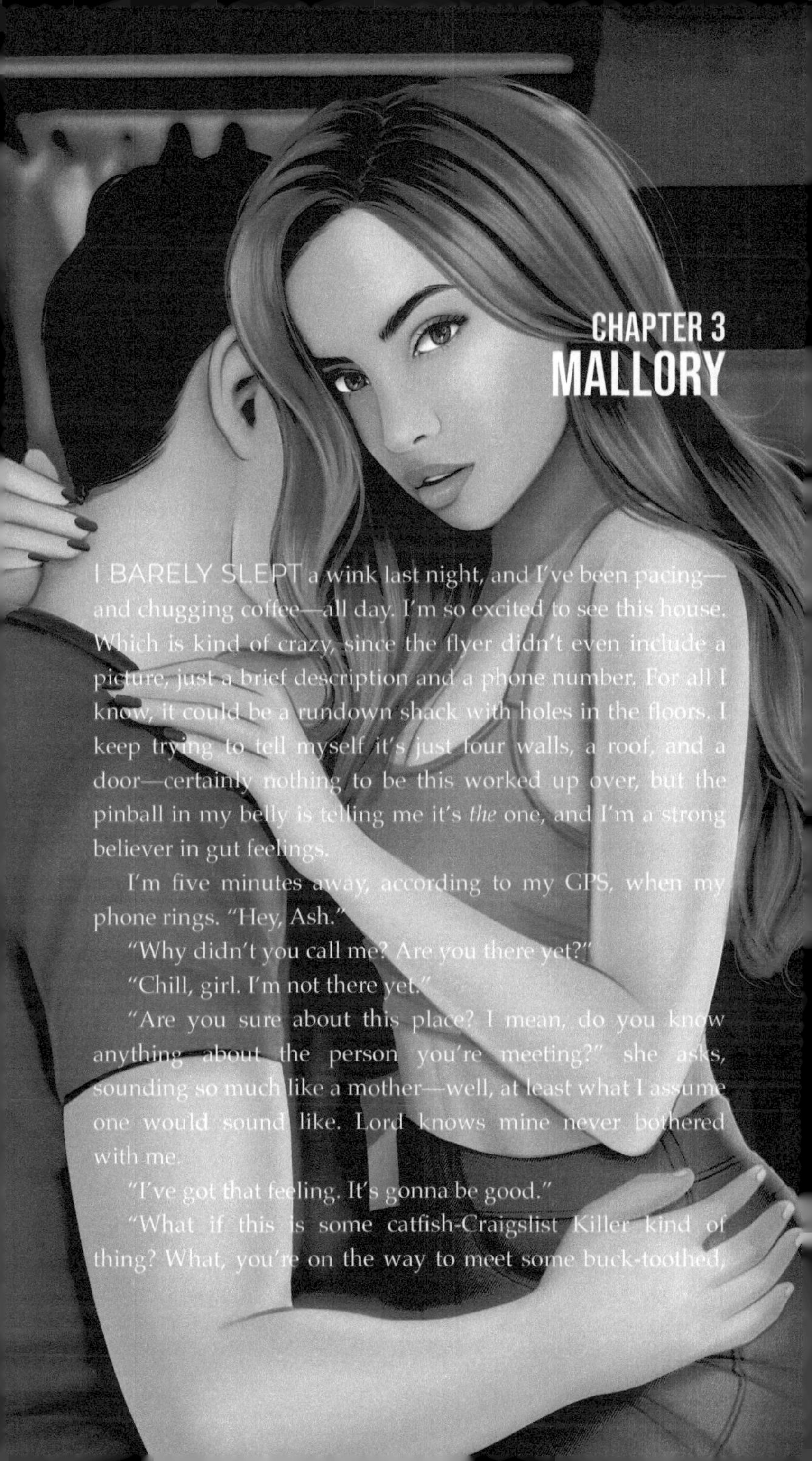

I BARELY SLEPT a wink last night, and I've been pacing—and chugging coffee—all day. I'm so excited to see this house. Which is kind of crazy, since the flyer didn't even include a picture, just a brief description and a phone number. For all I know, it could be a rundown shack with holes in the floors. I keep trying to tell myself it's just four walls, a roof, and a door—certainly nothing to be this worked up over, but the pinball in my belly is telling me it's *the* one, and I'm a strong believer in gut feelings.

I'm five minutes away, according to my GPS, when my phone rings. "Hey, Ash."

"Why didn't you call me? Are you there yet?"

"Chill, girl. I'm not there yet."

"Are you sure about this place? I mean, do you know anything about the person you're meeting?" she asks, sounding so much like a mother—well, at least what I assume one would sound like. Lord knows mine never bothered with me.

"I've got that feeling. It's gonna be good."

"What if this is some catfish-Craigslist Killer kind of thing? What, you're on the way to meet some buck-toothed, banjo-playing hillbilly who's gonna kill you, wear your skin, eat your meat, and sell your organs on the dark web?"

A burst of laughter passes my lips as I turn onto the narrow street listed in the address—a heavily wooded private drive from the looks of it. "Babe. I think you're mixing your murderers. Plus, my gut has never let me down."

She huffs in frustration. "I mean it, Mally. You shouldn't be going there alone."

"And who do you suggest I ask to come with? Maybe I'll just call up dear old dad?" My tone is pissy and I regret it instantly—she doesn't deserve my anger when all she's ever done is be there for me. "Crap. I'm sorry, Ash. I—that's why we're gonna video call, right?"

"Water under the bridge, girl. And yes. I may not be there in person, but I'm there in spirit…and in technology."

"You're ridiculo—oh my God!"

"What? What is it? Is there someone waiting for you with a chainsaw?"

I'd roll my eyes at her antics, but that would require me to look away from the most adorable little cottage I've ever seen. "No. What? No. I just pulled up to the house and it is, no lie, the cutest little thing I've ever seen."

"Oh! Swapping to video now!"

I accept her chat request, flipping my camera outward to show her my view. Together, we take in the crisp white paint job, small walnut-stained deck, and the deep blue front door of the miniature home's exterior. "Okay, Mally. That is…" She trails off, but I know what she's trying to say; it's freaking perfect.

"Well, here goes nothing," I murmur as I step out of my car and head toward the house. With my phone in my left hand, streaming, I knock with my right.

Footsteps sound from inside, followed by the front door swinging open to reveal a petite woman around my age. I'd find her beauty intimidating, if not for her kind, welcoming smile. She is practically the physical embodiment of sunshine —bouncy, soft, and kind—so much like Valorie it makes my heart clench in my chest.

"Hi! I'm Jenny," she says softly, extending her hand my way.

"Mallory." I grip her hand and shake it before awkwardly wiggling my phone in her face. "And this is my best friend."

"Best friend and virtual house hunter! The name's Ashley. It's nice to meet you."

Jenny's smile ratchets up a notch as she glances from my phone screen and back to me. "Nice to meet…y'all. So, off the bat, the rent is seven-fifty a month, utilities included. There's only one internet provider in the area, and they kind of suck, but…" She shrugs as if to say *what can you do.* "Wanna come in and take a look around?"

"Yes, please," Ashley chirps before I can even open my mouth.

"This is the living room—duh—and straight back is the kitchen; the appliances are a little smaller than usual, but it is fully equipped." She leads us to the back of the house, past a massive set of sliding glass doors that pretty much take up the entire left side of the house—which explains how the small space is so airy and light. "Up the stairs, you'll find the loft-style bedroom and beneath them is the bathroom. Oh! And the stairs all open to provide extra storage."

Ash is uncharacteristically quiet during the tour, but I can totally see myself living here. It almost seems too good to be true, so I have to ask, "What's the catch?"

"There's no catch, promise. I've lived here the past few years; truly, it's a great little house."

I'm still suspicious. "Then why are you moving out?"

A cheek-splitting smile lights up Jenny's face as she wriggles her left hand out in front of her. "I'm getting married, and while this place was perfect for just me, my fiancé has a larger home, so I'm moving in with him."

Ash squeals—the girl is a complete love-a-holic, hence her career as a wedding photographer. "Mally, move the phone closer to her ring!"

"Yeah, no, I'm not doing that."

My best friend hisses. "Yes. Do it! Now!" Jenny takes mercy on her and brings her hand in closer. "Oh, a sapphire, I love it!"

I zone out while they chat about her upcoming nuptials, only tuning back in when Ashley offers to shoot a free engagement session for them before rushing off the chat due to another call coming in.

"When can I move in?"

"I'm moving out this weekend, so anytime the following week. Does that work for you?" I nod and she continues. "Perfect. Let's meet one day this week, and I'll bring the rental agreement for you to read over and sign."

"Sounds good." Excitement swirls through me as we firm up plans to meet at Oh, Sugar Friday morning.

Moving back to a place so full of bad memories might not have been my first choice, but things are falling into place and looking up—the only thing missing is Val.

———

When I walk into Oh, Sugar, Jenny is seated at a little table by the door. Only she's not alone; there's an absolutely adorable little girl sitting with her.

"Hey," I call out as I approach their table.

Jenny looks up and grins my way. "Oh, hey. girl!"

"Is this your daughter? She's precious."

"Negative, that little monster would be mine," comes a voice from my left. Turning, I see a gorgeous blonde with the kindest eyes.

The little girl huffs. "I'm not a monster, Mama, I'm a princess; Daddy says so."

"That you are, Tater Tot."

"Grab a chair, have a seat," Jenny says.

"Sure, just let me order first."

I quickly return with my iced Americano, setting it on the table so I can pull up a chair. I suck down two gulps of the creamy, caffeinated goodness and introduce myself to Jenny's companions. "I'm Mallory—"

"Oh, Lord. I'm so rude!" Jenny exclaims, rushing to finish our introductions. Nodding my way, she says, "As she said, she's Mallory, and she's moving into my she-shed. Mallory, this is my best friend and soon-to-be sister-in-law, Natalie, and her daughter, Tatum."

"It's so nice to meet you," I say, meaning it.

Making friends has never come easy to me. Aside from going to school, my parents did their best to keep me isolated —out of sight, out of mind and whatnot. Up until I escaped Orchard Grove, my twin was the closest thing I had to a friend, though mommy dearest made sure to chip away at our relationship every chance she could until finally it crumbled altogether.

Having Ash assigned as my dormmate was probably the best thing that's ever happened to me—fate, if you ask her. Much like Valorie, she was bright and bubbly, my polar opposite. At first, I wanted jack-all to do with her, but she was relentless in her pursuit to befriend me and draw me out of my shell.

If she was here right now, I guarantee she'd make some smartass comment about being a proud mama bird watching her hatchling fly the nest.

"It's nice to meet you, too. What brings you to Bay Ridge?"

"Work. I'm a teacher, and the elementary school here offered me a job."

The little girl—Tatum—looks up at me and squinches her nose. "You're a teacher? You're too pretty to be a teacher."

"Tatum!" Natalie scolds, but it doesn't bother me. Kids her age only know what they've seen in movies and whatnot.

"Well, thank you," I say softly. "But I assure you, teachers—just like everyone else—come in all shapes and sizes. How a person looks doesn't define who they are or what they do." Tatum nods like I've just offered her sage advice. Natalie shoots me a grateful smile. Changing the subject, I ask both Jenny and Natalie what they do.

Natalie is the first to reply. "My husband, Alden, and I own Bayside Café."

"And I work there part-time when I'm not tending bar at Bennet's," Jenny adds.

"I'll have to check both of those out once I'm moved in."

"Speaking of…" Jenny trails off, leaning down and grabbing a manila folder from her purse. "Here's your rental agreement."

After giving it a thorough read-through, I sign and initial on the dotted lines and Jenny passes me the keys. "You can move in any time after Sunday."

"Do you have a lot to move?" Jenny asks, slipping the duplicate copy of the lease back into her bag.

"No, I sold most of my furniture before moving. Figured I could start fresh."

"What I'm hearing is you need to do some serious shopping," Jenny says, sounding all too excited by the prospect.

"Pretty much."

"Let us know if you want company."

"Yeah! I'm super-duper good at shopping!" Tatum declares proudly, causing us all to laugh.

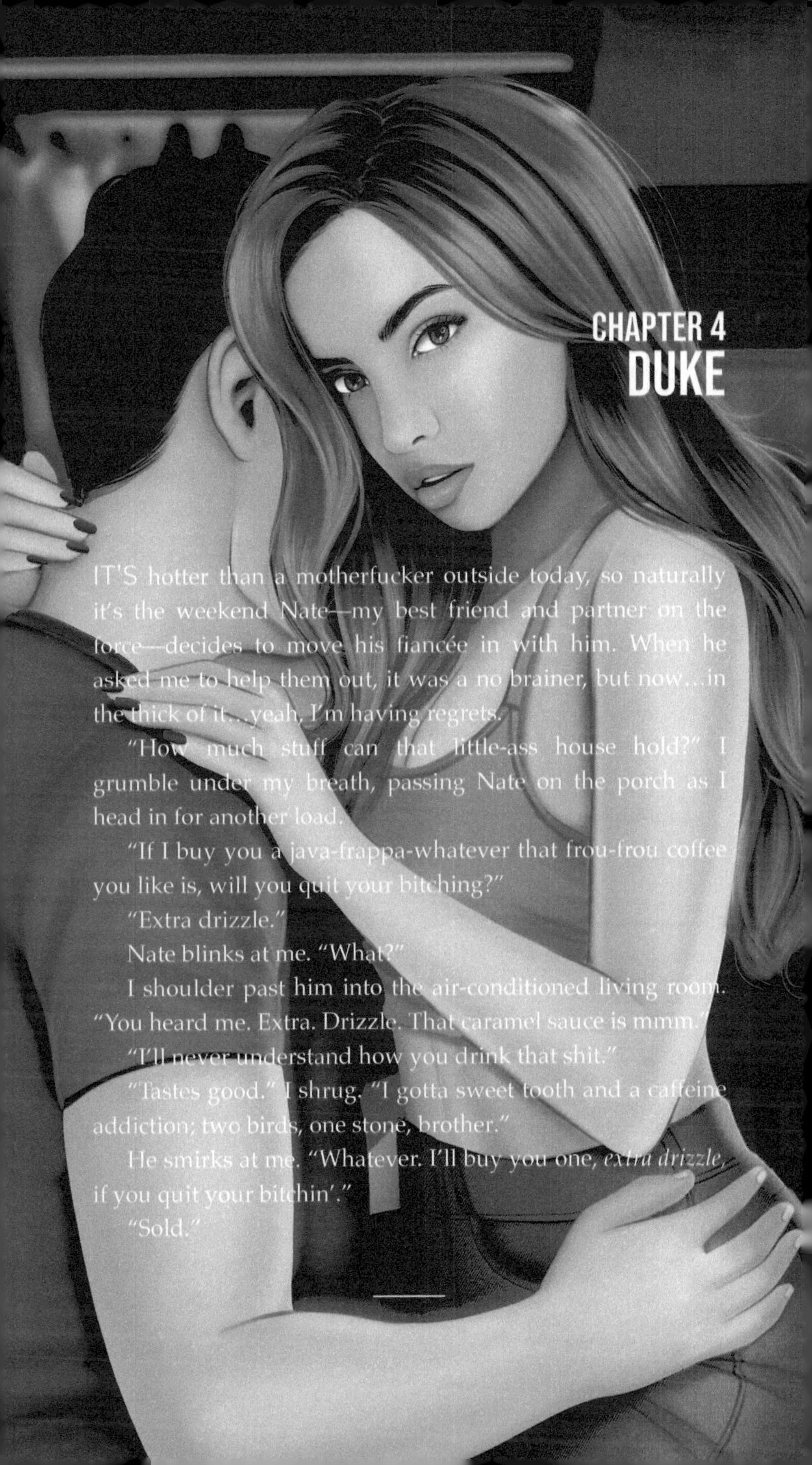

IT'S hotter than a motherfucker outside today, so naturally it's the weekend Nate—my best friend and partner on the force—decides to move his fiancée in with him. When he asked me to help them out, it was a no brainer, but now…in the thick of it…yeah, I'm having regrets.

"How much stuff can that little-ass house hold?" I grumble under my breath, passing Nate on the porch as I head in for another load.

"If I buy you a java-frappa-whatever that frou-frou coffee you like is, will you quit your bitching?"

"Extra drizzle."

Nate blinks at me. "What?"

I shoulder past him into the air-conditioned living room. "You heard me. Extra. Drizzle. That caramel sauce is mmm."

"I'll never understand how you drink that shit."

"Tastes good." I shrug. "I gotta sweet tooth and a caffeine addiction; two birds, one stone, brother."

He smirks at me. "Whatever. I'll buy you one, *extra drizzle,* if you quit your bitchin'."

"Sold."

Two hours and a hell of a lot of boxes later, we have everything loaded up into the beds of our trucks. I'm feeling pretty good until Nate opens his big ass mouth. "All right, now we just gotta unload it all at my place."

I groan. "Swear, y'all had to pick the middle of summer for this shit."

"Ah-ah," Nate scolds, wagging his finger at me like a schoolmarm. "Little boys who complain don't get fancy-ass coffees."

"You do realize I could just buy my own, right?"

My friend nods. "True, but we all know it tastes better on someone else's dime."

He's got me there. It's not just when someone else pays, either; my grandma made the best mashed potatoes this side of the Mississippi, and even following her recipe verbatim, Val couldn't seem to replicate them, and she knew her way around a kitchen.

A pang of sadness reverberates through me as memories of Valorie and I working around one another in the kitchen flit through my mind. As clear as day, I can see myself sidling up behind her at the stove, my hands on her hips and my face buried in the crook of her neck, breathing in her scent right alongside whatever she was making. I can still hear the way she would sing as she chopped vegetables, her tone sweet but slightly off key.

It's the memory of these simple, little things that drove me out of Orchard Grove, the only home I've ever known. Every room of my apartment was tainted with her essence; every restaurant haunted with her memory. All of these things that once seemed completely innocuous now haunt me, to this day. But that's what death does; it magnifies the mundane.

The second I heard the next town over—Bay Ridge—had an opening on the force, I sent in my application. Unbeknownst to me at the time, Cal was able to put in a good word for me with his uncle, who happens to be the chief of the Bay Ridge PD. And while I won't call coming here fate, because that would imply Val was meant to die and *fuck that*, luck was damn sure on my side when he partnered me with Nate. The two of us never had any weirdness or growing pains. We just…clicked.

Another hour and we have everything piled into Nate's foyer—I figure I'll let him and Jenny sort through it and unpack without me. I've more than earned my caramel macchiato float.

I'm about to head out when Jenny hollers from the kitchen. "You staying for dinner, Duke?"

"Depends, whatcha makin'?" I holler back, lying through my teeth; I'd eat anything Jenny whipped up. The girl can cook something fierce.

"Burrito bowls, nothing fancy."

Nate rolls his eyes, and I smirk. We both know Jenny could serve us chicken nuggets, and they'd be gourmet. Between his fiancée, his mama, his little sister and brother-in-law—who happens to also be his childhood best friend—he pretty much has an entire staff of chefs at his disposal; it's a wonder he's not the size of a blimp. If I had someone cooking good for me every day like this joker does, I'd have to double up on my workouts, that's for damn sure.

"Hell yeah, I'm staying. You know those are my jam." I venture farther into the house toward the kitchen. "You make any of that ball rice stuff?"

Jenny barks out a laugh. "For the last time, it's called quinoa, and yes, I made some. Fresh guac, too."

"You're too good to me, girl."

She bats her long lashes at me, and my hackles rise. That look says she is buttering me up for something. "Good enough you'd be willing to help with some more moving?"

My eyes widen. "More? You need to put some stuff into storage or something?"

Nate walks past me, going to stand at his woman's side.

"Nah, she has a renter moving in. She's new to the area and doesn't know anyone, so—"

"She doesn't know anyone here—literally no one. So, Natalie and I went with her to pick out some new furniture, and I offered to help her move in," Jenny says, speaking over her fiancé.

"Offered me to help's more like it," Nate grumbles good-naturedly.

"Oh, so you don't want any of the peanut butter fudge pie I made especially for you? Huh. Guess I'll have to send it home with Duke."

A panicked look crosses Nate's face. "Whoa, hold up. Let's not make any hasty decisions. I don't mind helping out. I mean, like you said, she's new here and all alone. I'd be remiss not to lend a hand. I mean, really, it's my civic duty."

My shoulders shake with silent laughter. "Laying it on a little thick," I say out of the side of my mouth, helping myself to a glass bottle Coke from their fridge. I pop the cap, take a swig, and turn to Jenny. "When does she need help?"

"This weekend."

"Yeah, I can do that."

Jenny slides the skillet of delicious smelling chicken off the stove before flitting over to me and wrapping me in a hug. "You're the best, Duke!"

"The fuck am I?" Nate barks. "Chopped liver?"

We break apart and she winks at me before turning to Nate. He grasps the front of her shirt in his fist and pulls her body flush to his. She pops up onto her tiptoes, sealing her lips to his. I busy myself with making my plate, not so much because I don't want to intrude on their moment, but because sometimes witnessing their intimacy and happiness feels like a testament to all I've lost.

We should be able to take our girls out on double dates and do couple-y shit together, but instead, I'm the third fucking wheel. While I'm happy as hell for Nate, watching my best friend and his girl only serves to remind me that I'm one half of a whole without Valorie. When she died, she took the best of me right along with her, leaving a shell of the man I was before.

Sure, I still joke and cut up and smile, but fake it 'til you make it, right? Only, how in the hell am I supposed to make it without the woman I love by my side?

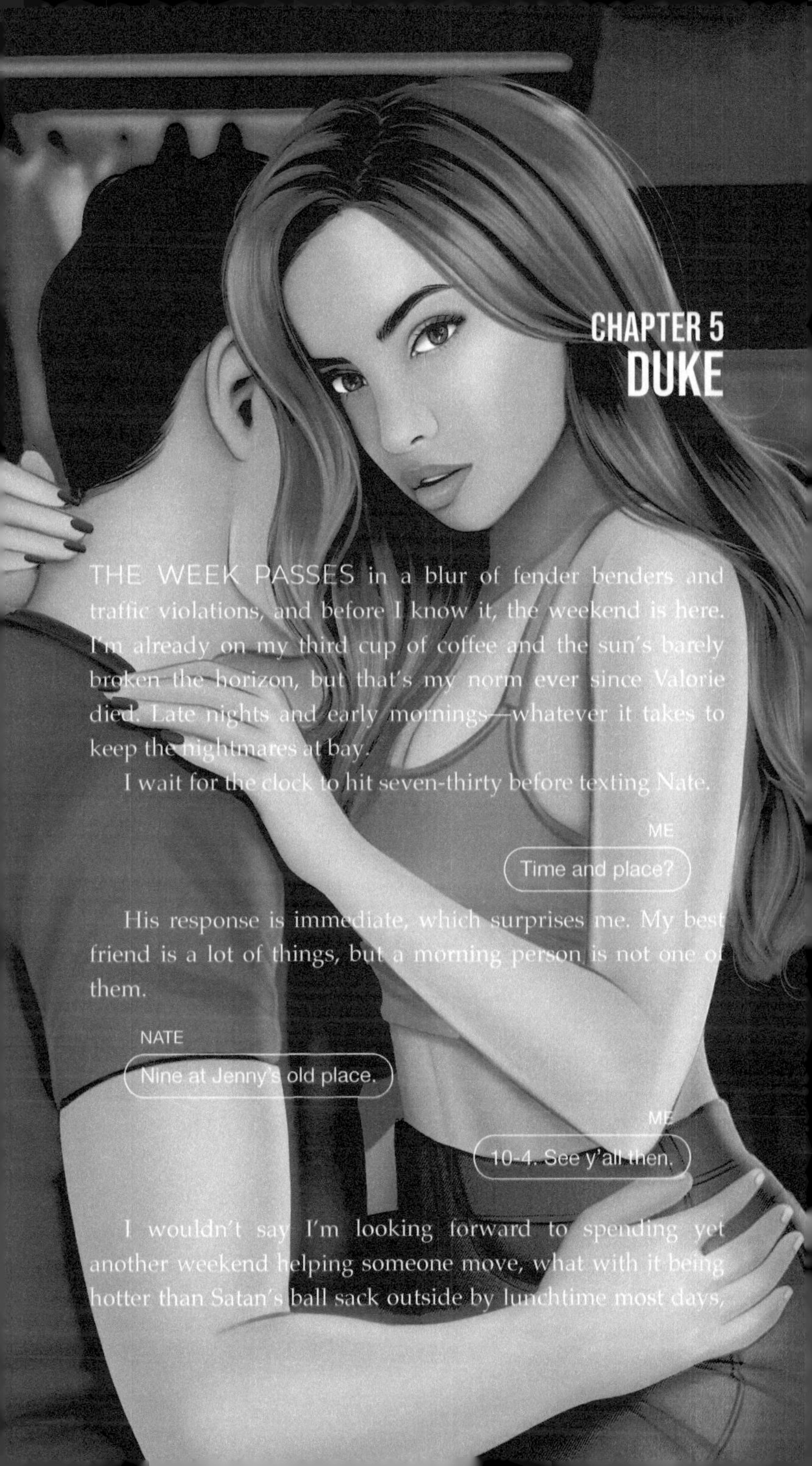

THE WEEK PASSES in a blur of fender benders and traffic violations, and before I know it, the weekend is here. I'm already on my third cup of coffee and the sun's barely broken the horizon, but that's my norm ever since Valorie died. Late nights and early mornings—whatever it takes to keep the nightmares at bay.

I wait for the clock to hit seven-thirty before texting Nate.

ME

Time and place?

His response is immediate, which surprises me. My best friend is a lot of things, but a morning person is not one of them.

NATE

Nine at Jenny's old place.

ME

10-4. See y'all then.

I wouldn't say I'm looking forward to spending yet another weekend helping someone move, what with it being hotter than Satan's ball sack outside by lunchtime most days, but it sure as shit beats being here alone, drowning in thoughts of the life I was supposed to have.

———

I'm on my way to meet Nate and Jenny when my phone buzzes in the cupholder with an incoming text, but I pay it no mind. There's too much traffic to not give the road my full attention. Two more messages come through before whoever's trying to reach me gives up on texting and calls. Twice.

I still drive the same truck I drove in high school; it's one of the only things from my life with Val that I didn't give up. The memories in this beast are far too precious, even if they cause me pain. However, an old-ass truck means no fancy Bluetooth, so whoever keeps calling is just going to have to wait for me to find somewhere safe to pull off.

About a mile or so down the road, I pull into the Piggly Wiggly parking lot and check my phone. All three texts and both missed calls are from Valorie's dad, Darryl. "Fuck," I groan, spearing my left hand through my hair. "What now?"

Valorie's parents, her mother especially, have never been my favorite people, but since her death, things have been worse than ever with them. At least two or three times a month, Darryl calls me to come out and help him manage his wife. To say she's handled her daughter's death poorly would be an understatement. I try my damndest not to judge her though, because her pain must be tenfold what mine is. Only instead of at least trying to cope, Nancy drowns herself in prescription pills and booze.

With great trepidation, I return Darryl's call. He answers on the first ring. "Duke. Can you—"

I grip the steering wheel so hard my knuckles turn white and my nails bite into the leather, trying like hell to keep my frustration to myself. "I'm on my way." I hang up before he can reply and immediately dial Nate.

"'Sup, brother?"

"Nancy," is all I say.

And it's all he needs to hear to get it. "Shit. What now?"

"No clue, but I've gotta go. Sorry to bail."

"You're good, man. I'll let Jenny know, but be prepared for her to give you shit."

Rolling my eyes, a small smile tugs at my lips as I imagine Nate's little five-foot-nothing spitfire of a fiancée reaming me out for canceling. It's like what that Shakespeare dude said… she's little, but damn she's fierce.

"Tell her to go easy on me, yeah?"

Nate barks out a short laugh that says *don't count on it.* "Keep me posted with what happens with Nancy and let me know if you need backup."

"Will do, brother, will do."

I make the fifteen-minute drive to Darryl and Nancy's house in Orchard Grove in a little over ten, worry over what I'm going to walk into churning in my gut like the ocean during a storm.

Judging from the outside of their meticulously kept ranch-style home, you'd never know anything was amiss, which isn't surprising since appearances mean everything to the Parsons.

Warily, I exit my car and head up the paved path leading from the driveway to the front door. I give two loud knocks before trying the knob; it's unlocked. "Darryl? Nancy?" I holler both of their names as I step into the house.

The house is quiet—too quiet; my senses immediately go on high alert. Suddenly, the sound of glass shattering, followed by an ear-piercing wail, reverberates through the house. Instinctually, I take off toward Valorie's childhood bedroom at the back of the house.

As I draw nearer, I realize the commotion is actually coming from the one room in the entire house I've never been in—Mallory's room. *What in the hell?* I pause just outside of the door, listening for any clues about what could have set her off this time, because while these breakdowns aren't anything new, they're always over Valorie.

Hell, no one's seen or heard from the other Parsons daughter since the day they graduated. Mallory collected her diploma, packed her shit, left, and hasn't been back since—not even for her own sister's funeral. *Some twin she was*, I think bitterly, recalling all of the times Val talked about her sister after she left, all the times she cried over her, how much she missed her. I know shit between Mallory and Nancy has always been strained, but that's no excuse, at least not in my book.

Then again, Valorie and Mallory were never all that close —they definitely weren't the stereotypical twins you see in movies, finishing the other's sentences and shit. I mean, for the first four months of our relationship, I assumed Mallory was her younger sister, not her fucking twin. Talk about a shocker when I showed for their Thanksgiving dinner and met her…I'm pretty sure my jaw hit the floor.

Nancy's broken sobs penetrate through the door and into the hall where I'm still lingering. I move to open the door when something heavy hits it from the other side. "It should have been you!" she screams, bitter pain and cold resentment lacing her every word.

"Nancy!" I punctuate her name with two loud knocks. "I'm coming in."

The room is a total disaster. The bedding appears to have been torn from the mattress and tossed around the room. The curtains are ripped from the wall. There is clothing strewn haphazardly through the small space along with little rips of paper.

"Nancy," I say her name softly, hesitantly, as though I'm approaching a wild animal. She looks up at me, her eyes red-rimmed and glazed. "What's going on?" I ask, still not entering the room.

She stares at me blankly before returning to…whatever it is she's doing, muttering under her breath all the while. "Stupid. Worthless. Never should've been born."

"What are you doing, Nancy?"

"Erasing her."

"Erasing who?"

"HER!" Nancy shrieks, tangling her fingers into her matted hair.

"Where's Darryl?"

She once again lifts her gaze to me. "He left. No-good traitor. Everyone's against me."

I step into the room, my hands held loosely at my sides in an effort to show Nancy I'm not a threat. "Nancy, I need you to calm down—"

I know I've messed up the second the words pass my lips; her guttural roar only confirms it. She hauls herself up from the floor, and I take a step back. "How can I calm down when *she's* back?" she hisses.

"Who? Who's back?"

"Thinks she can come back and take her place. She can't. Stupid girl should know she's not welcome here." Her voice grows with her anger, and before I know it, she's all out yelling. "She should have died! HER!" She screams the last word, slamming her balled fist into the mirror on the wall, cracking the glass.

She draws back to hit it again, a crazed smile lighting her features as the cracks splinter out farther from the point of impact. The sight of blood trickling down Nancy's arm spurs me into action. I rush her, wrapping my arms around her frail body, pinning hers to her sides. Nancy screams and howls like a caged beast, but I don't release her. Usually when Darryl calls me out here, she's drunk or high, wanting to relive the past. Today though, something's different. Today, she's a danger to herself.

I haul her from the mess that is Mallory's room out to the

living room. Her adrenaline must be fading because she makes no move to fight me when I deposit her onto the couch. Even still, I stand guard as I dial up her husband, just in case she tries anything.

"Where are you?" I grit out, pissed he left me here to deal with this shit alone.

"I-I had to go, Duke. She was—she was in a bad way. I just…couldn't see her like that."

I pinch the bridge of my nose and pray for patience. "You need to come home. I've got her calmed down, but you need to come home and someone needs to explain to me what in the hell is going on before I have to Baker Act her."

"I'll be there in five."

I hang up the phone and address Nancy. "I'm gonna go get a rag. Don't move, you hear me?"

She nods once, the movement nearly imperceptible it's so small.

When I return to the living room, Nancy hasn't shifted from where I left her, not even an inch. She's nearly catatonic, with her eyes trained on her lap, save for the way she's rocking herself back and forth, much the way you would a baby.

Crouching down before her, I gently draw her hand into mine. I wipe the blood away before pressing the towel to the gash in her hand, applying pressure. "Got yourself real good there, Nancy."

At the sound of my voice, her gaze darts up to mine. "Duke," she whispers my name. "What happened? When did you get here?"

"Nance?" Darryl's voice rings out from the garage.

"Living room," I call back, and he rushes in, gathering his emotionally frail wife into his arms. I give them a minute as he whispers encouragements and calming words into her ear, trying not to be angry that he took the coward's way out and called me to deal with this shit.

"I'm gonna need you to tell me what happened, okay?"

Darryl grabs his wife's hand and gives it a gentle squeeze. "I-I'd like to know, too."

Oh, even better. He didn't even bother to figure out what caused his wife to breakdown before bailing out and calling me.

"I...I ran into Cherrie at the Piggly Wiggly, and sh-she said that Mallory moved back."

Darryl shifts uncomfortably at his wife's words, and my brows knit in confusion. *Why on earth would having her only living child come home be a bad thing?*

After a prolonged and uncomfortable silence, Darryl speaks. "Well, you know how Cherrie is. Loves to run her mouth. I-I'm sure it wasn't *her*. Maybe just someone who looks similar."

With wide eyes and downturned lips, Nancy slowly nods. "Yes. Maybe. Yes, that's it." She nods several more times, as if she's trying to convince herself to believe her husband's words. Eventually, a calm settles over features, completely erasing all traces of her previous mania. It's jarring, the way she went from foaming at the mouth like a rabid dog to as docile as a baby bunny.

"Her hand is gonna need some attention." I pivot on my heel and head back down the hall, calling out to Darryl over my shoulder. "I'll let you handle it while I clean up the mess."

Stepping back into Mallory's room is like walking into a brick wall, as all of Nancy's hate-filled words slam into me. *Why would Mallory being home set her off like this? Why would she say all of those horrible things about her child—her own flesh and blood? Why did she destroy her bedroom? And why is her room half the size of Valorie's? Why? Why? Why?*

After remaking the bed, I gather up the strewn clothing and toss them on to it. I begin gathering up the scraps of paper littering the floor, using my fingers to push the scraps into a pile. I'm not really paying attention to the task at hand, that is, until my fingers brush over what feels like an emboss-ment of some sort. That catches my attention, and I make quick work of fitting together the jigsaw-like remnants.

Holy. Shit. It's a birth certificate. Mallory's. She destroyed her daughter's birth certificate. *Why?* For what purpose, other than to hurt her? I mean, honestly, that's the only semi-feasible reason, because it's not like replacing it is all that difficult.

I rush to finish tidying up the rest of the small room, wanting nothing more than to get the hell out of this toxic-ass house and away from these toxic-ass people.

Nancy's nowhere to be seen as I stalk back toward the front door, but Darryl is waiting for me in the living room and that's just fine, because I've got shit to say to him—shit I should have said a long time ago.

"Duke, thank you—"

I cut him off, not wanting to hear his empty platitudes. "Save it. You wanna thank me? Thank me by getting your wife some professional help. She's a danger to herself, and one of these days, she's gonna take things too far. And then what, Darryl?"

He has the decency to look ashamed. And he damn well should. When you take vows, you honor them—you don't just cut out when it gets tough. "You're right." He nods, his eyes clouding with tears. "I will."

I step outside onto the porch and take what feels like my first full breath all day. Only, it's not day anymore; it's damn near sunset. *Did I really spend that long here?* I dial Nate as I walk to my truck, content to sit for a minute and gather my bearings. Being around Nancy is emotionally draining—I need some kind of reset to get back in the right frame of mind.

"You just now leaving?" Nate asks by way of greeting.

"Unfortunately."

"Everything okay?"

"Define okay," I deadpan.

"Seriously, are you okay?"

"I...I'm fine. It was just a really long day. How'd moving go?"

"It was fine. She had more stuff than I anticipated, and it was hotter than hell, but we got it done. But you totally owe me."

I smirk. "I owe you, huh?"

"Sure enough, and Jenny's already got it all planned out."

I roll my eyes. Of course she does. "What's the plan?"

"You'll see," Nate says cryptically as he ends the call, and I swear to God, it's like I can hear his grin through the phone.

Groaning, I toss my phone into the cupholder, crank the engine, and head home, where an ice-cold drink and a steaming hot shower are waiting on me.

"DO you remember seeing a box marked sex toys?" I ask.

Jenny chokes on her reply, her short sputters coming across the line. "Y-your what?" she finally squeaks out, causing me to grin.

I've settled in nicely over the past week. Heck, I'd almost call this house a home at this point, but something's missing —I just can't quite put my finger on what it is just yet. Either way, this roof and four walls is the closest thing I've ever had to a real home, and I absolutely love it.

"Kidding! But for real, I can't find my kitchen utensils. I've been eating with the chopsticks I got from the takeout place all week!" I readjust the phone, holding it with my shoulder as I, yet again, scan the small kitchen for my missing box.

Jenny and I have been chatting for the last twenty minutes, and it's kind of surreal. If someone would've asked me if I liked talking on the phone a month ago, I'd have emphatically said no. Then again, aside from Ashley, I don't think I've ever had a friend call me for no real reason, and we didn't start talking on the phone until I moved here. So, when Jenny called *just to talk,* I about fell out.

"Now that you've almost caused me to choke and die, I've

gotta go redo my makeup for dinner tonight. We'll meet you there at six?"

"Sounds good!"

"Sweet! Oh, and check the laundry room for that box. I know Nate stuck some stuff in there."

Sure enough, the box is exactly where she says, which is a relief. I don't think my handy chopsticks could've lasted one more meal, and I'm far too stubborn to just go out and replace my cutlery.

By the time I finish unpacking my lost box, I only have half an hour to get ready and to the restaurant. Even for a low-key girl like me, thirty minutes is cutting it close when it comes to getting ready for a night out.

I don't have time to shower, so a healthy dose of dry shampoo, some bronzer, mascara, and lip gloss will have to do.

I'm excited to take Jenny and Nate out to dinner tonight to thank them for helping me move in. Even though, technically, they invited me to dinner, I'm going to pay, and that's that. "Can't pay if you never get there," I grumble to myself as I haul ass up the stairs to my loft to get dressed. I have less than five minutes to be out the door and on my way. I toss on the first thing I see, which happens to be a short blue and white tie-dye linen romper with long sleeves and a deep V neckline. I slide my feet into a pair of coral-red espadrille wedges, grab my oversized hobo bag, and dart out the door.

Luckily, I don't hit any traffic on my short drive to the Black Sheep. Jenny swears up and down it is delicious, but going off of its non-descript exterior, I'm not so sure. Then again, I guess they say not to judge a book by its cover, so I'll withhold any and all judgment until after our meal.

Stepping into the dimly lit space, I'm blown away. Clearly the plain brick exterior and single red-painted door in no way do the Black Sheep justice. Inside is an effortless mix of industrial modernism and old-world charm. The warm wood of the floors and ceiling meet cool steel beams. The tables are also metal, but they have a patina to them that just screams vintage, and none of the chairs match. All in all, it's unlike anywhere else I've ever eaten before, and if the flavors wafting through the air are anything to go on, it's going to possibly be even better than Jenny said.

At the hostess stand, I give her Nate's last name, and she leads me straight back to them. They're seated at a four-top with the two of them facing the door. Nate stands as I approach, and I can't help but smile.

"Such a gentleman," I murmur to Jenny, waggling my brows.

"Damn straight he is. His mama would skin him up one side and down the other if he wasn't."

"That's the damn truth," Nate grumbles, but his smile tells me that he loves his mother and that her intentions are pure. I can't even begin to fathom what that's like. Lord knows, most days, my mother did her best to pretend I didn't exist.

"So, you found the place okay?" Jenny asks, breaking me out of my morbid thoughts.

I laugh. "This town has like three streets and two stoplights. I don't think it's possible to get lost."

Nate grins. "You'd be surprised."

"What's good here?" I ask, grabbing one of the menus from the table.

"Everything," Jenny says, her voice dead serious. "Also… I-may-have-invited-one-of-Nate's-friends-to-join-us."   She says that last bit all as one word, so it takes me a second to figure it out.

But when I do…*that little wench is trying to set me up!* "Did you now?" I ask blandly, trying not to let the panic inside my chest bleed out into my words.

Nate rolls his eyes. "Just ignore Cupid over there. My buddy was supposed to help us move you, but he got called away. So, Jenny figured since y'all didn't meet then, that now was as good a time as any. It's not a set-up, so don't worry. Duke's a good guy."

I freeze at that name. *Duke.* It's not exactly common. But… it's not *him.* It couldn't be, right?

As if on cue, Nate's gaze cuts to something—or someone, more likely—behind me and he grins. "There he is now."

I don't turn and look. I couldn't, even if I wanted to; I'm completely glued in place. In my peripheral, I see a large, tatted-up hand reach to pull out the chair next to me. The sound of the chair sliding against the floor is like nails on a chalkboard, causing me to cringe. The large form lowers into the seat next to me and his scent—something dark and heady and addictive—immediately envelops me.

A small tremor works its way through me—a premonition, like something terrible or life-changing is about to happen. I do my best to shake off my crazy before slowly turning to face the man seated next to me, ready to introduce myself. "Hey, I'm—" My words dry up faster than a puddle in the Sahara, because right next to me, close enough to touch in all of his hulking, brooding glory, is the man my sister loved up until her dying breath, Duke Kincaid.

MY VISION BLURS BEFORE TUNNELING. Cold sweat runs down my spine as I stare straight at a ghost. I want to look away. To blink. Something, anything. But I can't, and she's all I see. The noise and chatter surrounding me fade away until all I can hear is my own shallow breathing as I desperately try to send oxygen to my lungs. *In, out. In, out.* From the corner of my eye, I see Nate's mouth moving, but his words don't penetrate the haze blanketing me.

What the fuck? Those three words play on a loop as I choke back the bile creeping up the back of my throat. I want to run, to flee and pretend this never happened, but I'm rooted to the spot. "Val…" Her name passes my lips like a curse, bitter-tasting and vile, because as much as I want it to be her, it's not; my girl's gone, dead and buried.

What a cruel twist of fate for me to end up here not even two years after her death, staring at a woman that looks so much like my stolen forever that my heart feels like it's going to beat right out of my chest.

My stare never wavers as I drink her in. She's so right it burns my eyes to look at her, yet I can't look away. Seeing her is like coming home, even though logically I know she's really so wrong. Her skin's too tawny, and her hair's too dishwater. Her eyes are more honey and less whiskey. Her clothes are all wrong, quirky where Val was pure class.

My lips part, but no sound comes out. It's like I'm in the Twilight Zone, trapped and staring at an alternate version of the future I could've had.

A waiter rushes past, sending her scent my way; she fucking smells like vanilla and honey, like Valorie...*exactly* like Valorie. It's too much, and somehow, not enough. I can't handle it. On instinct, I reach for her before shoving away from the table and jumping to my feet. I can't be here. *I can't fucking be here.*

I haul ass out to the parking lot, Nate hot on my heels.

When the warm nighttime air hits my skin, I suck it greedily into my lungs, damn near choking on the humidity as I try and clear her scent from my skin. But like the memories of Valorie, that sweet vanilla clings to me, taunting and teasing me in the worst way.

I'm pacing the sidewalk like a caged animal, my hands tugging harshly on the ends of my hair as my partner approaches. "Wanna tell me what just happened?" he asks cautiously, curiously.

I give my hair one last tug before dragging my fingers down my face, keeping my mouth firmly shut. If I try to talk right now, I'm either going to fucking cry like a baby or vomit at Nate's feet.

My chest heaves as I try and regain control of myself, but the harder I try, the more panicked I get. My knees buckle, but before I can hit the concrete, Nate's there, catching me with a firm arm around my middle. He guides me to an iron bench near the parking lot and forces me to sit before shoving my head down between my knees. "Breathe," he commands. "Deep, even breaths."

I do as he says, each inhale ripping through my lungs like lighter fluid. After a few more painful inhales, my racing heart starts to even out and the pain in my chest dissipates a little, enough for my head to clear. "Fuck," I mutter on one last inhale before sitting upright.

"You okay, brother?"

"No." I don't elaborate. I'm not ready. Seeing her after so long was completely unexpected. Back in the day, thanks to Mallory's goth-phase, they looked so different no one ever would've thought they were twins. But now, with her hair long and light and her face soft and pretty and not covered in dark, heavy makeup, she looks so much like my Val that I... *fuck, I feel like I'm going insane.*

"Talk to me," Nate urges. But I don't know what to say or where to even start. Seeing Mallory is stirring up all kinds of feelings in me, with anger and longing being front and center. Anger over her leaving and never coming back—if she would've been here all the while, seeing her wouldn't have been such a shock to my system, and she could deal with Nancy's delicate mental state. But she ran away the second she could. And longing, because she looks so much like Val, which only serves as another reminder that she's gone.

After a prolonged silence, Nate plays his trump card. "Partners."

I inhale deeply. "That's...she's Val's sister. Her *twin* sister."

Nate whistles through his teeth. "Well, ain't that some shit." He wraps an arm around my shoulder and squeezes once before releasing me. "I can't imagine how hard this is for you. But try and remember she lost someone, too, okay?"

I know he's right, logically. But, right now, in the thick of it, it's hard to take her feelings into consideration. She's pretty much the physical embodiment of the life I lost, of the love I lost, which makes her the last person on earth I want to see, much less welcome into our friend group.

I'm about to rebuff Nate's statement when a hand comes down on my shoulder. A spark ripples through me at the touch, catching me wholly off guard. I spring up from the bench and whirl around, dislodging the unwelcome touch, shocked as shit to find *her*. "What?" I bark through clenched teeth.

Mallory's eyes glisten as she takes a half step back, her shoulders hunching before she steels her resolve. "Duke." She nods as if to reassure herself. "I-I was hoping we could talk."

At least their fucking voices aren't the same, I think bitterly. "Got nothing to talk to you about."

"Please?" she asks, and even though I want to be as far away from Mallory Parsons as possible, I find I'm helpless to deny her.

MY HANDS TREMBLE as I wait for Duke's reply, but my question is met with staunch silence from him. After a minute or two, a humorless laugh escapes me as I turn to address Nate, who has been watching us with a look of morbid fascination coloring his features. "Tell Jenny I'm sorry for just leaving. I-I can't be here."

I turn to flee toward the parking lot when Duke grabs ahold of my wrist. "Why are you here?" His voice reminds me of boots on gravel, turning my skin to gooseflesh.

"A job," I whisper, trying like hell to ignore the way his skin feels touching mine. He's Valorie's, and his innocent touch affecting me like this feels like a betrayal to her memory.

"What. Job?" His hands are balled into fists at his sides as anger pours off of him in waves. His back is ramrod straight, his eyes narrowed in accusation, though of what I'm not sure, and his lips are pressed into a thin, firm line.

"At the school. As a t-teacher." Back in the day, once he realized Valorie had a sister, Duke always made it a point to speak to me when I was around, to include me, even though mother dearest always found some asinine reason to prevent me from actually being a part of anything other than her misery. But the man in front of me right now, he looks like he despises my very existence, like he, too, thinks the wrong twin died. It's an arrow to my already fragile heart.

Out of the corner of my eye, I see Nate hedging his way past us. "I'm gonna let y'all talk. Duke, play nice."

"Do you wanna sit?" I take a hesitant step toward Duke, inclining my head toward the bench he was seated at.

I can tell from the way his mossy green eyes are shooting daggers at me that he wants to deny me; I just wish I knew where this animosity was coming from. I can imagine seeing me is like a slap in the face, but it's not exactly sunshine and roses for me either. His presence calls forth every ounce of guilt buried within me.

Maybe…maybe he knows the truth, that I'm the reason Valorie is dead. Maybe he hates me for it. Maybe he really does wish it would've been me that died instead of her. Lord knows, he wouldn't be the only person to feel that way.

Finally, he grunts out a nod.

"Why are you really here, Mallory? You and I both know you've got no business being here."

I lace my fingers together and place them in my lap to keep from fidgeting. Or maybe it's to keep from smacking him for implying that I'm somehow up to no good or have nefarious intentions. "As I mentioned, I'm here for work. Bay Ridge Elementary offered me a job. It's not like I knew you were here."

He sneers. "You sure about that?"

"Absolutely positive." I use the same voice I do in the classroom when a student is acting unruly: calm and placating.

He grunts again. Apparently, while the rest of the world is moving forward in some way or another, Duke Kincaid has regressed to a caveman.

"You got something you wanna say, Duke?"

He cracks his knuckles, working his jaw back and forth.

"Yeah, I do. I think it's bullshit you ran away after high school. Your sister missed the hell out of you, and you pretty much abandoned her to y'all's crazy-ass mother. She spent nights on end crying over missing you, and you couldn't even be bothered to fucking call or text. And don't get me started on her funeral. What kind of heartless bitch skips her own twin's funeral?"

My cheeks are damp with tears by the time he's finished. I shake my head, sadness engulfing me. "You have no idea, do you?" He couldn't, not if he thinks I ran away from my family out of selfishness. Hell no, I ran out of self-preservation. By the end of our senior year, Nancy's outbursts were getting progressively worse. I almost missed our high school graduation ceremony because she went ballistic the morning of when she found my acceptance letter from Knight U…

I walk into my bedroom, shocked to find it in utter disarray, like a tornado had torn through. Only the tornado has a name: Nancy. She stands in the center of the mess, seething, with papers clutched in her grasp.

"What are you—" I don't even get a chance to finish the question before her closed fist connects with my cheek. Holy crap, she just hit me. Like honest to God hit me. She's slapped me plenty of times over the years, but this…this is new territory.

"You stupid little bitch. You think you're so special because you got accepted to college? Your sister got accepted into twenty! She has pick of the litter, and you have what? One? One that you can't even attend, because over my dead body are we paying for it."

"I got a full ride," I whisper, immediately regretting it when she strikes me again. My cheek and jaw throb, but I refuse to give her an outward reaction.

"For what? What could you have possibly done to earn a scholarship? You're dumb as a box of rocks, unlike your sister, who is Valedictorian. You're useless, a waste of space."

That altercation ended with me having to cake on five layers of foundation and concealer to cover my bruised cheekbone. She also broke two of my fingers, but she didn't break my spirit.

"No idea about what?" Duke's cold voice brings me out of my memories and back to the here and now.

"She always was good at hiding it," I mutter to myself. Why is it that the crazies of this world are also the cleverest? They're crafty and manipulative and charming when they need to hide their monstrous nature from the rest of the world. And to outsiders, Nancy Parsons was the most charming of all. My whole life she used her silver tongue to hide her wrongdoings. For almost eighteen years, she had me convinced I was so stupid that no one could ever love me, all the while, convincing the rest of the world that I was simply a troubled loner who preferred keeping to herself.

"Hiding what?" Duke demands, his temper rising. "Enough of this cloak and dagger bullshit. If you've got something to say, spit it out."

My own anger threatens to burst forth and I pinch the bridge of my nose, trying to tamp it down. "Nothing. Forget it." I stand from the bench, my body shaking with a strange mixture of embarrassment, anger, and more than anything else, sadness. "This was obviously a mistake. I'll...yeah, I'll just go. It was...have a nice life, Duke."

I make it to the sidewalk before the first tear falls. I wipe it away and turn back to face him. There's something I need to say. "Hey, Duke?" He looks my way, his features shockingly blank. "I love my sister very much, and I miss her every day."

Satisfied with having the last word, I hightail it to my car and back to the safety of the four walls of my little cottage.

———

It's been a week since my run-in with Duke and, much to my dismay, he's still at the forefront of my mind. I should be focusing on my lesson plans and the fast-approaching school year. But nope, I'm too busy replaying our conversation from last weekend, picking it apart, dissecting every single word.

Jenny's been after me to talk about it, too, after the way I rushed out of the Black Sheep like the Hounds of Hell were nipping at my heels. I've managed to put her off, but my luck ran out this morning when she called and said she was on her way, Natalie in tow. I mean, I haven't even talked to Ashley about what happened—how can I, when I'm still trying to process it?

Maybe talking it out with someone who knows Duke as the man he is now will help; however, not going to Ash first feels like a betrayal of our friendship. *Maybe she'll be down for a video chat when the girls arrive?* I hope so, because if nothing else, it'll be nice having her in my corner in case this turns into the Spanish Inquisition. Especially seeing as I have no clue as to what Duke may have told Jenny and Nate about me and how we know each other. *What if he said something to turn them against me?*

Before I can deal with any of that, I need coffee, and a lot of it. Luckily, my Black Rifle Coffee Company order arrived yesterday—their Murdered Out roast gives me life. As it brews, the scent of the dark Colombian beans permeates the air, making my mouth water and my worries about Jenny's visit wane.

Once the carafe is full, I pour myself a mug, adding a generous splash of heavy cream. One sip in and I'm already feeling more confident about today; with this brew running through my veins, I can handle anything. On sip two, the sound of the doorbell echoes back to the kitchen, and my nerves return full force. *So much for being able to handle anything.*

I trudge to the front door, swinging it open to reveal two grinning blondes. "I brought chocolate croissants," Natalie says as she passes me.

Jenny follows after her. "I brought myself. But I gave her the recipe for the croissants, so they're from me, too."

I can't help the giggle that slips out. These two are the definition of squad goals.

"Sounds good to me. I just made a pot of coffee."

Jenny does a little shimmy. "Now you're speaking my language, girl."

I tell the girls to get comfy while I plate up the baked goods and pour our coffee. I grab a tray and load it down, adding a little dish of cream and bowl of sugar. "I hope y'all don't want some fancy flavored creamer," I say as I lower the platter down onto my coffee table.

They both assure me they're fine, and the three of us dig into the buttery, flaky, chocolate-filled goodness. "You made this?" I ask, in utter disbelief.

Natalie's cheeks turn rosy. "Do you like it?"

"Like? More like love." I polish off the rest of mine, licking the remnants from my fingers.

"Enough chitchat," Jenny says, ripping the proverbial Band-Aid off. "I need answers about last weekend. Pronto."

"This is gonna sound really lame, but could I try video calling my friend Ashley, so she can hear this, too?"

Jenny assures me she's cool with it, and I try calling her. Unfortunately, she doesn't answer. "Well, guess I'll have to catch her up later." I wring my hands in my lap, searching for the right words. "Duke and I…we have a history."

"History how?" Jenny asks. "I thought he was with the same girl since—"

"Valorie," I say, cutting her off with a nod.

"Yeah. You know her?"

I nod. "All my life. She's my sister. My twin sister." It's so quiet in my living room after I drop that bomb, you could hear a pin drop. I honestly think I've shocked them silent.

"Wait. What? Really?" Jenny's voice is tinged with incredulity.

"Really."

"Well, then why did he lose his ever-loving shit when he saw you? I mean, y'all should be pretty well acquainted, right? What gives? Because Nate said he was in a bad way and that he's been a total pill all week at work."

"They work together?"

"Yup. Partners and all."

"He…um…we…the last time I saw him—and my sister—was eight years ago."

Both of their eyes widen, and Natalie all but shouts, "What? You went almost a decade without speaking to your twin? I can't even go two days without talking to Nate. I…what?"

Even though I understand it, I cringe at her confusion, wondering how best to explain our complicated relationship. I give them the bare bones, watered-down version. "Val and I never had much in common growing up, and I went to school out of state on a scholarship. We just…kind of…grew apart." The half-truth tastes bitter on my lips, but I'm not ready to share the ins and outs of it with them just yet.

From the way Natalie's brow furrows, I can tell she wants to ask more about how we could've simply grown apart; thankfully, she doesn't. Most people hear the word twin and automatically assume we have that *Parent Trap* bond kind of thing where we can finish each other's sentences and feel the other's pain. But our mother made damn sure that never happened.

"That's intense, girl." Jenny drains the last of her coffee. "I'm an only child, but damn. I can't even imagine."

I eye her skeptically. "You're telling me Nate didn't fill you in? Really?"

She rolls her eyes. "That jackass pulled the bro-code card on me and wouldn't say anything. I even threatened him with no sex, and he still wouldn't spill. Joke was on me, though. I ended up none-the-wiser and horny as hell." A quick glance at Natalie and I can tell we're both trying to hold back our laughter at her rant. Then she mutters under her breath, "Damn jackass," and we both lose it.

Once our laughter subsides, Jenny adds, "Speaking of that jackass, our engagement party is three weekends from now, and we'd love for you to come."

Smiling, I nod my agreement. I know I haven't known them long, but I definitely think this is the beginning of two beautiful new friendships.

TWO WEEKS later and *she* is still on my mind. Her big, sad amber eyes and quivering, plump lower lip are taking up way too much real estate in my brain.

Fourteen damn days of trying to dissect what about her sets my teeth so on edge, aside from the obvious. Was it the surprise of seeing her? Or is it something more?

Three-hundred and thirty-six hours of fighting myself on the answer to the last question. My body is at war with all of the conflicting thoughts and feelings running through me faster than Usain Bolt during a one-hundred-meter sprint.

Logic says it's because she looks so similar to Valorie and is a stark reminder of all that I've lost. My inner Neanderthal wants something I'll never voice, because it's wrong. So. Damn. Wrong. My heart is angry and hurt because she should have been here all along to help with the fallout of her sister's death—and with her crazy-ass mama.

And my dick…well, that jackass must be in cahoots with my caveman brain, because every time I picture her wide, innocent, golden-hued eyes, and tight, lithe body—that I'll deny noticing until my dying breath—he does a half-mast salute.

Clearly, he's a traitorous SOB and has gone rogue. The very thought is a betrayal to the woman I love—*right?*

After a shitty shift on day seventeen post-Mallory, thanks to being called out to a domestic with minors in the home—it ended in two arrests and the children in state care—the only thing on my mind is a hot meal and a cold beer.

Problem is, my fridge and my pantry are empty. I could probably talk Nate into taking me home with him, but even Jenny's cooking isn't worth the four-billion questions they'll ask. As far as Nate knows, I reacted poorly out of shock, but God knows what Mallory has told his fiancée. And even if she is still in the dark, Jenny will pepper me with questions until I crack like an egg. Which means I can either hit up the Piggly Wiggly or a drive-thru.

Seeing as I have no desire to really go anywhere other than home, a drive-thru it is. Only, when I pull into the parking lot, there's a sign taped to a caution cone in front of the menu, saying that the speaker box is broken and to order inside. *If that ain't just my luck.* Shaking off my irritation, I steer my truck into a parking spot next to a sporty little blue crossover. Going into the dining room still beats going to the actual store.

I'm looking down as I walk toward the door, not really paying attention, so it's a total jolt when I collide with a small, feminine body. Instinctually, I reach out, my arm banding around her waist while her hands fly to my shoulders. To an outsider, our position is downright intimate—a lover's embrace.

"Oh!" she gasps. "I am so sorry!" I drag my eyes up to her face, my green eyes meeting her golden brown—Mallory. Subconsciously, I squeeze her tighter to my chest, pressing all of her soft into my hard, before stepping back and placing much-needed space between the two of us.

"Don't worry about it," I mutter, trying to step around her.

Seeing her, touching her, has my brain whirring, my blood fizzing, and my heart beating double-time.

But she matches me step for step, blocking my path. "Um, don't you want to apologize as well?"

She's right. I *should* apologize, but there's something about this girl that evokes a visceral response in me, and as much as it pains me to admit, I don't think it's because she reminds me of Val. And that sets me on edge. She's a virtual stranger to me; I shouldn't feel anything for her other than disdain for her not being around the past eight years.

"Sorry."

Mallory rolls her eyes, which I'm now noticing are several shades lighter than Valorie's. "Anyone ever tell you that you really have a way with words?"

I shrug and move to go around her again. "I've heard it a time or two."

"Whatever." She lets me pass. "Have a nice night, Duke."

But I can't, not now. Seeing her is the cherry on top of the shit sundae that was today. And hearing her say my name in that sweet, honeyed voice of hers...it's the extra fucking sprinkles.

———

I'm up bright and early the next morning, as per usual. I used to be able to sleep in until at least eight in the morning on my off days, even later if Valorie was curled into my side. My lack of sleep hardly bothers me anymore; it definitely beats the dreams of her that plague me. Sometimes it's visions of her bruised and bloody body that haunts me; other times, it's memories of the life we were building together. The worst ones, though, are dreams of the future we could've had— dreams of our wedding day and of her belly rounded out with our first child. Val wanted two kids, a boy first and then a girl.

As fucked up as it was, right after her death, I was so desperate to have more time with her that I used the sleeping pills my doctor prescribed just to catch a glimpse of her smiling face. Thankfully, I realized how unhealthy that was and put a stop to it before it became a habit I couldn't break—*too bad Nancy didn't do the same.*

I fly through my morning routine, wanting to get to the gym and the grocery store before either get too busy. After a thorough workout, I hit the showers and head to the Pig. I detest grocery shopping, but I'm too set in my ways to try the online pickup. I mean, how do I know they'll do a good job? Plus picking out ripe melons is one of my superpowers.

Inside the store, I grab a cart and head toward the meat section. I know most people do produce first, but I don't like everything sitting on top of my veggies. There's a method to my madness. I load up on lean proteins before hitting the dairy section. A carton of eggs, some butter, cheese, a gallon of milk, and a bottle of that bomb-ass Reese's-flavored coffee creamer and chocolate whipped cream, and I'm on my way. I grab a few snacks and drinks from the inner aisles before making my way to the bakery—there's nothing better than those big-ass loaves of French bread toasted and drenched in butter.

Finally, with my cart damn near overflowing, I mosey over to the produce section. I go to stock up on my usual veggies, reaching for a crown of broccoli with one hand while trying to shake the little plastic baggie open with the other. Only, instead of a cold and waxy green stalk, my fingers meet warm, smooth flesh that sends a zing up my arm and to my chest—almost as though I've touched a live wire. I yank my hand back; my eyes dart up, once again bringing me face-to-face with Mallory fucking Parsons.

"We have to stop meeting like this." She offers me a weak smile, her thumb rubbing small circles over the patch of skin I just touched on her wrist.

"That implies it's intentional." My voice comes out gruffer than I intend, and when she shrinks back, I cringe internally. Something about this girl brings my inner-asshole out in full force.

"Actually, it's the opposite. It's a stock phrase, typically used when two characters keep meeting in awkward or dangerous situations." She nibbles her pouty bottom lip, and I'm wishing I wasn't wearing workout shorts, because they hide nothing—especially not the inappropriate reaction I'm having at the moment.

I shift behind my cart to hide said reaction when she adds on, "Though, we're definitely more awkward than danger-ous." If only Mallory knew just how dangerous she really was to my mental, physical, and emotional health. I've worked hard to build up a suit of armor since losing Val, and here her damn twin is, all soft words and sweet smiles—a chink in my armor. A weakness. A threat, and I don't do well with threats.

When I offer her nothing more than a stony blank stare, she draws in a shaky breath, grabs the crown of broccoli we were both after and scurries away, leaving a sinking feeling in my gut.

———

Two days later, I've finally managed to shake thoughts of Mallory loose from my mind—mostly. Nate is content, for now, to keep talks of her in our no-fly zone, which has made our shifts thirty times more enjoyable. There's nothing worse than working with a pissed-off partner. I know eventually he'll push for details, and *eventually*, I'll give them. But for now, I'm still at a loss on how to even broach the subject. There's no good way to explain our past, much less that I suddenly find myself having thoughts about her that leave me feeling all kinds of twisted up inside.

"You want burgers today?" I ask as he pulls us back into the station parking lot for our thirty-minute lunch break.

"Actually, I've got plans with Jenny today. I must've forgotten to mention it." He kills the ignition and we both get out. "You…can join us," he offers politely, but his tone implies otherwise. Sounds to me like Nate has plans for some afternoon delight, and that's definitely *not* something I want to be invited to.

"Nah, I'm good." I give him a smirk. "You have fun though."

He winks and heads off toward his car with a skip in his step. *At least one of us is getting some.* I mean, I haven't been totally celibate since losing Val, but I haven't actually slept with anyone either. I've had exactly three bedmates since if you could even call them that since we never ended up in a bed and I never sealed the deal…with any of them. We'd get hot and heavy, usually in the back seat of their car, and I'd make sure they got off and then I'd bounce. It's like my brain is totally on board with providing pleasure, but something about actually fucking someone other than Valorie makes me feel dirty.

With half an hour to spare, I find myself hitting up my favorite little café, Oh, Sugar. They make an out of this world caramel macchiato float. I'm talking two scoops of homemade vanilla bean ice cream, topped with two shots of espresso, milk, and enough caramel drizzle to hype up an entire classroom of kindergarteners. Basically, it's a giant sugar-fest that's so bad for my body but so, *so* good for my soul.

I place my order at the counter and step off to the side to wait for it. I'm scanning the space for a free table when my gaze snags on a certain golden-skinned blonde tucked away in the back corner. *She's fucking everywhere.*

Irrational anger thrums beneath my skin. How is it I managed to go over eight years without ever seeing her, and now I can't catch a break? It's like the universe said, *Oh, you're struggling with your loss still? Here's some more shit to wade through.* Mallory's my own personal brand of torture, and yet, she sparks something to life in me that I thought died with her sister—*hope*—and that just pisses me off all the more.

I march over to her table. Over the din of chatter, she doesn't hear me approach, and like the asshole I am around her, I demand to know, "Are you fucking following me?"

Her doe eyes fly up to mine, and she chokes on a sip of whatever she's drinking. "I'm sorry, what?" She pats her chest a few times. "Oh, it's you."

I quirk a brow at her cavalier attitude.

"No, you pompous ass, I'm not stalking you. In case you failed to notice, you came in *after* me. Last I checked, psychics aren't real, and if they are, I certainly don't harness any of their powers. *And* if I did, I'd certainly use them for something better than following you!" She ends her rant on a shriek, causing more than a few patrons to look our way.

Luckily, I'm in uniform, so their stares don't linger. They probably assume she's some crazy woman and I'm just a humble officer of the law, doing my job, putting my life on the line at the hands of her insanity. The thought makes me grin, which I belatedly realize is *not* the appropriate response.

Looks like Mallory is batting 2-2 at eliciting inappropriate responses in me.

"Are you seriously smiling? Like the thought of me *not* wanting to stalk you is so freaking absurd?"

My grin morphs into a full-blown smirk at the outrage in her voice. Something about this encounter has me feeling lighter than I have in a long time. Who knows, maybe it's me finally having the upper-hand. "I mean, I'm pretty awesome." I wave my hand up and down my body as if to demonstrate said awesomeness.

Mallory's eyes follow my hand, and I don't miss the hunger in her eyes as she takes in the way my uniform hugs my taut muscles; the fact that she pauses on my handcuffs has me feeling some kind of way. It takes every ounce of my self-control to not imagine her cuffed, bare, and at my mercy, something Valorie was never into. *Nope. Stop. It's wrong to think of her that way, and it's especially wrong to compare her to her own fucking twin.*

My good mood evaporates, my smirk turning to a scowl. Of course, Mallory catches it. She rolls her eyes and asks, "What? What have I done to offend you now? Did I breathe wrong?"

I want to yell and scream, *Yes! Everything you do is wrong. Even when it's right, it's wrong because it makes me want you and I have no goddamn business feeling this way!* Luckily, the barista calls out my name and I stalk back to the counter without another word.

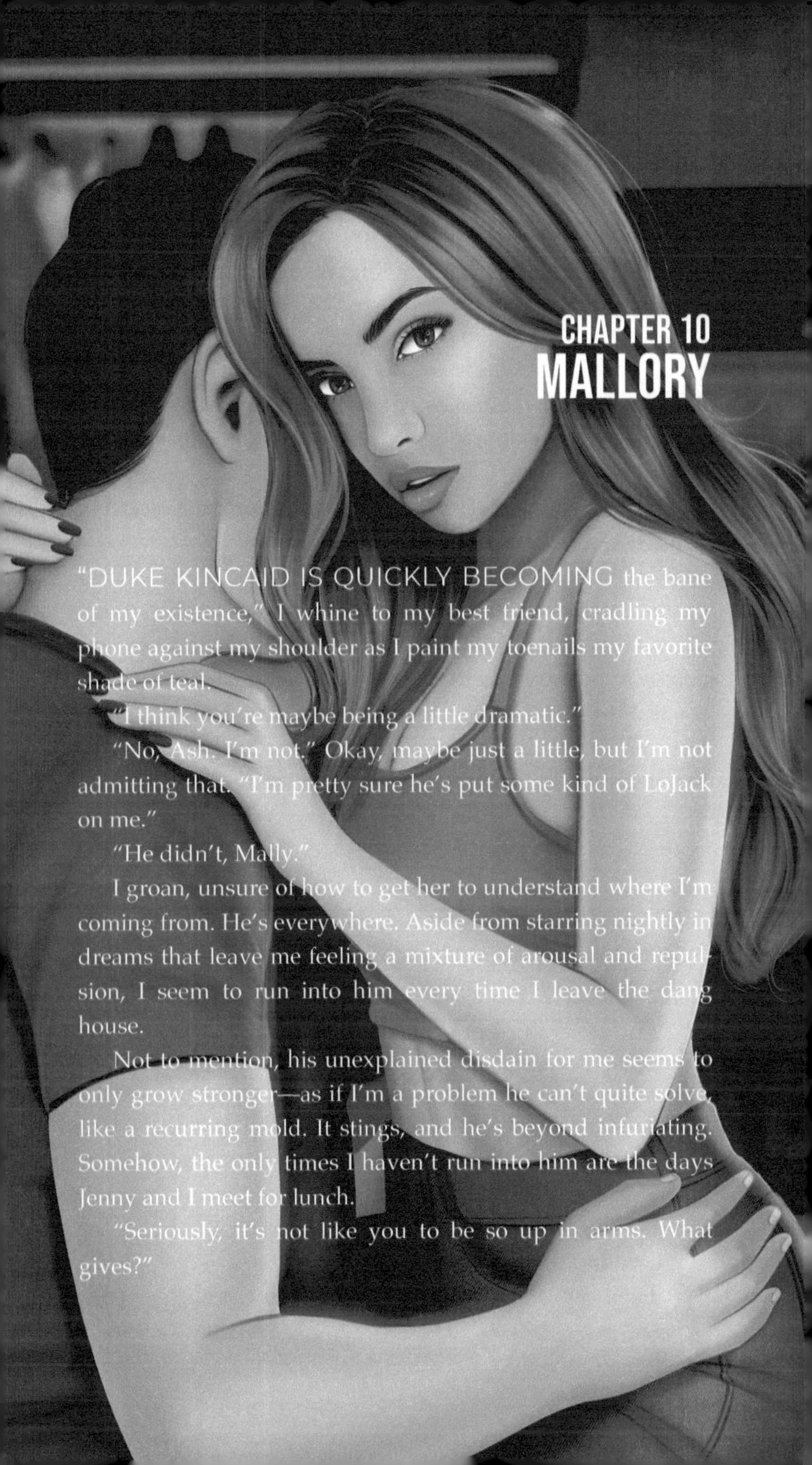

"DUKE KINCAID IS QUICKLY BECOMING the bane of my existence," I whine to my best friend, cradling my phone against my shoulder as I paint my toenails my favorite shade of teal.

"I think you're maybe being a little dramatic."

"No, Ash. I'm not." Okay, maybe just a little, but I'm not admitting that. "I'm pretty sure he's put some kind of LoJack on me."

"He didn't, Mally."

I groan, unsure of how to get her to understand where I'm coming from. He's everywhere. Aside from starring nightly in dreams that leave me feeling a mixture of arousal and repulsion, I seem to run into him every time I leave the dang house.

Not to mention, his unexplained disdain for me seems to only grow stronger—as if I'm a problem he can't quite solve, like a recurring mold. It stings, and he's beyond infuriating. Somehow, the only times I haven't run into him are the days Jenny and I meet for lunch.

"Seriously, it's not like you to be so up in arms. What gives?"

A small sigh escapes me. "I don't know. Maybe it's just the stress of the move and the approaching school year?"

"Maybe," Ashley says slowly. I can tell she thinks it's something else—something more—but thankfully, she doesn't voice it. She always knows when to push me and when to let me stew. Honestly, some days I think she may know me better than I do. Which makes it all the more absurd that I thought she would possibly see me talking to Jenny and Natalie about Duke before her as a betrayal. Nope. Instead, she squealed and made a comment about me finally blossoming—*such a smartass.*

Desperate for a subject change, I add, "Meet the teacher is in a few weeks."

We chat for a few more minutes as Ashley catches me up on her latest string of awful dates. I seriously don't know anyone—well, scratch that, I really don't know enough people to compare her luck to. It seems bad to me, but Ashley is steadfast in the belief that the right guy will come along— for both of us. Too bad I'm pretty sure the guy my heart thinks is right is the absolute physical embodiment of wrong.

———

A few days after the coffee shop incident, I realize Jenny and Nate's engagement party is this weekend, and I still don't have a gift. Since Jenny invited me after invitations were sent, I don't have their registration information. Luckily, with a quick text to Natalie, I have all I need to know at my fingertips, and I'm out the door.

The store the happy couple registered at is a few towns over. Upside, my chances of running into he who shall not be named is significantly lower. A wide smile blooms across my face as I merge onto the highway; today's going to be a good day, I can feel it.

I have my sunroof open, my windows down, and the

music cranked as I head toward my destination. Everything's going fine and dandy until I see flashing red and blue lights in my rearview. "Shoot, I hope everything's okay," I mutter as I pull off to the shoulder to let the cop car pass. Only, it pulls off right behind me. *What the...*

I pop on my flashers and gather up my license and registration while I wait. I know I wasn't speeding, at least not any more than five over.

The cop doesn't keep me waiting long, and I roll my window down upon his arrival. "Ma'am, do you know why I pulled you over today?"

I don't even have to look up to know who has pulled me over. *Duke. Freaking. Kincaid.* This can't be happening, truly. I have to be dreaming. I pinch my thigh to test the theory. "Ouch!"

"Ma'am, are you..." He lowers his aviators and looks down. "Oh, shit."

"Mmhmm, oh, shit." Duke stares at me for a few seconds, his eyes searing me like lasers over the rim of his sunglasses as he stands there unmoving, unspeaking, completely unwavering. Finally, I can't take the silence another moment longer. "So, you wanna tell me why you pulled me over, officer?"

Duke clears his throat. "You have a taillight out."

"Do I? Okay, well, I'll stop somewhere and replace it."

Duke leans down into my open window, crowding me... invading my space. "You'll replace it?" he asks, disbelief evident in his tone.

"Well, yeah. I would have already done it had I known. So...thanks?"

He shakes his head, biting down on the left corner of his lower lip. "No, I mean, *you'll* replace it, or you'll get someone to do it?"

My nose scrunches at his question. "Me. I'll do it. It's not like it's difficult."

An incredulous laugh slips past his lips. "You sure, Cricket?" Anger simmers in my veins. *This asshole just called me a freaking bug,* and *he's implying that he thinks I'm too helpless to do something as simple as swap out a taillight.* "I can recommend a good shop to do it for you." *I'm going to go to prison for murder.*

Done listening to his bullshit, I ask, "Do you need my license and registration or are we done here?"

"You don't want the name of the shop then?"

My fingers curl around the side of my seat, squeezing until my knuckles turn white. "Nope. Contrary to what you seem to believe, I'm no fucking damsel. Not only can I handle this all on my own, I can also change my own tire and my own oil. But thanks anyway. So, I'll ask you again, are we done here?"

Duke smirks, and I'm torn between wanting to claw his eyes out or wanting to draw his chiseled face to mine for a kiss. *Nope. Definitely the first.* I'm pretty sure there's an unwritten rule somewhere—girl code, sister code, you name it—that you don't think about kissing your sister's man. What in the hell is wrong with me? This man, somehow, has me tied in knots and thinking crazy.

"Guess we're done here," Duke says, taking a slight step away from my car. I'm about to roll up my window when he tacks on, "Be sure and get it fixed today; if it's out next time I see you, it'll be a ticket."

I raise two fingers to my forehead in a salute, leaving only the middle up as I draw them away. "Yes, sir, officer." It's probably my imagination playing dirty tricks on me, but I swear Duke groans under his breath when I call him sir. How strange.

———

The morning of the party, I'm a tangled-up mix of excitement and apprehension. Excited, because for the first time in my life, I feel like I've found my place in the world. I have a great place to call home, a good job, and a great group of people to call my friends. It's the *friends* part that astonishes me the most. For so long, I convinced myself that I was fine on my own…that I didn't need anyone. Then Ashley gave me a taste of friendship, and now, well—now my plate is full, and I couldn't be happier.

Which brings the apprehension. I guess, in a way, I'm still waiting for the other shoe to drop. What if they decide they don't like me? Or what if my weird tension with Duke causes issues? I worry this will all be taken from me and I'll end back at point zero; and now that I know what a full life feels like, that emptiness would quite possibly break me.

Dressed in a light floral maxi over my swimsuit, I grab my bag and my gift for the happy couple and hop in my car. Their party is actually a poolside get-together at Natalie's house, and I'm excited to try some of her and her husband's food. Here's to seeing if it's as good as the hype.

———

It's better…so much better, I think as I pop another sesame-ginger meatball into my mouth. I mean, how can a meatball be this freaking good? Honestly, the food Natalie and Alden prepared for this party could put a Michelin-starred restaurant to shame.

I've been laid back in one of the many pool loungers, snacking and mingling, for the last twenty minutes, discreetly scanning Natalie's well-appointed backyard for Duke, but so far, he's a no-show. A thread of worry works its way through me; I can't imagine him missing his best friend's engagement party. I hope I'm not the reason for his absence.

I've moved onto the pork dumplings when a shadow falls over me. Looking up, I see it's Nate. "Having a good time?" he asks, lowering himself to sit on the end of the lounger next to me.

My mouth is full, so I nod until I can speak. "Yeah, I am." I wrack my brain for something to say, finally settling on, "Congrats, by the way. On, you know, being engaged."

Amusement swims in Nate's eyes. "We've never really talked one-on-one."

I clear my throat a little. "Um, no. We haven't." Where on earth is he going with this?

He cranes his neck from side-to-side, scoping out the back-yard as if he's looking for something—or someone. After a few more passes, he seems satisfied. "About the other night, at dinner…"

I gulp. This can't be good. "What about it?" I ask, surprised at my level tone.

"Look, I'm gonna cut to the chase; Duke's got a lot on his plate. He's been stuck in this…limbo…for a long time. Most days are good, but some are harder than others. And he's been having a lot more hard days since seeing you. He tries to play it off like everything's fine, and to someone who doesn't know him like I do, it's believable. But he's been moodier, a little withdrawn."

My hackles rise. Is he seriously blaming me for Duke's surly ways? I'm ready to call him out, not caring one bit that this is his party or that in doing so I'll most likely lose the only friends I have outside of Ashley.

Nate must read my intent on my face, because he rushes to add, "I'm not saying it's your fault." I take a breath, waiting on him to explain further. "Well, not really. It's nothing you're doing, it's just…you. Honestly, I think you being here is good for him. It's forcing him to face a lot of things he just kind of shoved down deep when he lost Valorie. For so long he's been teetering on the brink of living, but most days he's just going through the motions. I…I think you could be the push he needs to really start living again. But, Mallory, be careful with him; don't hurt him."

I stare at Nate blankly, taking him in as I chew up and

digest his words. His handsome face is open and honest; the fool truly believes everything he just said.

"I think you have the wrong idea about the nature of mine and Duke's relationship; mainly believing that there is one. We're not even friends. We're two people who share a dead loved one. That's it." But even as I say it, it tastes like a lie, bitter on my tongue and difficult to swallow. A tiny, quiet, hidden part of my heart screams that he could be more.

Nate studies me, looking for the fib. Finally, he says, "I think you're wrong. Maybe you don't know it. Hell, maybe he doesn't either, but there's something there, tying the two of you together, and it's more than a common loss."

I shake my head in denial, though I'm not sure which of us I'm trying to convince more, me or him. "No. You're wrong."

"Nah, I don't think I am, Mal."

I suck in a sharp breath. Ashley is the only other person to ever call me by anything other than my name—my mother's insults notwithstanding—and hearing someone else do it stops me in my tracks. But Mal—it's a little too close to Val for my liking.

When I don't say anything back, he asks, "Is it okay to call you that?" This dude must be awesome at his job if he can read everyone as easily as he can me.

"It's...um..." I search for the right words. "Mally, call me Mally. It's what...my friends call me." I almost snort at my use of the word *friends*, though I guess it's not really a lie, not anymore.

Grinning, Nate nods. "Okay then." A warmth, *a very platonic warmth*, sparks in my chest; it feels weird, but nice all the same.

He's about to say something more when Jenny walks up, plopping herself down onto his lap. At first I worry she may be upset that Nate and I are talking alone, but instead of being angry, she smiles brightly. "Mallory! I'm so glad you're here!"

"Thanks for inviting me."

"Of course. Hopefully this guy's not boring you too terribly." She leans farther into Nate, nestling her head into the crook of his neck. He looks down at her, pure affection for her lighting his eyes. My God, what I wouldn't give to have someone look at me like that, for someone to love me so absolutely. But I already know love isn't in the cards for the likes of me. I've never been enough for anyone—not for my ex, not even for my parents.

Nate huffs. "As if I could ever bore anyone. C'mon, GG, you know better. Mally and I were having a heart-to-heart—"

"Oh, so y'all are on a nickname basis now, huh?" My worry that Jenny's upset with me returns tenfold but dissolves just as quickly when she shoots me an exaggerated wink.

"Hell yeah, we are. She said her friends call her Mally. Catch up, girl." The playfulness between Nate and Jenny warms me. Sadly, they're one of the only examples of a healthy relationship I've ever seen, which makes them the very definition of *couples' goals*. Too bad it's an unattainable goal.

"Okay then, cutie, catch me up on what you and Mally here were gossiping about."

"We were talking about Duke."

"Ohhh." Jenny grins. "Yeah, he wants you. Bad."

My face heats at her words. I part my lips to refute them, only instead of speaking, I somehow suck air down the wrong pipe, causing me to choke up a storm. As I hack up a lung, tears trail my cheeks and I wish a freaking hole would swallow me up to end this embarrassment.

To add insult to injury, Jenny leaps from Nate's lap and rushes to me, patting my back with enough force to shake loose my teeth. I shake my head rapidly in reply to her earlier statement and in an effort to get her to stop.

We must be making quite the spectacle, because Natalie and Alden both rush over. Natalie passes me a bottle of water, and with shaky hands, I uncap it and take a sip. The cool liquid soothes my coughing but not my humiliation. Literally every guest is staring at me like I'm the entertainment instead of a guest. *Seriously, a sinkhole would be really great right about now...*

I CAN'T BELIEVE I'm fucking late for Nate and Jenny's engagement party. But big surprise, Nancy had another meltdown. I figured now that Mallory was home, I could pass that particular baton to her, but nope. The burden still falls to me.

Don't get me wrong—I know Mallory and Nancy don't have the best relationship, but, *damn*, you'd think the girl could at least make an effort; I mean, it is her mother after all.

At least this time wasn't as bad as the last. She didn't wreck the house or try and hurt herself; today was her usual drink and reminisce. Which means not only am I late for the party, but I'm also in a shit mood after looking at every picture ever taken of Valorie. She was so damn beautiful and full of life, and now she's so damn gone. Too bad she took my heart to the grave with her.

When I finally make it to Alden's house, I'm half an hour late and in desperate need of good company, some great food, a cold drink, and a dip in the pool to unwind. Except, when I step out into the backyard, the first thing I see is Mallory reclined back on a lounge chair, like a fucking queen, surrounded by all of *my* people.

The sound of their laughter reaches me clear across the yard; it grates on my ears, making me clench my teeth. While

Mallory's been here laughing it up, without a care in the world, I've been taking care of her mother. *Ain't that some shit?*

I grit my teeth, steel my resolve, and make my way over toward where they're gathered. As I approach, I hear my name slip past Mallory's luscious lips, asking where I am. The hell is she asking about me for? And why the fuck am I noticing how tempting her lips look?

Nate glances down at his watch. "I haven't heard from him. Let me shoot him a text."

"No need," I say, announcing my presence.

Like it was choreographed, they all turn to look at me simultaneously. "Where've you been?" Nate asks.

I cut my eyes over to Mallory. "Nancy." Neither Alden or his wife react to my single word reply, but Nate and Jenny both nod knowingly.

Mallory, on the other hand, scrunches her nose and shoots a questioning glance my way. "Why—" she starts to ask, but I turn and stalk away toward the cooler. My patience with her is a frayed thread on the verge of snapping altogether at this point.

Not shockingly, Nate follows, hot on my heels. "Everything okay?"

I tip my chin. "About like always." Leaning down, I grab a frosty beer from the cooler, using the ledge of the food table to pop the top. I bring the bottle to my lips and tilt it back, relishing the feel of the cool liquid. I'm not much of a drinker, but sometimes—especially after dealing with Nancy—it's nice to take the edge off.

Nate allows me a good three sips before he starts in on me. "Listen. What's up with you and Mally?"

"Mally, huh?" I pop a brow at him, trying to mask my annoyance. "It's like that?"

"Yeah, man, it is. The girls really like her. The only holdout is you. It's obviously more than you being surprised to see her. So, what gives? What is it about this girl that gets you so riled up?"

I polish off the rest of the bottle and scrub a hand over my face, trying to buy myself some time.

"She…makes me…*feel*." The words pass my lips in a low mumble. Somehow, my admission makes me feel both lighter and more weighted than ever, all at once.

I'm expecting him to laugh or to dog me out, but I should've known better. Serious-relationship-Nate is far more mature than the man-child-player he was a few years ago when we met. "You ever think that maybe the two of y'all should sit down and talk?"

I glance over his shoulder, toward Mallory, just in time to see her step out of the long dress she was wearing, giving way to what has to be the smallest bikini of all time. Two teal-colored triangles conceal her breasts—just barely—and the measly bottom is supported by nothing more than two thin strings tied at her hips.

The sight of all of her smooth, bronzed skin on display has my mouth feeling like it's full of cotton, and as shameful as it is, the only sitting I want to do with her right now involves her on my face, and the only talking I want to hear is her screaming my name as she comes.

Nate follows my line of sight and smirks. He may be my best friend and partner, but damn if I don't want to knock that smarmy-ass look right off his face. And when he opens his mouth, the feeling intensifies. "It's okay to—"

I shoot him a withering glare before stomping off toward Mallory.

I don't stop until I'm close enough to feel the heat of her body. She has to tilt her head back to see me, and when our eyes meet, my name topples from her lips on a breathy sigh. "We need to talk." My tone is all business—my cop voice, as Nate calls it—as I wrap my fingers around her forearm, prepared to drag her along behind me if necessary. Luckily, she comes all too willingly—*so why am I still holding on to her?*

The feeling of her soft, sun-warmed skin beneath my palm sends little zaps of electricity under my skin, into my muscle. Her nearness has me strung taut like a drawn bow. *Here's to hoping like hell I don't snap.*

Deep down, like really fucking deep, I know I'm acting like a colossal asshole, but much like a prepubescent boy picking on his schoolyard crush, it's the only way I know how to deal with all of the conflicting feelings she stirs in me.

By the time I navigate us through the back door, down the hall, and into Alden's laundry room, my grip has somehow slipped, and I find my fingers are gently cradling hers. *What in the hell? I haven't held a woman's hand since…*I shake off the thought as well as her hand, taking a step away from her so that she's positioned with her back to the washer and mine to the door.

Even with a solid three feet separating us, my skin hums at the memory of Mallory's hand in mine. What is it about this woman that elicits such a physical reaction from me? My fingers itch to explore the rest of her skin; my body begs to know what the rest of her would feel like. Would she be soft and sweet beneath me, our bodies moving in complete harmony together? Or would she be a little hellcat, wild and untamable, determined to be in control?

An uneasy silence settles over us as we stare one another down, Mallory's eyes narrowed on mine while I fight to keep my gaze from dropping down to rove over her exposed skin. After a few tense moments, Mallory speaks, her words short and punctuated with frustration. "Is there any particular reason you brought me back here?"

My original plan was to confront her about Nancy, regardless of this being neither the time nor the place. However, after seeing her swimsuit, my plans changed. "Yeah, I wanna know why you're prancing around all of my friends half-naked."

She scoffs. "You've got to freaking be kidding me."

I make a big show of running my eyes all over her body, my gaze unwillingly lingering on her breasts and the sweet little dip in her waist. The longer I stare, the more I notice the subtle differences between her and her sister. Where Val was all long lines and lean muscles, Mallory's lush, with curves in all the right places. "Not even remotely."

"It's a swimsuit, Duke. Surely you've seen one before."

"I've seen fucking strippers wearing more than you are."

Her eyes spark with humor. "Strippers, huh? Gotta thing for paying for it?"

Her mouth—swear to God. "That'd be a prostitute, not a stripper, Cricket."

She snorts out a laugh, which only serves to frustrate me all the more. "Guess you'd know, huh?"

I take a step toward her. "You are the single most frustrating woman I've ever met."

She drops her cheek to her shoulder. "Takes one to know one," she murmurs before sticking her tongue out at me. In this moment, she looks so young, so sweet, so…mine.

Before I can think it through, I'm on her, crowding her small body with my much larger one, forcing her up against the washing machine as I capture the tip of her tongue between my lips, sucking gently before shoving back away from her.

An animalistic roar bursts forth from my lips as I pace, my hands tugging on the ends of my hair. Mallory Parsons is clearly a witch, and she's cast a spell on me; sure, it sounds crazy—*I sound crazy*—but I can't think of a single plausible reason for my inexplicable behavior.

"What on earth is wrong with you?" Mallory whisper-screams, her voice tight with anger. "One second you're looking at me like I'm a bug you want to squash, and the next you're kissing me! You're…you're freaking mental."

I'm not sure what kind of response she's expecting, but I know a half-hearted shrug isn't it. Too bad it's all I have to offer, because she truly does make me feel like I'm losing my ever-loving mind. "I don't know what you want me to say."

"I want you to explain why you've been acting like a goddang lunatic."

Against my better judgment, I find myself right back in her space, my hands tangling in her hair and my mouth hovering over hers. "Because of you." I press my lips to hers, not in passion but anger. *How dare she make me feel this out of control.* I nip at her bottom lip, and the sexiest damn sound I've ever heard slips from her mouth to mine before her hands fly to my chest and she pushes me away.

"You make me fucking crazy!" I roar without a single thought to our surroundings or who could overhear. "Every time I see you, I…FUCK!" I resume my pacing, feeling like a caged lion.

"I what?" Mallory asks, her voice soft, timid, and my eyes cut to her. She has a bewildered look on her face, with her eyes flared wide and her lips slightly parted. Her hands tremble as she wraps her arms around herself, gooseflesh covering her exposed skin. She looks like terrified perfection —and I can't help but want to wrap her in my arms and shelter her—from me.

Expecting her to lay into me, I brace for impact. Only instead of chewing me up one side and down the other, she shocks the shit out of me by demanding I give her my phone. Too confused to argue, I pass it to her. She taps around for a few seconds before handing it back to me. "Call me when you pull your head out of your ass; obviously we have a lot to talk about."

Stunned, I watch as she maneuvers past me, her lithe body

brushing against my rigid one, completely unaware of her effect on me. Well, maybe not completely unaware; after all, my dumb ass did just kiss her twice.

MEET THE TEACHER IS TONIGHT, and while I'm crazy excited to meet the little angels in my class, thoughts of Duke steal my excitement, leaving me feeling…well, just plain crazy. How is it that the one person on this planet who couldn't possibly be more wrong for me is the one that has my insides twisted up like a rubber band ball? Somehow, he takes my feelings—both good and bad—and stretches them, pulling and tugging until I reach my breaking point, only instead of absorbing the emotions he pulls from me, he always steps back at the last second, leaving them to snap back into me.

In the week and a half since my laundry room run-in with Duke, the two quasi-kisses we shared have been looping in my mind—pathetic, I know. Truly, it's unhealthy how often I find myself thinking about the way he gently sucked on the tip of my tongue, the way he tugged at my hair, the way he nipped at my lower lip. Lord knows, kissing my ex was like kissing a fish—*open, close; open, close*. Duke though, with just those two small, barely anything kisses, managed to raise the bar so high I doubt any other man will ever reach it.

Which really pisses me off. I mean, how unfair is that my first *good* kiss is from him…the love of my sister's life? And just like every time that little reminder crosses my mind, my lusty thoughts evaporate into a swirl of shame and disgust. Maybe I am as awful as my mother says—I mean, what kind of good and decent person has the kind of feelings I'm having?

Worse than all of that, though, is the fact that I gave him my number and I haven't heard from him. Not a text, not a call, heck…not even a butt-dial. Whether he likes it or not, though, we're going to have to clear the air, because I'm not willing to give up the only friends I've ever had because of some inane issue he has with me.

The sound of voices echoes from the hall, alerting me to the fact that parents and students are about to start trickling in. I take a quick glance around my classroom, making sure everything is ready—from the students' desks adorned with a personalized bookmark and cupcake to the reading nook in the corner filled with every kind of story a kid could ask for.

As footsteps and voices draw nearer, I position myself near the classroom door. As the families begin to trickle in, I introduce myself and direct the parents to sign-in on the clipboard. I have signs up all around the room, directing them where to stash the supplies they brought along with them.

I'm in the middle of discussing the ins and outs of afternoon pickup when I hear a loud, excited squeal. Before I can source the sound, two pint-sized arms are wrapped around my legs, hugging me. "Ms. Mally! Are you my teacher? Please say yes! This is the best day ever!"

I smile down at the tiny little tornado and her use of my nickname. The second she heard her mom and Jenny call me that at lunch the other day, all bets were off. "Sure am, Tatum. We're gonna have a lot of fun this year!"

She bounces on her toes, still holding me. The sensation makes me jiggle, but her enthusiasm is catching, and I quickly find myself bouncing right back as I shoot the parent I was speaking with an apologetic smile. Luckily, they seem to find her antics as cute as I do.

A second later, a frazzled Natalie bursts through the door with Alden hot on her heels. "Tatum! You cannot just run off!"

The precocious little girl rolls her eyes. "I didn't run off Mama; I ran to Ms. Mally."

"You'll have to call her Ms. Parsons during class," Alden tells her, at the same time his wife says, "I am so sorry—"

I wave a hand in the air, dismissing her apology before taking a knee so I'm eye-level with Tatum. "I love that you're so excited for big school. I'm just as excited to be your teacher. But you can't run away from your mom and dad, okay?"

Tatum mulls over my words, weighing the pros and cons before finally nodding. "Okay. I won't run off again. Unless I'm really super, *extra* excited."

I arch a brow. "Nope, not even then." Her button nose scrunches in displeasure, but she ultimately agrees.

I direct Tatum to her desk, and she grabs her dad's hand and beelines to it. Natalie, however, stays behind. "We've been really nervous for kindergarten, but you being her teacher really lessens that worry."

"It was definitely a pleasant surprise to see her name on my roster. I would've told you, but we're not allowed to."

Natalie smiles. "No worries. So…have you heard from Duke lately?"

I study her face, searching out her intentions. "Nope."

She tilts her head to the side. "Hmm. Give him time."

Time for what? I think without giving voice to it. Instead, I change the subject, diverting Natalie's attention to my Kids are the Future station, where I have postcards for each child to fill out with their name, age, and what they want to be when they grow up, with plans to repeat the activity at the end of the year and compare their replies.

The rest of the evening passes quickly as I chat with parents and students alike, and by the time I flip the lights off and close my door, I'm so excited for the first day of school that even thoughts of a certain hot, broody cop can't dampen my mood.

———

Apparently, it seems I spoke too soon, because when I get home and check my phone, there's a text from an unknown number waiting for me.

UNKNOWN

When can we meet?

I know it's Duke, and my stomach churns. I don't know if it's anticipation, anger, or nerves that has me so keyed up— probably a little of all three. He kissed me—twice—and then has the balls to wait ten days before contacting me. *Seriously, who freaking does that?* Duke Kincaid, that's who. Quickly, I save his number and reply.

Me

Did you get an enema?

Duke

...the fuck?

ME

I'm just saying. Your head was pretty far up there. I figure you had to have help dislodging it.

DUKE

Ha ha, you're a real riot, Cricket.

ME

And you're a real charmer, calling me an insect.

DUKE

Well, you do *bug* me.

ME

Who's the comedian now? Oh, wait, no, not you.

DUKE

I swear to God, you make me crazy.

ME

HA! You're one to talk, Mr. Hot and Cold. How you can go from semi-normal to a raging dick in the blink of an eye is beyond me.

DUKE

All I'm hearing is I'm hot and you think about my dick.

I almost drop my phone after I read his last text—but really, he's only proving my point that he's unhinged. I mean, who says that kind of shit to someone they hardly know? While he's not unsolicited-dick-pic bad, his texting etiquette leaves much to be desired. I'm in the middle of tapping out a text, tearing him a new one when an incoming message pings through.

DUKE

JFC, ignore that last text. Nate took my phone. Jackass.

ME

A likely story—or maybe your true colors are shining through.

ME

And by true colors, I mean, your CRAZY is showing.

DUKE

You know what, never mind.

I sigh, knowing I'm going to have to be the bigger person, because while Officer Kincaid can dish it, he certainly can't take it.

ME

Okay, okay. I'm sorry. I'm free all week and this weekend, just let me know when and where.

DUKE

Saturday, my place, noon.

ME

Uh…your place?

DUKE

Yes, Mallory. My place. I'll text you the address.

I know sometimes tone can get lost in a text, but his annoyance is coming through loud and clear. The thought of going to his house kind of terrifies me. But walking into the lion's den is a small price to pay for us to try to clear the air.

AS PROMISED, Duke sent me his address this morning. Now, here I am, idling in his driveway, trying to convince myself that this isn't a bad idea, that everything's going to be okay, that it's totally logical to meet here, where we'll be secluded and alone.

From the safety of my car, I take in his house. It's so different from what I imagined that I'm kind of speechless. In my mind, Duke lived in some kind of ultra-modern bachelor pad. In reality, he lives in a charming modern farmhouse. Painted white brick at the base gives way to wide planks of the same hue. The window frames and gutters are black, creating a pop of visual interest. The house also has a large brick paver-style porch that wraps around the left side of the house. The front door is a gorgeous mahogany color with a large transom window.

All too easily, a picture forms in my mind of Duke and me relaxing in oversized rockers, sipping on sweet tea while our children play in the generously sized front yard. *What the heck? Where did that come from?*

I try my best to shake off the weird thoughts filtering through my brain. Several deep breaths and a pep talk later, I exit my car and head up the little paver path toward the front door. The whole way there, I can't help but feel like agreeing to meet him here might just be the beginning of the end. The only question is, will it be a happy ending or one of those messed-up ones that leaves everyone feeling displaced and disgruntled?

I ring the bell and wait—impatiently. I'm more than ready to get this show on the road. After a few seconds pass and he doesn't come to the door, I ring it again. Still, no answer. *I swear to God, if he had me come out here just so he could stand me up, I'm gonna freaking scream, and then I'm going to hunt him down and kill him.* It doesn't escape my notice that a lot of my thoughts about Duke center around his fictitious demise—when I'm not lusting after him that is. I'm also astutely aware that it's beyond morbid to even joke—internally—about killing my dead sister's boyfriend. Clearly, I have issues.

I give the bell one last ring, punctuating it with two sharp knocks. Finally, the door swings open, revealing Duke dressed in only a pair of low-slung jeans with the button undone. He looks as though he's cut from stone, and my eyes greedily eat him up, feasting on the way his ink-adorned skin stretches taut over his corded muscles. His hair is damp and pushed back from his face, and little rivulets of water drip from the end of his hair and streak down his chest. The urge to follow one with my tongue hits out of nowhere. My thighs clench involuntarily, and heat pools low in my belly as I fantasize how his warm skin would taste.

Duke clears his throat, halting my slow perusal. My eyes fly up from his defined pecs to his eyes; they glint with an almost feral sort of amusement, like he can't decide if he wants to pounce or play. My traitorous libido pulses with want, telling me she'd be down with either.

"Are you gonna invite me in? And if so, put on a god-dang shirt."

He smirks. "Whatever for? Surely a little bit of skin

doesn't bother you? I mean, a swimsuit would show more, right?"

My lust transforms to indignation. "Are you freaking kidding me right now?"

Duke steps back and opens the door wider, making room for me to pass. "Not at all. It's just a little skin, right, *Mally?*"

My fists clench at my sides. "Don't call me that. Only friends call me that."

His stupid smirk widens. "You wound me."

Ignoring him, I march right past his arrogant ass and into the house, only to draw up short. "How long have you lived here?"

Duke closes the door and steps up behind me. "Bought it shortly after—" He doesn't finish the sentence, but I know how it ends; he bought this place after my sister died. Meaning he's called this place home for almost two years, and yet the space is so bare it looks completely unlived in.

His living room consists of a threadbare couch, an over-turned pallet turned coffee table, and two mismatched, sagging armchairs. Oh, and there's a massive seventy-five-inch flat-screen mounted on the wall.

Why on earth would he invite me here? Why would he live like this? A million questions swirl through my mind, but I refuse to give voice to any of them; he already seemingly resents me and I don't want to make it worse.

He unceremoniously drops down onto the couch, his broad chest still very much on display. I head for one of the chairs but he pats the cushion next to him. Against my better judgment, I claim the seat next to him. The cushion sags, angling me close enough that I can feel the heat from his skin. "Bet you've got a lot of questions, huh?"

I laugh through my nose. "I can definitely think of a few."

Duke nods. "Then let's play a game. A question for a question. You only get one free pass, so use it wisely."

My eyes widen at his proposal. "You're being serious?"

"As a heart attack."

"Okay. I guess you can go first," I tell him, that way he can set the tone of this little game we're playing.

———

DUKE

If Mallory thought she'd ruffle my feathers by asking me to go first, she's sorely mistaken. We both have questions, and I'm damn ready to get some answers. I know if I start strong right out of the gate she'll clam up, so I begin with something small, slow, and easy.

"What's your favorite color?"

She eyes me dubiously. "Teal." I'm expecting her to ask something similarly mundane, but as it turns out, Mallory's not pulling any punches. "Why don't you have real furniture?"

I twist my head from side-to-side, cracking my neck. "I do. It's..." I hesitate, unsure if I want to share so much of myself with her. She eyes me expectantly, and I decide to just roll with it. "It's in storage. Val and I bought it together for the house we were going to buy back in Orchard Grove."

Mallory stares at me intently, her expression giving nothing away. "Your turn." Even her voice is carefully neutral.

I decide to stick to my original plan of light and easy. "What made you want to be a teacher?"

Unconsciously, she rakes her fingers over her thighs, drawing my attention to the fact that she's wearing a pair of slick galaxy-print leggings that cling to her like a second skin. My eyes then move to her shirt, a flowy black tank that reads 'So long, and *thanks for all the fish*' with a pod of dolphins leaping through space above planet earth. *She really is an odd girl.*

"Um. I wanted to be able to offer light to kids stuck in darkness. Kids with bad home lives, kids who are bullied and misunderstood. I just...wanted to be able to...I thought if I could help at least one kid, make one of their lives better, then my pain would've been worth it."

My initial reaction is to brush her off. What in the hell does Mallory Parsons know about pain? So what if she and her mom don't get along...ninety-nine percent of teenage girls and their mothers don't. The only difference is most people fucking grow up at some point. Not Mallory, though. Here she is, over twenty-five and still mad at her mommy for God knows what. Don't get me wrong, Nancy's a piece of work, but what mother wouldn't be after losing a child? I'm about to call her on her bullshit, but when I see her eyes are glassy with unshed tears, I bite back the words. Instead, I grunt out an unintelligible response, gesturing for her to take her turn.

"Did you and Val live together?"

Jesus. She's not messing around. It's like she has a direct line to my unresolved issues and is picking at them one by one. I give a terse shake of my head. "No. She wanted us to at least be engaged first. I had an offer in on our dream house and had planned to..." I let my words fall away as the pain of losing her consumes me.

I'm sucked back out of my misery just as quickly when Mallory mutters, "She was right."

"I'm sorry, what? Who was right?"

Sweat beads her hairline, and her breaths are shallow but rapid. She's hiding something.

"Who was right?" I ask again, leaning forward, crowding her space just a little.

She shakes her head. "No, I, um...no one. I-it's nothing."

"It's obviously something, Mallory. Tell me. Who. Was. Right?"

"Pass," she whispers, her voice rough with some kind of emotion. Judging from the inward curl of her shoulders and her refusal to meet my eyes, I'd say guilt. The question is, what is she guilty of?

"Just remember, you only get one pass and you just used yours all up." Which suits me just fine, because now I can get down to the nitty-gritty and there's not shit she can do about it. "Take your turn, Mallory."

"Why did you kiss me?"

There are a million different lines of bullshit I could feed her. I could say she reminds me of her sister, but I won't because it's a damn lie. Sure, when I first saw her, all I noticed were the similarities, but over the course of our run-ins, I started seeing all of the differences, too. And I don't just mean in the way she acts. Their shape is different; Mallory is all curves while Val was straight lines. While they're both blonde, Mallory's hair is a darker shade. And their eyes... Val's were a deep, dark chocolate, whereas Mallory's are specked with gold and caramel.

I could tell her it was simply to shut her up, but that'd also be a lie. The truth of the matter is, I kissed her because she is, hands down, the single most frustrating and fascinating woman I've ever met. So, I settle with something close to the truth. "Because I wanted to."

She scoffs. "You wanted to? Riiiight. And that's why you acted like I'd done something to personally offend you after *both* times and then proceeded to ignore me for the rest of the party, and the next ten days. Sure, Duke, that makes complete and total—"

Before I can stop myself, my lips are on hers again. While our last two kisses were fairly benign, this one's ravenous and wild—a violent clash of lips, tongue, and teeth as we both release our pent-up anger and desire, letting it engulf us.

I haul her from her spot on the couch onto my lap, and she instantly bears down on me, both of us moaning at the sensation of the seam of my jeans lining up perfectly with the apex of her thighs. Unable to relinquish control to her, I palm her hips to guide her movements, but like the little minx she is, she fights me, determined to set her own pace.

That just doesn't work for me. I flip her onto her back, settling myself between her thighs. She claws at my chest—in passion, not protest—as I thrust my denim-covered erection against her. The pain of her nails digging into my skin is gasoline on the fire that is us, but I'm not ready to combust just yet. I press against her again and drop my lips to her neck, distracting her just enough to pin her wrists above her head, leaving her breathless and at my mercy. Too bad I'm not feeling particularly merciful.

She jerks her arms against my hold, but the way she wiggles her pelvis against mine tells me she doesn't want me to let go, not really. I capture her lips in a bruising kiss, and when she parts them, I suck her tongue into my mouth, relishing the taste of her.

"Oh, God, Duke," she pants, her voice wanton and pleading.

"Tell me what you need, Cricket."

She bucks against me. "More."

I trail kisses from her lips down the right side of her jaw and neck, stopping at her collarbone. "More what?" I ask before nipping at the protruding bone.

A soft, needy moan passes her lips at the feel of my teeth marring her flawless skin, and she wraps her legs around my waist, holding me to her. "More of you."

All too eager to please, I kiss and nip my way across her chest, giving her other collarbone the same treatment before sliding my free hand beneath the fabric of her shirt to tweak her left nipple. "Yesss," she hisses. "More. I need more."

That makes two of us, I think as I draw back, releasing my hold on her wrists. "Lose the shirt," I command. Mallory sits up and strips it off, baring her braless tits to me.

Like a man possessed, I dive for them, drawing the tight bud into my mouth. I lavish her breasts with attention, and all the while she runs her hands all through my hair, over my chest, shoulders, back, and abs—anywhere she can reach. Her fingers burn a trail, and I fucking love it.

This is the most alive I've felt since Valorie's death.

And just like that, my desire, my need, my aching want for Mallory, withers under the memory of who she is—of how wrong these feelings simmering between the two of us really are. I mean, how fucked up is it for me to even entertain the idea of *more* with my dead girlfriend's twin sister? Pretty sure that makes me the lowest of low. Being with her, in any capacity more than friends, is plain wrong…but goddamn it feels right, and that makes me sick to my stomach with guilt.

What would Val think about this? How would it make her feel to know that her sister's touch sets me on fire or that at night, when I can't sleep, instead of counting sheep, it's visions of Mallory playing behind my closed lids?

Do I think she'd want me to find happiness without her? *Absolutely.*

With her fucking sister? *Hell-fucking-no.*

I jump up from the couch and grab her shirt, tossing it her way. "Get dressed."

She blinks up at me, chest still heaving and her lips swollen from my kisses. "What?"

"You heard me. Get dressed."

I turn away from her, giving her my back while she rights herself. "You really are an asshole, Duke Kincaid." Her voice is hoarse, like she's trying not to cry. I feel like a dog, but I know I have to put a stop to this before we go too far. Were it not for that terrible day, she'd be my sister-in-law, for God's sake. How fucked up is that? That the one woman I want is the one woman I absolutely can't have.

I shrug, trying to act unaffected. But when I turn to face her, the sight of her tear-dampened cheeks is too much for me to take. "Just fucking leave. Go home," I mutter before stalking out of the room.

I asked her here for answers, and instead I find myself with balls so blue they're purple and more questions than ever.

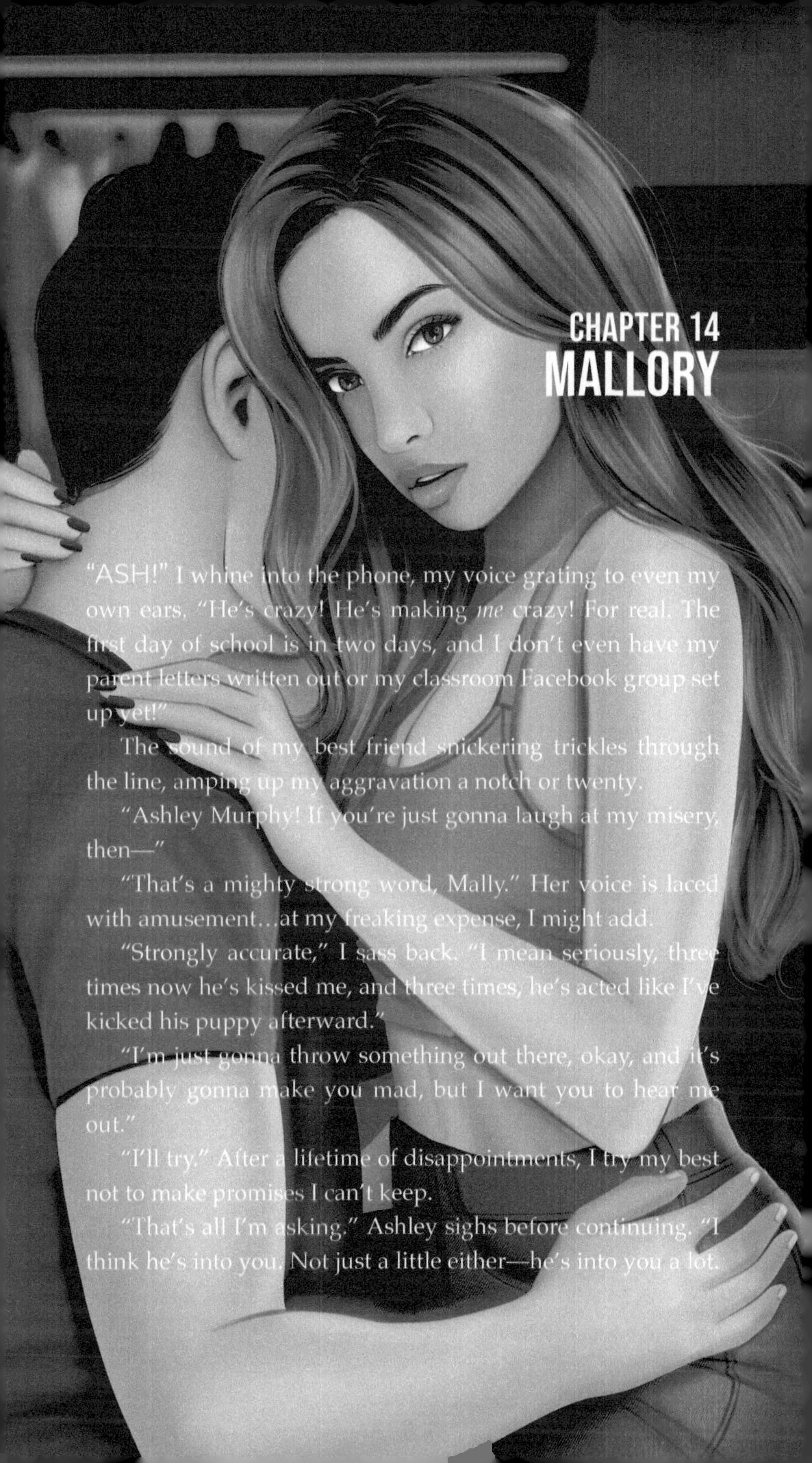

"ASH!" I whine into the phone, my voice grating to even my own ears. "He's crazy! He's making *me* crazy! For real. The first day of school is in two days, and I don't even have my parent letters written out or my classroom Facebook group set up yet!"

The sound of my best friend snickering trickles through the line, amping up my aggravation a notch or twenty.

"Ashley Murphy! If you're just gonna laugh at my misery, then—"

"That's a mighty strong word, Mally." Her voice is laced with amusement…at my freaking expense, I might add.

"Strongly accurate," I sass back. "I mean seriously, three times now he's kissed me, and three times, he's acted like I've kicked his puppy afterward."

"I'm just gonna throw something out there, okay, and it's probably gonna make you mad, but I want you to hear me out."

"I'll try." After a lifetime of disappointments, I try my best not to make promises I can't keep.

"That's all I'm asking." Ashley sighs before continuing. "I think he's into you. Not just a little either—he's into you a lot.

And I don't mean you as Valorie's twin; he has feelings for *you*, Mallory, and it scares him shitless."

"Riiiight, okay." I try to brush her words off, but they push beneath my skin like porcupine quills, the barbs burrowing into me.

"You can only treat your feelings like a joke for so long before you have to own them."

"You're wrong."

"I'm not; you know I'm not. Furthermore, his feelings aren't one-sided. You want him every bit as much as he wants you. Only, you think it's wrong, so you feel guilty and that guilt—which I can guarantee he's feeling as well—is practically drowning the two of you, causing you both to lash out. Y'all need to talk it out. Not fight. Not bicker. Not make out. But T-A-L-K talk. Do you hear me?"

I roll my eyes even though she can't see me. "I hear you."

"Good. And, Mally, I'm gonna follow up on this, so you better make an effort. Now, go write your letters and make your group. You're gonna be the best kindergarten teacher Bay Ridge Elementary has ever seen!"

"Yeah, yeah. Love you big."

"Love you bigger," she replies before ending the call.

———

The first week of school passes in a blur of ABCs, 123s, shapes, and colors. I'm pleasantly surprised by the lack of tears from my kindergarteners.

These little humans are so incredibly brave; I know on my first day of school, I bawled my eyes out. Though, that could've had a lot to do with my parents walking Valorie to class the entire first week while leaving me to fend for myself.

Heck, I even had to make my own lunch because my mother neglected to load any money into my lunch account. Even at five, I knew that wasn't right. I also knew better than to question it, so when the lunch lady questioned me on it, I laughed it off and fibbed about forgetting that I was actually a lunchbox that day.

In hindsight, I don't think she believed me, but she never said anything, seeing as every day after I came to the cafeteria with a brown paper bag in hand, even if it only had an apple and string-cheese inside of it.

I'm also blown away by how bright the kids in my classroom are—especially Tatum. That little girl is next-level smart—not that I'd ever show her favoritism.

It's six o'clock on Friday night, and instead of being out celebrating the first week of a new school year in the books, I'm home binging *Hart of Dixie* and working on my lesson plans for the coming month. If I were still in Cottonwood, Ashley would've made me go out to celebrate. And it's not that I was averse to going out tonight, but Jenny and Nate are having a date night, Natalie and Alden are catering an event, and Duke…well, who the hell knows what he's up to—probably staring at a voodoo doll crafted in my likeness as he contemplates new ways to aggravate me.

Regardless of what he's up to, everyone is busy tonight, leaving me to fly solo. I guess it's a good thing I'm pretty used to being alone.

I'm re-upping my snack supply between episodes when I hear my phone trill in the other room. It's probably Ashley texting me pics of whatever poor sap she has her sights set on tonight. God love her, she's determined to find Mr. Right, even if it means working her way through a thousand Mr. Wrongs. Fro-yo pop in hand, I meander back into the living room, ready to start the next episode. As I'm settling back into my spot on the couch, my phone sounds again, reminding me of the unread message.

I wolf down the mint chocolate chip goodness, licking the stick clean, and snag my phone from where I left it on the coffee table. I tap the screen a few times, navigating to my texts, only to drop the phone onto my lap when I see it's actually Duke and not Ashley.

DUKE

8:00, The Gilded Goat. Be there.

I read the message twice, just to make sure my eyes aren't playing tricks on me. Why on earth would he want to meet up? Also, who does he think he is, telling me where to be and when? I'm about to reply when another text comes through.

DUKE

We need to talk. For real this time. Please?

It's the please that does me in, because Duke Kincaid doesn't seem like the kind of man to plead for anything.

ME

Yeah, sure. See you soon.

As I back out of my text screen, the time catches my eye. It's already almost seven, and I'm dressed in jammies with my hair up and a mask on my face. Lord Jesus, I've got to get dressed—and fast.

I peel off my mask, moisturize, and apply some makeup, focusing on a subtle smoky eye and a bold fuchsia lip—battle armor, if you will. After releasing my bun, I give my hair a quick tousle, shimmy into a pair of distressed jean shorts and a black Johnny Cash shirt. A pair of Doc Martens later, I'm out the door.

The Gilded Goat is actually located in the next town over, but with my handy-dandy GPS, it's easy to find. The parking lot is packed to the brim, with some cars even parked on the curb. I guess that's not necessarily a bad thing though; the more people we're around, the less likely we are to end up mauling each other again.

I'm out of the car and approaching the entrance before I can give myself time to rethink it. Swinging open the metallic gold door, I scan the ridiculously crowded space for Duke. Shockingly, I find him in a matter of seconds, as if my eyes somehow already knew where to look. Just as strange is that he was already looking my way, and the intensity of his gaze, full of dark promises, steals my breath, heats my core, and almost crumbles my resolve.

Straightening to my full height—a whopping five-foot-seven—I flip my hair and stalk his way. I radiate a confidence I don't truly feel through my stance, face, and body. As long as I keep up the façade, I should be fine. There's no need for him to know that with one glance I'm imagining the scrape of his five o'clock shadow or the way his kisses drown everything but the way he makes me feel. Nope, no reason at all. Because regardless of what Ashley and the others say, there's no way in hell this man wants me the way I want him.

I NEVER TRULY UNDERSTOOD THE saying *'stuck between a rock and a hard place'* until now. Countless times over the last week, I've warred with myself over whether or not I should reach out to Mallory to try to settle our differences. I'm torn between burying the hatchet and clinging to my resentment—God knows, resentment is easier to stomach than the other feelings she stirs in me. But when I think about the way her eyes get all soft whenever she looks at me, combined with the way my entire body feels electric when she's near, makes it hard to ignore.

I don't know why I asked her to meet me here.

Okay, that's a lie. I do. The only problem is, I'm lying about the reason. How can I expect us to have an honest conversation when I can't even be straight with myself?

Mallory knows my every button to push and damn if she doesn't seem to actually enjoy pushing them. With one look, she can have me hard as steel or pissed as hell and ready to go toe-to-toe with her. And don't even get me started on her smart mouth. She's under my skin, and I don't want her there.

At least this time I was smart enough to ask her to meet

somewhere public. Then again, I also asked her out to a bar, so maybe I'm still an idiot. Only time will tell.

I made sure to get here early, mostly because if I was already here, I'd be less likely to back out. I've been chilling at the bar, nursing the same drink, for about forty-five minutes when the entire atmosphere of the room suddenly changes—for me at least.

My gaze swings to the door, and sure enough, there she is, looking like every dark desire I've ever had as she scans the space for me. Her golden-hued gaze finds me with alarming speed and accuracy, and for a minute, we simply drink each other in.

Fifteen seconds of looking at her in those tight little shorts hits me harder than any drink ever could. She may not know it, but Mallory Parsons is the walking definition of sex appeal. Hell, the fact that she's clueless to the way she affects most men only serves to make her hotter.

Valorie, on the other hand, knew she was a looker, and many-a-times used it to her advantage. Be it charming a male teacher when she forgot to do her homework, a free latte at Starbucks, or getting a discount on her oil change, the girl knew how to wield her looks like a weapon. Until this very moment, I never realized just how much Val using her looks like that bothered me. *Huh.*

Unsure of what to do with that revelation, I tuck it away to dissect when I'm alone.

I track Mallory as she walks toward me, the crowd parting as she moves through it. She looks like a warrior princess, her hair all wild and her lips painted pink. For a flash, I imagine that bright shade ringed around my dick, but just as quickly, I shake it away. Now's not the time for thoughts like that—hell, is any time the right time for sexual thoughts of your dead girl's sister?

She hoists herself up onto the stool next to me, and the bartender rushes over to take her order. She goes for a rum and Coke. I tip my bottle toward him, letting him know I'd like another beer. We sit in silence, absorbing the noises of the bar while we wait for our drinks. When the bartender returns, Mallory tries to pay him, but I swat her hand away and tell him to put it on my tab.

"I asked you here. I'm paying."

"That makes it feel date-ish." Her eyes widen and her cheeks pinken, making me wonder if she wishes this were a date.

"It's just me being a gentleman."

Mallory giggles. "Never pegged you as gentle."

My pulse thrums. As wrong as it is, I'd love to show her just how rough I am.

Seeming to realize what she said, she rushes to add, "Not like that! I just mean…like you're so big and strong and broody, and you have this whole tatted-up bad boy vibe going for you and—oh my God, I'm just making it worse. Please ignore everything I just said."

I bring my drink to my lips, taking a slow sip to let her sweat it out a little. "Nah. There's no way I can forget that, Cricket." I wink at her and she scowls. I'm sure she means to look threatening, but really, she looks cute as hell. I guess glaring, golden-eyed dark-blondes just do it for me. The thought makes me cringe, because not that long ago, the only girl to really rev my engine was a certain brown-eyed, pale-haired one. *Fuck.*

Somehow, the more time I spend around Mallory—even if we're not directly interacting—the more I find myself inexplicably drawn to her. She just has this goodness about her, this light that shines like a beacon, calling to my darkness. Ever since Val's death, I've been like a sailor stranded in a tumultuous sea, and Mallory…she's the lighthouse guiding me home.

After a beat, she says, "So, you wanted to talk? Let's talk."

I pick at the label on my beer bottle. "Where do we even start?"

"How about with what exactly your issue is with me." Her words are blunt and to the point, catching me completely off guard. It seems as though the gloves have come off for this round.

I scrape a hand over my scruff. "You want me to be honest? I'm talking no sugar-coating, no bullshit or half-truths honest?"

Mallory nods. "Always."

"You left. The second you had your diploma, you hauled ass out of Orchard Grove and never looked back. You couldn't even be bothered to show up for her goddamn funeral. What kind of person does that?"

Mallory's eyes glisten, and her throat works as she swallows. "You…you don't understand. My parents…"

I wave a dismissive hand in the air. "Yeah, yeah, y'all don't get along. Do you know how many nights Valorie sobbed to me about missing you?"

I watch as her sorrow morphs into righteous indignation. "Do you know how many times my mother hit me? Not spanked me—beat me. How many times she belittled me? Made me feel unworthy and unloved? Do you know she continuously compared me to Valorie and that she always found me lacking? Do you, Duke? So, yeah, I left after high school. I was lucky enough to score a full ride, and I took it. I wanted more…better. No one deserves to be told they're stupid and ugly and unlovable day in and day out. *No one.*

"And you know what else? It took a long time to realize that all of the things my mother drilled into my head weren't true. It took even longer to realize that Valorie loved me in spite of the way our mother always pitted us against one another. And then it took even longer for me to sort my feelings and work through forgiving her for never sticking up for me. In hindsight, I realize she was either scared or didn't know the extent of it—or hell, maybe she was just glad it wasn't her on the receiving end of our mother's vitriol. I don't really know. What I do know, is it took time.

"It's hard to move past years and years of abuse. It's hard to forgive. It's hard to heal. But I'm not a victim anymore. I'm a survivor. A warrior. And I'm not about to let you or anyone else reduce my suffering at the hands of the people who were supposed to love me unconditionally to *not getting along*."

By the time she finishes, her eyes are red and glassy, and her makeup is streaked from her tears. I clench my fist around my beer bottle, torn between outrage and disbelief. I was with Valorie for over a decade, and not once, ever, did she mention that her parents abused Mallory. Did she truly not know or was she willfully ignorant? My mind is racing with a million questions, but when I open my mouth to speak, nothing comes out.

I mean, what do I fucking say back to all of that? I want to comfort her, but I have a feeling if I tried, she'd either pour her drink in my face or backhand me—hell, probably both.

"Oh, and by the way," she adds, draining her glass. "I was absolutely at my sister's funeral. I just figured it was best to pay my respects from afar. It's not as if our parents wanted me there. Plus, how do you face someone when it's your fault they're dead?"

She sucks in a sharp breath, realizing what she's just said. My heart pounds frantically in my chest. "What?"

Wide-eyed and trembling, Mallory shakes her head. "No, I…" She shakes her head again, hard enough to send her long locks whipping through the air.

Before I can say another thing, she spins her stool away from me and flees. Luckily, foot chases are par for the course in my line of work. I quickly drop two twenties on the bar and take off after her.

If Mallory thinks she can drop the kind of bombs she did just now and not deal with the fallout, she's dead fucking wrong.

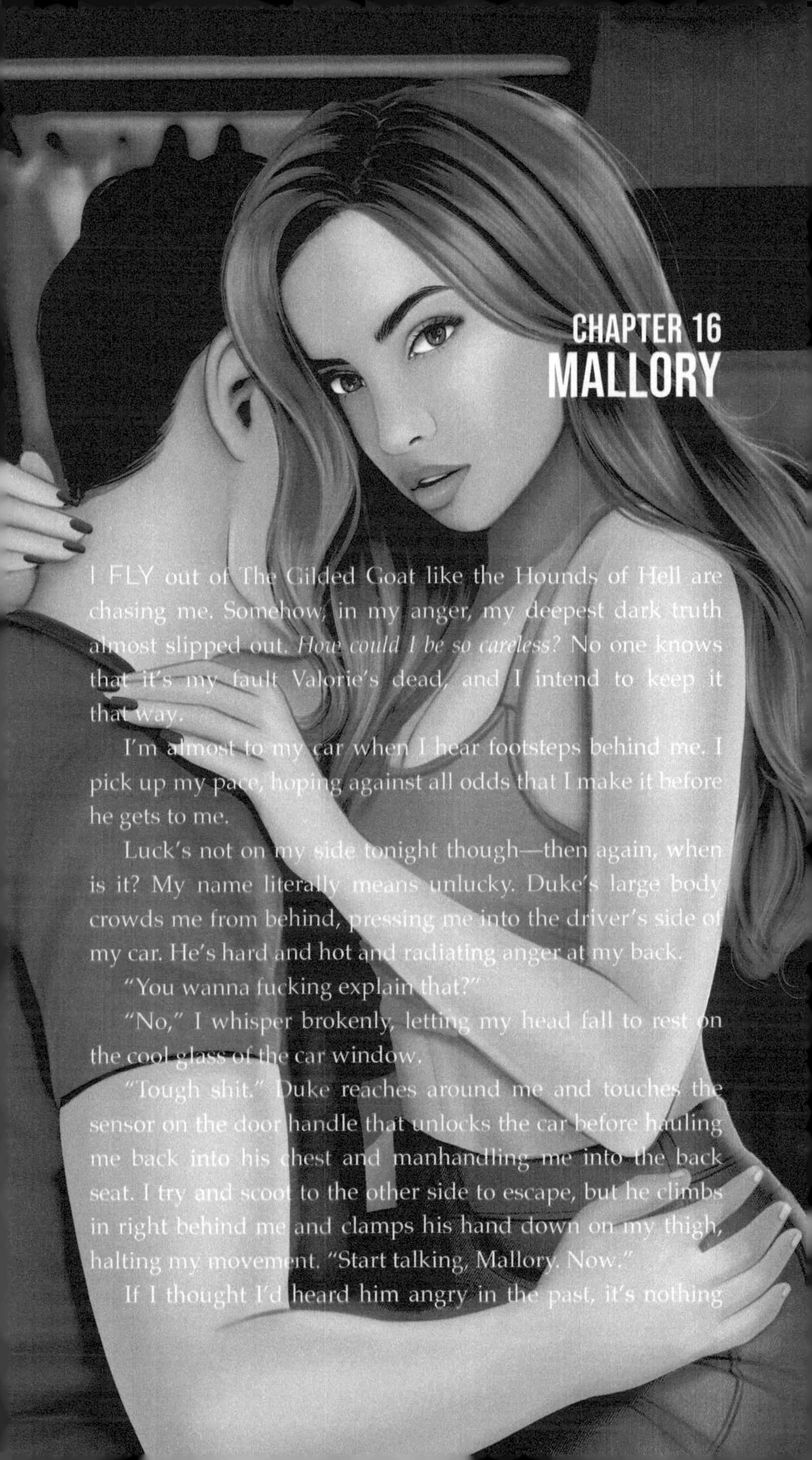

I FLY out of The Gilded Goat like the Hounds of Hell are chasing me. Somehow, in my anger, my deepest dark truth almost slipped out. *How could I be so careless?* No one knows that it's my fault Valorie's dead, and I intend to keep it that way.

I'm almost to my car when I hear footsteps behind me. I pick up my pace, hoping against all odds that I make it before he gets to me.

Luck's not on my side tonight though—then again, when is it? My name literally means unlucky. Duke's large body crowds me from behind, pressing me into the driver's side of my car. He's hard and hot and radiating anger at my back.

"You wanna fucking explain that?"

"No," I whisper brokenly, letting my head fall to rest on the cool glass of the car window.

"Tough shit." Duke reaches around me and touches the sensor on the door handle that unlocks the car before hauling me back into his chest and manhandling me into the back seat. I try and scoot to the other side to escape, but he climbs in right behind me and clamps his hand down on my thigh, halting my movement. "Start talking, Mallory. Now."

If I thought I'd heard him angry in the past, it's nothing

compared to the cold bite of his tone now. If I thought he barely tolerated me before, this revelation will surely be the straw that broke the camel's back.

Nervously, I fidget, wringing my hands and bouncing my knee. How on earth am I supposed to look at this man—this amazing man—and tell him I'm the reason the love of his life died? That I'm the reason for his pain and suffering; that I'm the reason for his unhappiness?

I guess since it's dark, I don't. With my head tilted down toward my lap, I tell him everything. "A few weeks before… before she died, she started texting me. Nothing big, just a simple *hey*. But it was enough to get the ball rolling. She said she wanted us to have a relationship, and I desperately wanted that, too." Tears drip from my cheeks to my thighs, and my throat clogs with emotion.

"The day of the wreck, we were texting. I-I didn't know she was driving. I swear. I swear I didn't know. She was giddy, telling me she thought you were about to propose. She asked me if I'd be in y'all's wedding if you did and I…" I trail off again, my self-loathing practically swallowing me whole. "I told her I'd have to think about it, but she n-never replied."

I'm all out sobbing now, expecting Duke to yell and scream, to call me a murderer, and to leave. Only he does none of that. Instead, he wraps an arm around me and pulls me close, tucking my body into his. "Oh, Mallory. Jesus. Fuck."

"I-I'm sorry. I'm so sorry," I wail, repeating my apology over and over into his side until my words are nothing more than an unintelligible garble.

"Cricket, baby, I need you to listen to me, okay?"

I sniffle but nod. *Is he about to push me away? To tell me he hates me?*

"It's. Not. Your. Fault. It was an accident."

I immediately try and push away from him, but he only clings tighter to me. "No! You…you don't understand! If I wouldn't have been texting her...she'd still be here. You'd still be happy. I-I ruined everything. It's all my fault."

Duke presses his lips to the top of my head before resting his chin in the same place he just kissed. "She was hit by a drunk driver who crossed the lines and veered into her lane. That has nothing to do with you—nothing." His tone is soothing but firm, but he's still wrong.

"If I hadn't been texting her, she wouldn't have been distracted and looking down. She could've seen the car coming and swerved to miss it."

It's then that Duke pushes me away, and I know. I know he realizes that I'm right—that it's my fault.

So imagine my surprise when he frames my face with his big hands and tilts my head back so our gazes meet. "I need you to not only listen but to *hear me.* It was an accident. A horrible, awful accident. Knowing your sister, you weren't the only person she was texting, so removing yourself from the equation doesn't change anything. She could've been looking down to change the radio station. She could've sneezed. Hell, she could've seen the car coming and not had time to react. But, baby, trust me when I say *it wasn't your fault.*"

I notice through my cry-induced stupor that he's called me *baby* twice now tonight. But this isn't the time to deal with that.

I exhale a shaky breath, and Duke pulls me back into him, so close it's like he's trying to absorb some of my pain into himself. "I hate that you've been living with this, that you've been blaming yourself. Have you...have you ever considered talking to anyone about this?"

I shake my head as best as I can with my face pressed into his chest. "I saw a therapist for a little while in my sophomore year, which helped me get through the stuff with my parents, but not since."

"I think it would help. The OGPD made me see a therapist afterward, and while it didn't miraculously heal me, having someone to talk to who wasn't going to judge me or my grief helped."

I draw back just enough to look at him. "You really don't blame me? Not even a little?" My voice slurs with exhaustion; tonight really took it out of me.

"Not even at all." Duke leans down and presses a chaste kiss to my lips. "Let me drive you home?"

I'm too emotionally spent to question him on how he'll get home, so I nod. He exits the back seat and helps me into the passenger seat, and before he can even start the engine, my eyes are drifting shut.

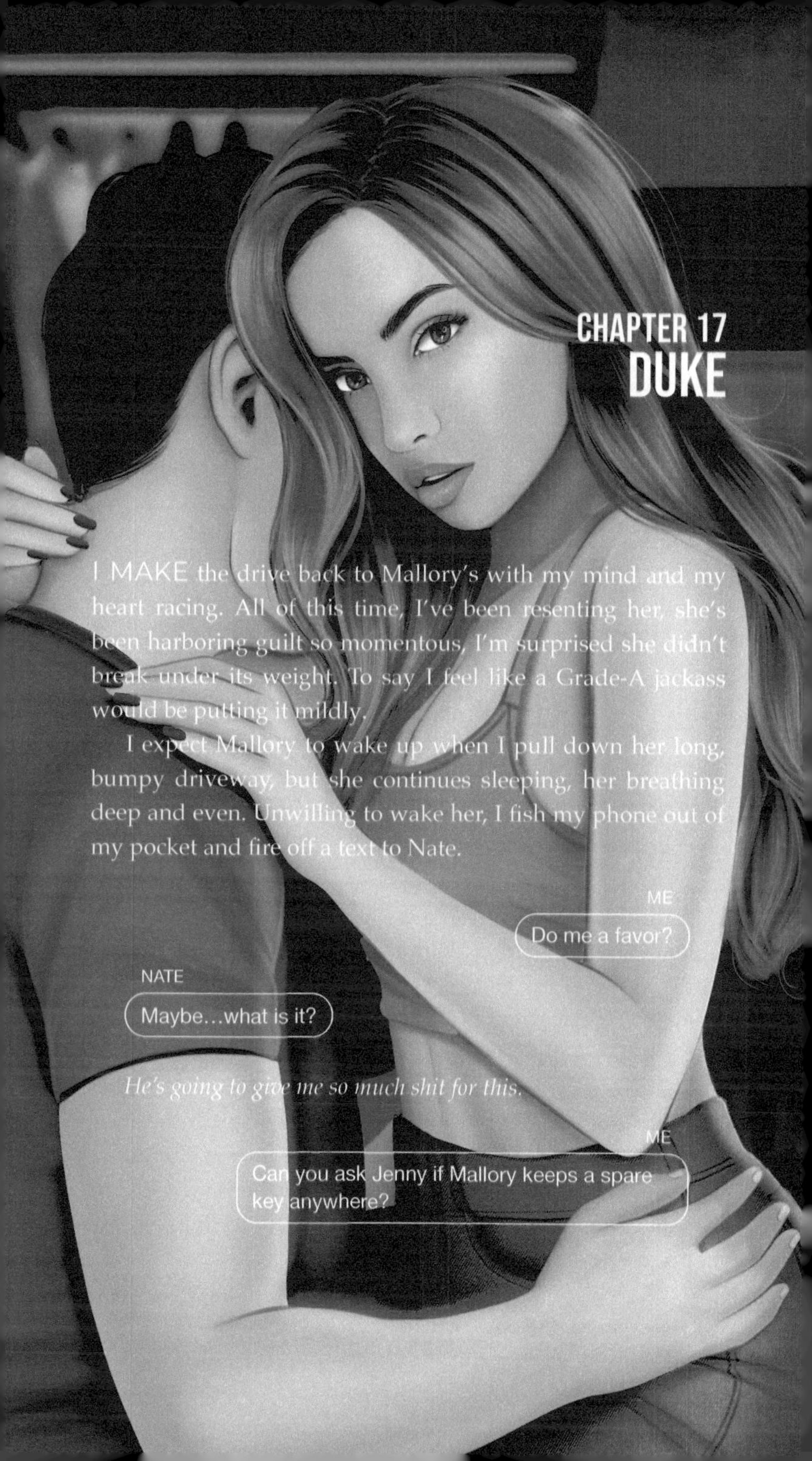

CHAPTER 17
DUKE

I MAKE the drive back to Mallory's with my mind and my heart racing. All of this time, I've been resenting her, she's been harboring guilt so momentous, I'm surprised she didn't break under its weight. To say I feel like a Grade-A jackass would be putting it mildly.

I expect Mallory to wake up when I pull down her long, bumpy driveway, but she continues sleeping, her breathing deep and even. Unwilling to wake her, I fish my phone out of my pocket and fire off a text to Nate.

ME

Do me a favor?

NATE

Maybe…what is it?

He's going to give me so much shit for this.

ME

Can you ask Jenny if Mallory keeps a spare key anywhere?

NATE

I'm sorry. What? Why are you at her house? Are you trying to break in? You know that's against the law. Don't include me in your fall from being a sworn officer.

ME

Okay, drama king. No, I'm not breaking in. She's right next to me. She fell asleep on the drive home, and you know I'm not going through a woman's purse.

NATE

Wtf! I have so many questions. Jenny says there's a key under the potted succulent.

NATE

When I call your ass tomorrow, you better answer.

ME

I'll do you one better. Pick me up around lunchtime, and I'll tell you everything on the way back to my car.

NATE

SO! MANY! QUESTIONS!

I read his last texts with equal parts mirth and dread. He's going to be like a dog with a bone over this—unrelenting until he's positive he has every last detail. And then he's going to be a smarmy little jackass, throwing about twenty *I told you so*'s in my face. It's safe to say, our next few shifts are going to be fun...*for him.*

With the car still running, I exit and dash up the front steps and unlock the front door. I switch on a small lamp by the couch and dash right back out to get Mallory. I hit the power button, killing the engine before unbuckling her seat belt and lifting her gently into my arms.

With her small body cradled to mine, I'm struck with a sense of rightness—like she belongs with me, *to* me.

I take the stairs to her loft slowly, not wanting to jostle her. But when I reach her bed, I find myself facing a whole new conundrum. Should I wake her up so she can change or just let her sleep fully clothed? After a few moments of debate, I settle on pulling off her boots before tucking her under the covers.

Back downstairs, I kick off my shoes, shirt, and shorts, making myself at home on her couch. It's definitely not built for someone my size, but I make the best of it. Our conversation from earlier lingers until finally, my body succumbs to sleep.

———

MALLORY

I stretch awake with a crick in my neck and painful indentations around my ribs from sleeping in my bra. My first question is...*why did I sleep in my bra?* Followed quickly by *why did I sleep fully clothed? How did I even get home?* I'm baffled—like I really don't freaking get it. I know I didn't have but the one drink and Duke—*oh my God, Duke!* Suddenly all of last night comes rushing back at me.

We straight up hashed it out and had a come-to-Jesus kind of talk. I confessed my deepest, darkest secret to him, and instead of hating me, he comforted me. But if he drove me back here in my car...then how did he get home? I guess he either called an Uber or had a friend pick him up.

After stripping out of last night's clothes, I toss on a short, silky black and white striped robe, grab a clean towel and head downstairs, desperate for coffee and a hot shower.

I'm passing through my small living room when something catches my eye. And by something, I actually mean a bare-chested, tatted-up piece of male perfection snoozing away peacefully on my way-too-short-for-him couch. The sight is completely drool-worthy, the way he's laid back with one strong arm tucked behind his head and the other resting, I assume, on his lower belly, though it's impossible to say with my bright magenta throw blanket covering him from the waist down. My inner dirty-girl is all too eager to imagine his hand a little lower, wrapped around himself, stroking.

My thighs squeeze together at the thought, and when I see his hand move slightly beneath the blanket, a squeak passes my lips. I pinch my eyes shut, sending up a quick prayer that he stays asleep before attempting a hasty retreat to the kitchen.

"Good morning, Cricket," Duke murmurs as I move past him, his voice thick from sleep.

"Hi. Bye. Coffee!" I speed up, practically running to the kitchen, dropping my towel along the way. I know I should pick it up, but that means facing him again, and that's not going to happen—at least not yet. *Way to go, Mally, you finally manage to reconcile with him only to act ten shades of crazy.*

His throaty laugh follows in my wake and I'm cursing myself for being so lame. But, really, who can blame me? Even when my ex spent the night, he was always gone long before I woke up, so this whole morning after—*can you even call it that without sex?*—is completely foreign to me.

I start a pot of coffee with my cheeks still flaming hot, hoping against all odds he'll let my awkwardness slide. But when he struts into the kitchen, my towel draped around his neck, clad in only his boxer briefs with a noticeable bulge in the front, I know he has no intentions of that.

The coffee maker stops percolating, and I whirl around to retrieve two mugs—and to hide my embarrassment and arousal. But he steps up right behind me, crowding me, his firm body brushing mine. I arch away from him, trying to avoid any skin-on-skin contact, but all that does is push my ass directly into his pelvis. Duke groans at the contact, and his right hand comes around, landing on my hip, clamping me to him in a possessive gesture that sets my heart on fire and my blood speeding through my veins.

With his left hand, he reaches above us to the cabinet and extracts two mugs. He places them on the counter, keeping me pinned to him for a second or two longer before stepping away.

Unconsciously, I glance down at his package as I turn to face him. My blush deepens to atomic red when I notice his bulge has turned to a full-on erection. And from the looks of it, he's freaking packing. Like, there's-no-way-it-could-fit huge.

I audibly gulp and he laughs. "Eyes up here, Cricket."

"How about that coffee? Do you want some coffee? I definitely want some coffee." I fill both mugs with trembling hands and push one his way. "Mmm, coffee!"

Smirking, Duke says, "Why don't you say *coffee* one more time?" His teasing dispels some of the lust hanging in the air, and a small giggle passes my lips.

I move past him to the fridge, keeping an almost comical amount of space between us, and reach for my carton of heavy cream. "How do you take your coffee?"

"Sugary."

I quirk a brow at him. "Really?"

"Hell yeah. As sweet as humanly possible. Preferably with chocolate and caramel. Oh, and whipped cream."

I stare at him in disbelief. I know, I know. I'm totally stereotyping him based on his appearance. But this big, broody, hulking man is the last person I ever envisioned drinking such frilly coffee.

"Well, I've got heavy cream, chocolate syrup, sugar, and… vanilla ice cream."

Duke shoots me a crooked grin that hits me right in the gut, and…other places. "I can definitely work with that."

I wave him forward. "Be my guest."

I grab the sugar bowl while he gathers up the ice cream and chocolate syrup. I'm torn between incredulity and horror as he adds two spoonfuls of sugar to his still-steaming mug, followed by a healthy pour of both heavy cream and syrup. He then adds a scoop of ice cream, topping off his tooth-rotting concoction with a liberal drizzle of more syrup.

He takes a sip and sighs happily. I, on the other hand, shudder in repulsion. "That is…I have no words."

Duke shrugs unapologetically. "I like what I like." He eyes me long and hard, and I can't help but wonder if he's referring to more than just the coffee.

"Sooo," I address him over my mug, drawing out the word. "Last night…"

He takes another sip, licking away the liquid sugar clinging to his upper lip. "What about it?"

I take another gulp, buying myself some time. "It was a lot. You know, to take in."

"It was," Duke agrees. My stomach knots. *Did we cover too much ground too fast? Not enough? Has he had a change of heart?* As though he's attuned to my rioting thoughts, he abandons his sugary confection on the counter and steps into me, wrapping me in a warm, comforting embrace. "Chill out, Cricket, I can practically see your mind racing."

"Sorry."

"You didn't have anything to apologize for last night, and you don't have anything this morning either. If anything, I'm sorry I didn't man up and talk to you sooner."

I glance up at him from beneath my lashes. "You mean that?"

"One hundred percent." He releases me, and my body instantly misses his. "What are your plans for the day?"

My robe gaps open a little when I shrug and his eyes hone on the exposed tops of my breasts like two green heat-seeking missiles. Seeing my shot, I take it, tossing his earlier words back at him. "Eyes up here, Duke."

"Touché."

"I don't really have any plans. Saturdays are lazy days for me typically. Pjs and Netflix, that kind of thing."

He checks the time on his watch. "Sounds good; it's barely nine o'clock. Why don't you go shower and stuff while I whip us up some food and then we can veg out? You like true crime kind of stuff?"

Mutely, I nod.

"Sweet. You ever seen *The Confession Tapes*?"

I'm not positive, but I think I've been transported to some kind of alternate dimension. Still, I shake my head no.

He thrusts my towel toward me. "Perfect. Go on and do whatever you need to do and meet me at the couch when you smell the bacon sizzle."

I nod. *Definitely in an alternate dimension. I wonder if I'll get some kind of plaque in my honor for my inter-dimensional travel? Maybe a guest spot on Ellen?*

When I make no move to leave, Duke shoos me away. "Seriously, scram. Shower, brush your teeth." His eyes roam over my body. "But maybe put that back on?"

With flaming cheeks, I snatch my towel from him and scurry into the bathroom. As I start the water, I notice the towel now smells like Duke, and I have to fight the urge to melt into a puddle on my bath mat; it should be illegal for anyone to smell that delectable.

After my shower, I dress in a pair of cozy terrycloth shorts and a tank, much to Duke's disappointment. The breakfast he made the two of us—bacon, eggs, and toast—was delicious. Especially as I usually opt for cereal or a smoothie most mornings. Even better, he insisted on doing the dishes afterward.

We spend the rest of the morning on the couch, with him at one end with his feet kicked up on the coffee table and me lying at the other with my toes barely brushing against him.

We make it through five episodes of *The Confession Tapes* before Nate shows up to chauffeur him back to his car.

Unfortunately, he leaves without us making any kind of plans to hang out again, but at the end of the day, I can't be upset about it, not really. Honestly, I'm just relieved to know he doesn't hate me. Not to mention, there's little to no point in fantasizing over the thought of *more* with him, even though there is some definite chemistry between the two of us. I mean, my God, he was going to marry my sister. If that doesn't scream wrong then I don't know what does.

IT'S BEEN two days since everything Mallory really came to a head. Two days that I've let slip by without reaching out. Mostly because I'm scared, because what in the hell would I even say? *'Hey, I had a great time sleeping on your small-ass couch, and I can't stop thinking about you and all of the wicked things I want to do to you…with you. I know I was with your sister, but I want you, too.'* Yeah, that's a whole lot of nope.

"Dude," Nate says, knocking me out of my thoughts. He's driving on shift today, leaving me to wallow in the passenger seat.

"What?"

"You're pouting."

I scoff, straightening in my seat. "Am not."

Nate grins. "You sound like Tatum."

"Do not," I mutter as he slows to a stop at a red light. He turns to look at me and…*fuck, he's totally right.* We both start laughing—that is until a car flies through the intersection from the other side. "Shit!" I yell, thankful as hell the jackass didn't hit anybody. I flip on the sirens while Nate makes a U-turn to follow.

All too quickly, it becomes apparent the driver has no intention of pulling over. Nate calls in a 10-80—*chase in progress*—and hits the gas. I'm in constant contact with dispatch over the radio as Nate expertly pursues. They put out a call for any and all available units to assist.

As we near him, the driver increases his speed, which unfortunately lessens his control of the vehicle. We fall back a little—for our safety and theirs. By four miles in, the driver is swerving and sliding all over the two-lane road. My breath lodges in my throat when he crosses the double yellow lines, narrowly avoiding an oncoming SUV. Finally, the driver over-corrects and the vehicle flips twice before landing on its roof and skidding to a stop in a ditch.

I radio a 10-52—*ambulance needed*—as Nate pulls onto the shoulder. The two of us race from the cruiser, guns drawn; our firearms are a last resort, but in a situation like this, there are too many unknowns and it's better to be ready for anything. Though, the whole way, I'm begging God for us not to need them.

As we move toward the vehicle, we look for any sign of movement from inside, calling out our presence as we approach. "Driver, respond if you're okay!" Nate hollers just as two more units and a sheriff pull up, effectively blocking off a quarter-mile stretch of road. A firetruck and ambulance arrive shortly after.

When we reach the overturned vehicle, I cover Nate while he presses his face to the window, once again asking the driver if they're okay. Still no response.

The fire department medics end up having to do an extraction—the driver wasn't wearing a seat belt and sustained severe injuries. Turns out, he ran because he was hauling enough methamphetamines to take out a small country.

If he survives, he's facing a whole slew of charges, including felony possession with intent to sell, fleeing a peace officer in a motor vehicle, and reckless endangerment. Suffice to say, dude's in a whole lot of trouble.

The rest of our shift is uneventful—pretty much just paperwork, a lot of paperwork. But the chase and subsequent wreck left me on edge. Every single time I work an accident, regardless of the circumstances, it forces losing Val to the front of my mind.

I'm in a foul mood by the time we radio out. Though I can't pinpoint precisely why. If I had to guess, I'd say it's a combination of the events of today, memories of Val, and *everything* with Mallory. My temples throb as an ache forms behind my eyes.

"Just text her," Nate says quietly as he pulls into the lot at the station.

"Text who?" I ask, playing dumb.

He shoots me a look. "Mally." *Here we go again; he's been on me since he picked me up Saturday afternoon.* "You obviously want to, so man up and do it."

"You suddenly a psychic?" I'm being a dick and I know it.

Nate throws the car in park. "Listen, brother, when shit was a mess between me and Jenny, you told me that if I loved her—or even thought I *could grow* to love her—that I needed to buck up, because a girl like her only comes around once in a lifetime. I know you don't wanna hear this, that you're not ready to hear this, but it looks like life's giving you a second chance—don't throw it away."

His—well, *my* words—hit me like a punch right to my solar plexus. Could there be any truth in what Nate said?

———

Back at my house, the first thing I do is hit the shower and desperately try to wash away the day. Except no matter how hard I scrub, thoughts of today's wreck and flashbacks from Val's accident mingle, one blinking into the other like some kind of fucked-up nightmare tailor-made for me.

Once the water runs cold, I towel off and slide on a pair of sweats. I pad out to the kitchen and grab a water bottle and my phone before retreating back to my bedroom. This is the one room in my house that's fully outfitted with furniture and décor. As lame as it sounds, this room is my sanctuary; my safe place to escape when the weight of life gets to be too heavy.

I pitch myself down onto my bed, sighing in contentment as the plush foam envelops my body, making me feel weightless. After a few sips of water and a muttered prayer, I pull up my and Mallory's text thread and tap out a message to her.

ME

Come over?

MALLORY

It's almost 9 at night...and we haven't talked for 2 days...

ME

I...never mind. Goodnight, Cricket.

I roll my eyes at myself. I had a bad day so now I'm begging for Mallory to come comfort me. How much more pathetic can I get? I toss my phone down next to me, hating the way I feel in this moment. I feel desperate and clingy and just...needy. But only for her, which makes me feel even more on edge.

I resolve to be stronger, to be self-reliant. I won't let these possible feelings for a woman I can't have break me. Except when my phone dings, I dive for it like a cat going after a laser pointer.

MALLORY

I'm on my way.

Twenty minutes later, I'm opening the door for Mallory. She's loaded down with her purse, a duffel-type bag, and two stuffed-full grocery bags. Just seeing her, I feel lighter.

"Moving in?" I joke, but my tone is off.

She rolls her pretty eyes and moves past me, heading toward the kitchen. I follow behind her out of pure curiosity. She drops her bags in the middle of the floor and starts opening cabinets and drawers, gathering things until she has two bowls and two spoons. "Do you have an ice cream scoop?" she asks, hands on her hips.

"Nope."

"This'll have to do then," she mutters, grabbing a serving spoon. I watch with rapt fascination as she unloads her grocery bags, revealing two pints of ice cream—one plain vanilla and the other butter pecan—a jar of caramel topping, a bottle of Magic Shell syrup, chocolate sprinkles, and whipped cream.

She adds a generous scoop of each flavor with a layer of caramel topping between them that she heated in the microwave before covering it all with the Magic Shell. Once it hardens, she adds the whipped cream and sprinkles.

Wordlessly, she passes me a bowl and spoon and heads to the couch. I debate for all of two seconds before I say, "Let's go to my room."

She whips around to face me. "Excuse me?"

"Not like that. We both know my couch leaves a lot to be desired, but my bed is comfy as hell, and I have a TV in there, too."

Her pouty lips purse to the side for just a moment before she nods and gestures for me to lead the way.

Mallory claims the left side, which suits me just fine, seeing as I prefer the right. We both make ourselves comfy and dig into the sundaes she made. One bite in, and I know this is going to be a staple in my life. "Jesus, this is so good," I groan between bites.

"Right?" She grins and licks her spoon. "It's my best friend Ashley's creation. She calls it her *'Has the Sads Sundae.'*

She always makes it when she's feeling down. I figured you could use it."

"Wait, what? Why do you think I'm sad?" I mean, she's not wrong, but she doesn't know that.

"Your texts," she says. Shrugging as if that explains everything. Newsflash: it doesn't.

I eat the last spoonful and place the bowl on my nightstand. "I'm gonna need you to elaborate."

She polishes off hers as well and passes me her bowl. "Duke. We haven't talked in two days, which is fine. We're both busy and have lives. But for you to text *me* of all people, out of the blue at nine o'clock on a random Tuesday night… yeah, it's safe to say something's wrong."

Her intuitiveness blows my mind; I bet it really helps in the classroom. "It was just a rough day on the job."

Mallory licks her lips as she turns to face me, drawing her legs up under her. "You wanna tell me about it?"

My initial reaction is to say no. As amazing as Valorie was, she never really grasped how emotionally draining my job could be at times. She always expected me to move on from the traumas I deal with day in and day out in the blink of an eye.

But Mallory isn't her sister, and I decide to take a chance. I bare my soul to her, telling her about the chase and the drugs and how the driver was badly injured. Somehow, I end up lying with my head in her lap as she plays with my hair, listening patiently as I confess to her how every accident I work makes me think of Val. Through it all, she listens patiently, never once judging me. By the time I'm finished, I feel freer than I have in years.

She continues raking her fingers over my scalp, offering me silent comfort. We're both quiet for so long that it startles me when she speaks. "I-I think you're incredibly brave, Duke. To have loved and lost the way you have, to have experienced everything you have, the fact that you're still able to get up every day and put on that badge speaks volumes. You're a good man with a good heart, and I know we aren't all that close and that we don't really know each other all that well, but if the things you deal with start to weigh on you too much, just know I'll always be here to listen. That probably doesn't mean much—"

I fly up from her lap, spinning to face her in the process so that we're knee-to-knee. I clasp both of her cheeks, tilting her gaze to mine. "It means everything. Do you hear me? Everything."

She nods, causing my hands to fall away. "Thank you." Her words are nothing but a whisper.

"Why are you thanking me?" I ask, genuinely perplexed. I literally just ignored this girl for two days, asked her over out of the blue, and dumped all of my emotional baggage at her feet.

She reaches out and wraps her pinky around mine, the gesture equal parts surprising and soothing—*or maybe it's only surprising because how damn right it feels?* "Because out of everyone, you called me. You needed someone and you called me. Don't you get it?" Her amber eyes glisten. "I've never been anyone's first choice, but you. Called. Me."

The next thing I know, we're both leaning in, and sparks fly as our lips softly brush. Feather soft, she sucks my bottom lip into her mouth before opening to me. Our knees and lips are our only points of contact as our tongues dance together as if it's a choreographed routine, perfected over time. While our previous kisses have been fueled by lust, anger, and resentment, this one is a slow kindling built on connection and understanding. This kiss feels healing, like she's knitting the tattered pieces of my soul back together. If I'm being honest, it kind of terrifies me, but not enough for me to stop.

After several more torturous moments, Mallory pulls away.

"Stay?" I ask, reaching forward to tuck a wayward strand

of hair behind her ear. "Please. I'll take the couch. Just…stay?"

Her eyes seem to glow as she nods. "Okay, Duke."

I was totally prepared for her to argue, for me to have to beg, so her easy acquiescence throws me for a loop. "Huh?"

"I packed a bag, just in case."

"Then I guess you don't need one of my shirts to sleep in?"

A beatific grin splits her cheeks. "I brought sleep shorts, but I'll take a shirt if you're offering."

I hop up from the bed, retrieve the larger of her two bags and a shirt from my closet. "I'm insisting."

Mallory rises to meet me, and our fingers brush as she takes her stuff from my outstretched hand. She quickly fishes out her phone charger and plugs it in before she disappears into the bathroom. In her absence, I pace the room a few times, trying to rid myself of the nervous energy pulsing through me in waves.

I freeze when I hear the hinges of the bathroom door creak, trying to play it calm and cool. Too bad calm and cool goes right out the window when I see Mallory in my shirt. I bite down *hard* on my bottom lip, forcing my forbidden desire for her to remain unspoken.

Mallory moves past me, her lips tipped up in a mirthful smile as if she knows I'm on the verge of losing it. I'm frozen solid, wholly spellbound as she climbs back up into my bed, settling herself under the covers this time.

She fluffs the already-full pillow before snuggling down into it. "Aren't you going to bed, too?" Her question spurs me into action, and I grab the quilt draped over the chair in the corner. "What are you doing?" she asks.

"I said I'd take the couch."

"Don't be silly. Your bed is colossal; we can share."

I swallow hard. This simple decision feels momentous, like I'm standing at the precipice of what could be my future, but only if I take the leap. The thing is, even if things between Mallory and me stay completely—well, mostly—platonic, something tells me she's worth the leap.

I reclaim the right side of my bed, slipping beneath the covers, my body held rigid. Of course, Mallory picks up on my discomfort right away. "What's wrong?"

Embarrassment blankets me, and I switch off the table lamp, plunging the room into darkness before replying. "I…you…you're the first woman I've spent the night with since Valorie."

When stark silence meets my admission, I regret sharing it. Lord only knows what she's thinking right about now.

"Like, spent the night with as in sleeping or as in…?" Her words fall away, but my brain fills them in just fine.

God, this is humiliating. "Um." I cough. "I mean, I haven't been a saint, but I haven't actually slept with someone in any sense of the word since she passed away."

"Oh, Duke." Mallory reaches out in the dark and brushes her fingers over my brow bone and down my cheek. "There's no shame in that. Everyone grieves differently and heals at different speeds. There's no right or wrong way, and there's definitely no rulebook. You have to honor what feels right for you and your process. And if anyone judges you for it, then forget them. You don't need them anyway."

Where in the hell did this girl come from? "You know what? You're right." I grab her hand and press a soft kiss to her knuckles. "Goodnight, Cricket. Sleep tight."

She rolls to her other side so she's facing away from me. "Sweet dreams, Duke."

THE SOUND of an unfamiliar alarm rouses me from what has to be one of the best nights of sleep I've ever had. I'm not sure what time it is, but the fact that the sun rose before me speaks volumes.

As my body catches up with my brain, the reason for my great night's sleep becomes apparent. *Mallory.* I'm wrapped around her, with my knee wedged between her legs and my hand splayed across her lower belly, holding her to me as if she's the most precious thing.

Her alarm sounds again, and as she fumbles around reaching for it, her ass brushes against my morning wood. I hiss at the contact, loving it just as much as I hate it. I'm not sure if it's because I've gone so long without, but suddenly I'm so hungry for intimacy that my entire body is wrung tight with need. I want nothing more than to flip Mallory to her back, crawl between her thighs, thread my fingers through her long, unruly hair, and kiss her senseless.

Once she finally manages to silence her phone, she rolls to face me. "G'morning," she whispers, her morning voice so sexy it feels like a warm caress across my skin.

Unable to deny myself any longer, I reach over and brush her hair from her face. "Good morning, Cricket."

She smiles shyly, averting her gaze. The loss of her attention feels like someone stole the sun, leaving me in the dark cold. With two fingers beneath her chin, I bring her eyes back to mine. "You sleep okay?"

"I did. You?"

"Best sleep I've had in years," I tell her honestly, allowing a bit of vulnerability to bleed into my words.

"Really?"

I nod, reaching for her again, this time twining our hands together. For some reason, I can't stop myself from touching her. The feeling of her skin on mine is like a fucking drug, and I'm an addict, fiending for my next hit.

"Yeah, I-I haven't slept like this since before…" My words drop off, but we both know what I'm referring to. I haven't slept through the night since the day Valorie died. I can't decide if this breakthrough, with her of all people, is some kind of weird, cosmic stars-aligning thing or it's so far past fucked there's not a word for it. Either way, it's the sweetest kind of torture.

Now it's Mallory who's reaching for me, running her fingers over my scruff. She parts her lips as if to speak when her alarm blares to life again, effectively ruining the moment.

"Shit!" Mallory scrambles out of the bed, looking some kind of fine in my shirt. "It's almost six-thirty! I've got to get ready. Can…can I shower here?"

"Go for it. There are clean towels under the sink."

"Thanks!" She flits away, grabbing her duffel before locking herself into the en suite.

I hear her humming before the sound of water running through the pipes drowns her out. All of the sudden it hits me —she's bare-ass naked in there, and the only thing truly separating us is a flimsy-as-hell wooden door. The thought of busting it down, flinging back the curtain, and begging her to let me join her takes over.

My dick perks up as I envision water and suds sluicing off

her tight little body. Unable to bear it a second longer, I stalk into the kitchen. If I can't taste her, I may as well whip us both up some breakfast.

—————

MALLORY

Duke's bathroom is far more luxurious than I imagined it to be, with an oversized walk-in shower with a plethora of wall jets and one of those fancy rainfall showerheads. It's no soaker-tub, but it's a close second.

Even though I tossed my body wash into my bag last night, I find myself squeezing a dollop of his into my palm. He uses some kind of menthol-infused scrub that smells like heaven and makes my skin tingle—and while that's probably from the menthol, I'm tingling internally at the thought of smelling like him all day.

I try my best to keep my hair out of the water, but it proves to be no easy feat with all of these showerheads. By the time I finish, my ends are damp, so after I dry off, I weave it into a messy fishtail braid. I brush my teeth, apply a quick layer of tinted moisturizer, coat my lashes with some inky black mascara, and swipe some sheer cherry gloss across my lips and call it a day. I may not look runway-worthy, but my kindergarteners won't think twice about my laid-back look.

I emerge from the bathroom, bags in hand, dressed in a red A-line linen dress with a belted waist and a pair of flat sandals. I follow the smell of fresh coffee and bacon to the kitchen, where I find Duke scrambling up some eggs.

He grins as I join him. His kitchen is bright and light with stainless steel appliances, pale gray cabinetry, and white granite countertops. There's a picture window centered over the sink and a large island separating the space from the still-unfurnished breakfast area.

"You hungry?" he asks as he pours two mugs of

caffeinated goodness, adding heavy cream to mine before desecrating his with fifty pounds of sugar.

"Starving."

He passes me my coffee. "You're in luck; I made my specialty. Eggs, bacon, and toast."

Twice now this man has made me breakfast. "Sounds good to me. I usually have cereal, so this is a treat."

We eat standing at the island, making small talk between bites. This time I insist on rinsing our dishes, much to Duke's dismay. I dry my hands on a dishrag and cross the room to him. Rising up to my tiptoes, I wrap my arms around his neck. At first, he doesn't react, standing stock-still. Embarrassment curls around me, but when I try to step back, Duke bands his arms around my waist, finally returning my embrace. He holds me so close to him there's not even room for air to move between us.

We stay like this for what feels like an eternity, and yet when he releases me, it's too soon. In all of my life, I've never felt safer than I do in his arms. I know it's wrong for me to want him, for me to have feelings for him, yet I'm helpless to deny it. I know with certainty that if Duke Kincaid asked me to be his, I would unequivocally say yes, Valorie be damned.

He takes a step back from me, his fingers grazing my side. "Are you free on Sunday?"

I run my teeth over my lower lip and nod. "Yeah, I am."

"Good. I'll pick you up around eleven." The fact that he's telling and not asking has that little pinball in my belly bouncing around like someone is tilting the machine.

"Okay," I murmur, suddenly shy.

"C'mon, I'll walk you out." He presses a hand to the small of my back as we walk together to my car. I open the door and toss my bags into the back seat before situating myself behind the wheel and pressing the start button.

I expect Duke to shut my door and go on his way, but instead, he leans down into the car and, his eyes on mine, draws my seat belt across my lap, buckling it. "Safety first, Cricket." He presses his lips to my forehead in the briefest of kisses, barely a brush, before standing back to his full height. "Have a good day."

He shoulders my car door shut and saunters back toward his house, and all I can do is drool over the way his sweats sit so deliciously low on his hips and swoon over the events of this morning like a schoolgirl whose crush finally noticed her.

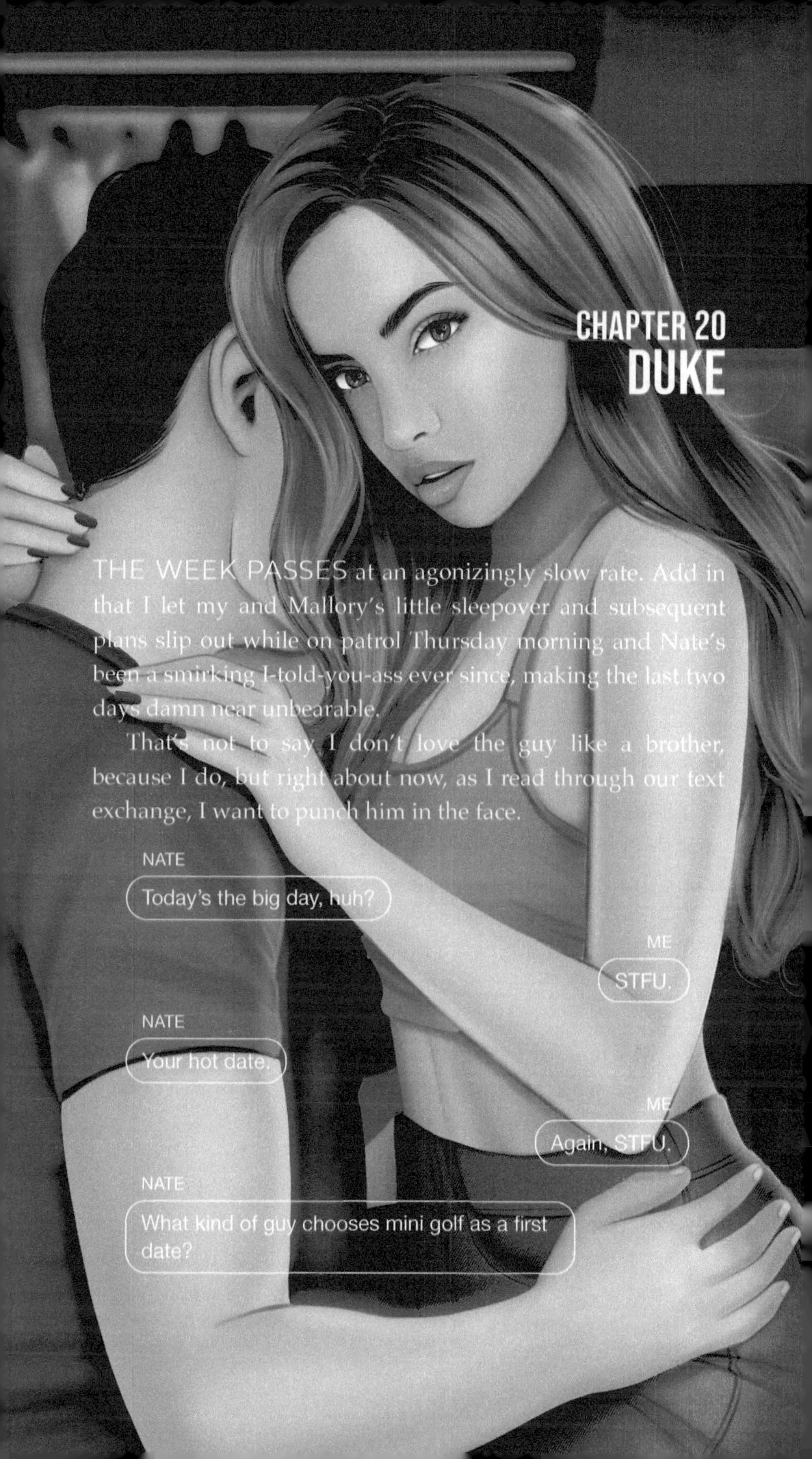

CHAPTER 20
DUKE

THE WEEK PASSES at an agonizingly slow rate. Add in that I let my and Mallory's little sleepover and subsequent plans slip out while on patrol Thursday morning and Nate's been a smirking I-told-you-ass ever since, making the last two days damn near unbearable.

That's not to say I don't love the guy like a brother, because I do, but right about now, as I read through our text exchange, I want to punch him in the face.

NATE

Today's the big day, huh?

ME

STFU.

NATE

Your hot date.

ME

Again, STFU.

NATE

What kind of guy chooses mini golf as a first date?

ME

Maybe the third time's a charm? STFU!

NATE

You gonna buy her a flat soda and some nachos from the concession stand?

NATE

Maybe y'all can hit up the arcade. Who knows, if you win enough tickets you can win her a friendship bracelet to commemorate the occasion.

ME

I hate you.

NATE

You love me. Hey! Maybe if you shoot a hole-in-one, she'll let you score?

ME

I'm requesting a partner change first thing tomorrow.

I know what he's doing. He's trying to take my mind off of the reality of the situation—that I'm taking my dead girl-friend's twin sister on a date. So, as obnoxious as he's being, I appreciate the levity his particular brand of humor brings.

I roll up to Mallory's at eleven on the dot to find her standing on the porch waiting for me, decked out in some sheer teal kimono-looking thing over a pair of frayed daisy dukes, a white tank top, with white Chucks on her feet. Her hair is tied up in a high ponytail, and visions of it wrapped around my fist as I pound into her from behind assault my mind.

She heads down the steps and toward my old truck, a wide smile painted across her kissable lips, and I swear, the sun pales in comparison. The passenger door sticks a little as she pulls on the handle. She tries again, this time throwing her weight into it, and the door pops open, causing her to stumble back a few steps.

"Shit! I'm so sorry, are you okay?"

"One hundred percent. Don't even worry about it." She emphasizes her words with a pat to my leg, and before I know it, I've clasped her hand in mine. I don't let go until we reach our destination.

When Mallory sees where we are, she does this little cute-as-hell wiggle in her seat. "I've been wanting to check this place out!"

I shoot her a cocky wink. "I aim to please."

She rolls her eyes and hops out of the truck. "C'mon, I'm starving!"

We meet at the front of the truck, and I take her hand in mine again, the movement as natural as breathing. We step inside the building and my mouth immediately starts to water when the scent of sizzling grease and toasted bread hits us.

At the counter, we both order cheeseburgers with fries and shakes—chocolate peanut butter for me and mint-chip for her —before claiming a seat near the door.

Not five minutes later, our number is called, and I run up to the counter to retrieve our order. Mallory's eyes widen to the size of saucers when she sees the amount of food. I guess I should've warned her that one burger alone can practically feed a family of four. *Okay, so I'm exaggerating—but only slightly.*

Mallory only finishes half of her burger, but my God, watching her eat it might just be one of the hottest things I've ever seen. Seriously, she puts that old Carl's Jr commercial with Kim K. to shame. After her last bite, she licks a gob of ketchup off her finger, moaning at the taste. "This might be the best thing I've ever eaten."

"Good," I murmur, discreetly reaching beneath the table to adjust myself. I can't say watching someone eat has ever turned me on before, but I'm finding Mallory calls forth a whole host of emotions I've never felt, which is all kinds of shocking since I was in love with her sister for over a decade. "You ready for me to kick your ass in some putt-putt?"

Her eyes twinkle as she scoffs. "As if. It's a well-kept secret, but I'm a mini-golf champ. I'm talking pro-levels, Masters worthy, Tiger-Tiger-Woods-y'all good."

I stare at her for a beat with a goofy smile plastered on my face before we both crack up laughing. "All right, Cricket, let's drive over and you can show me what you got."

The drive to the mini-golf place is less than five minutes, and as it turns out, Mallory wasn't joking—she's damn good. By hole nine, she's hit three hole-in-ones, whereas I'm so far over par it's not even funny. I don't care though, because even though she's absolutely kicking my ass, I'm having the time of my life.

At hole thirteen, she takes pity on me. "Do you want me to show you how to line up your shot and stuff?"

I appraise all five-foot-seven of her, wondering how on earth she plans to show me. I don't mind losing to her; not with the way she's smiling and carrying on, doing little finger-guns after every shot like she's Shooter McGavin. I say yes simply to see how she plans to show me.

She pockets her neon pink ball and nudges me out of the way. "First things first," she says, demonstrating the proper way to grip the club. Once I've mastered that, Mallory moves on to my posture. "Keep your feet parallel to the hole. Bend your knees. No, not that much. Good!"

Mallory tries explaining how to read the slope, but it's a lost cause. God bless her though—she has the patience of a saint; even going as far as dropping to her knees to show me. My concentration goes to shit when I see her practically kneeling before me, my mind swimming with all kinds of dirty thoughts. "Duke, are you listening?" she asks, looking up at me from beneath her long lashes.

I shake my head. "Nope, not at all." I reach for her and wrap my hand around her ponytail, just the way I envisioned when I picked her up. Only now I'm imagining guiding her movements in a whole other way, and judging from the way Mallory's eyeing the bulge in my shorts, she knows it.

"Moving on then," she mutters, springing back to her feet. She works with me on my stroke, but the only thing I'm interested in stroking right now is my dick. *She truly has to have cast some kind of spell on me—it's the only plausible explanation I can think of for wanting to haul her behind the gigantic windmill on hole sixteen and have my way with her.* With Val, I never would've even *thought* about doing something so naughty in public, but Mallory seems to bring all of my baser, more caveman instincts to life. It's like my brain knows wanting her is wrong, but every single square inch of my body is shouting, "Her! Mine!"

"The trick is not to lift your head after you take your shot. You want to hear it go in, not see it."

Before I can register her meaning, I say, "Bull. I damn sure wanna watch it go in."

"Uh...um..." Mallory sputters, and I swear to God, my cheeks have to be as red as a tomato. *Like I said, baser instincts.*

We make it through the last five holes without incident, even if I do linger at sixteen a little longer than necessary. All in all, today's been crazy good; the most fun I've had in a long, *long* time.

The drive to Mallory's is spent with the windows down and the radio up. When I pull up to her house, I step out and come around to open her door, helping her down from the truck.

I walk her up the steps to the front door. "I had fun today, Cricket."

She shoots me a lazy grin. "I did, too. Do you...um...want to get together again sometime?"

"I work earlies this week, so any evening will do."

"Wednesday?" she asks, and I readily agree. "Good. Can I pick what we do?"

If it were Val asking that, I'd know it was her way of passive-aggressively telling me she didn't have fun, but with Mallory, I know she genuinely enjoyed herself today and has something in mind she thinks I'll like. It's kind of crazy how well I already know her; it's almost as if my soul has a direct line to hers.

"Sounds good," I murmur, my voice thick and rough as I look down at her.

We stare each other down like we're in the schoolyard and the first one to blink loses. Or hell, maybe I'm just so entranced by the way the gold specks in her eyes seem to dance in the fading light of the sun that I can't look away. I don't know. What I do know is when her pink little tongue darts out and slicks across her bottom lip, I can't help but lean down and capture it between my lips.

She twines her arms around my neck and leans into me, into my kiss. She opens to me, and I groan in delight as I thrust my tongue into her mouth, tasting her.

Mallory kisses just like she lives, with all of her heart and soul, and here in this moment, I know she's claiming a piece of both of mine.

THE START of the week passes in a blur of teaching, grading, Netflix-ing, texting with Duke, and second-guessing almost everything.

On Monday I woke up to a good morning text from him, and my brain almost went into hyperdrive. Did he text me because I was at the forefront of his mind first thing in the morning, or was he just being nice?

On Tuesday I mentioned that I forgot my lunch at home, and at eleven on the dot, the front office called my room to tell me I had a delivery; he had called in lunch for me from the little sub shop in town. Once I reconstituted myself from the puddle of goo I dissolved into, I sent him about forty-million *thank you* texts. Honestly, I was floored; it's the nicest thing anyone—Ashley aside—has ever done for me.

It's crazy really, how Duke and I went from being at one another's throats to being in each other's arms, metaphori-cally and literally. But I wouldn't trade it for anything—except having Valorie back, even if it meant there never being an us.

I mean, not that there *is* an us. We're just…Duke and Mallory…two people with a complicated history, navigating the waters of life and trying not to get swept away in the tide.

At least, that's what I tell myself when the guilt creeps in. I feel like I'm constantly toeing the line between crushing guilt and a happiness so profound it has wings. While my guilt is rooted solely in my growing feelings for Duke, my happiness stands on its own, ingrained in the life and friendships I'm building here. For the first time in my adult life, I feel whole, like I'm on the path I was meant to be on. And dang it, contentment feels good.

That's not to say I wasn't happy in college. Ashley worked wonders in helping me become my own person; out from under my mother's watchful eye and razor-sharp tongue, she showed me I could be anyone I dared dream to be. But then I got with my ex and he stuffed me right into another box, molding me into who he wanted me to be.

It's finally Wednesday and I'm still in bed, just waiting to see what will come first, my second alarm or his text. My phone vibrates, and I snatch it off the nightstand.

DUKE

Good morning, Cricket, did you have sweet dreams?

ME

Hi. How did you sleep?

DUKE

Not as good as when you spent the night.

ME

Haha. Are we still on for tonight?

DUKE

Yup. Want to tell me what we're doing?

ME

evil laugh Heck no! Meet me at 5? I'll text you the address later.

DUKE

I'd rather pick you up.

ME

Nope. We're meeting. Be safe today.

DUKE

Always. Text you later.

My belly flutters with nerves; I really hope he likes what I have planned for tonight. To some, it might be corny, but only time will tell what Officer Kincaid thinks.

However, before I can find that out, I have young minds to shape, and I certainly can't roll up to my classroom dressed in cat-print pajamas with hair in a ratty poof on the top of my head.

If it weren't for the rambunctious five– and six-year-olds, the day would've passed like molasses. Tatum especially kept things interesting by announcing that she was going to marry Ben Thompson and didn't care if he wanted to or not. Personally, I thought it was funny and imagined Natalie would, too —Alden on the other hand, probably not so much.

But now, I'm on my way home to get ready for my date— at least, I think it's a date. Would it make me seem super lame if I asked for clarification? My plans for us are incredibly low key, so I don't have much to do in the way of prepping, just a fluff of my hair and a spritz of body spray, really. Oh, and cuter shoes. I learned the hard way that a kindergarten class-room is no place for heels, at least not for me. My kids are far too active for me to be able to keep up in anything other than flats.

Not even twenty minutes after getting home, I'm heading back out to meet Duke. I text him the address before heading for the little locally owned bookstore in town.

The closer I get, the more my doubts start to creep in. *What was I thinking? I don't even know if he likes reading.* As I park, I send up a quick prayer that I don't make a fool of myself tonight.

Even though I arrive a few minutes early, I find Duke

waiting for me near the entrance. "Books, huh? You a big reader?"

"I love it. Probably because fictional characters were the only friends I had growing up." My cheeks heat with my overshare, but Duke doesn't seem to mind.

"I'm glad you had at least that." He places his hand on my lower back and chills ripple through me—how is it that even the simplest touches from him affect me so much? "So, what's your plan?"

"First, coffee," I tell him, grabbing his wrist and tugging him toward Oh, Sugar, which is only three stores down. Somehow, we end up walking hand-in-hand like a real couple. The thought makes me giddy.

We take turns ordering at the counter, but when I try to pay, Duke refuses to let me. Coffee in hand, we snag a table in the back. "You wanna tell me what we're doing now?"

I take a deep sip of my iced Americano before answering. "Okay, you're probably going to think this is super lame, but I was thinking we could go over to Page After Page after this and do a kind of blind-date-with-a-book thing."

"A what?"

I bury my face in my hands. "Oh, God, you think it's totally lame."

Duke's warm, rough hands come down on mine, prying my fingers away. "Not at all, Cricket. I've just never heard of this book date thing. Explain it to me."

"Okay. So basically, we'll split up, and I'll pick out a book for you to read and you'll pick one for me. Normally you go in knowing the genre and whatnot, but I figured we could each pick something we like, something that will teach us a little bit more about each other. Does...does that sound okay?"

"Hell yeah. I think that sounds awesome." My heart soars. "On one condition." Then, just as quickly, it plummets.

"Wh-what's that?"

"You let me take you out to dinner after."

And we're cleared for takeoff. "I see your dinner offer and would like to counteroffer with takeout at my place and a movie."

"Only if I get to pick the movie."

I pretend to think about it for a second, tapping my index finger against my chin. "Deal."

Inside Page After Page, we go our separate ways. As I peruse the shelves, I can't help but wonder what he's going to pick for me. I doubt he's a romance reader, so who knows how he'll feel about my selection for him, but this genre has played such a huge part in my life—it's pretty much all I read.

A lot of people like to tease or belittle women who read romance, but throughout my adolescent and teen years—a time when I needed it the most—romance books gave me hope that one day I, too, could have a happily ever after.

I'm shocked by how diverse their shelves are, with indie and traditional authors sitting side-by-side in equal amounts. The sight makes my heart soar. My eyes about bug out of my head when I see a copy of *Doppelbanger* by Heather M. Orgeron. I read this book a year or so ago, and laughed so hard I almost peed myself. It's one of those books I suggest anytime someone asks for recommendations. I highly doubt it'll be Duke's cup of tea, and I can't wait to see the look on his face when we exchange books.

When I get to the checkout, I'm shocked to find him kicked back in one of the reading chairs near the front window, his bag resting at his feet. "You're already finished?"

"Oh, yeah, it was a no-brainer for me." He taps the face of his watch twice. "You took forever." There's a playful quality to his tone that makes me smile. The more time we spend together, the more I see behind the broody mask he shows the world. He's thoughtful and kind and funny and a total softy at his core.

"What do you want to eat?" I ask him after I pay.

"Hopefully you don't mind, I called in an order to Bayside."

I snort. "Um, I'll never turn down food from Alden and Natalie's kitchen."

Duke boops my nose. "Smart girl. I'll pick it up and meet you at your place."

"Sounds good. Drive safe."

Duke brushes his knuckles over my cheekbone. "I will. You, too."

WITHOUT EVEN TRYING TO, Mallory Parsons has me damn near wrapped around her little finger. I'm not even sure when or how it happened. Suddenly, she's my last thought before bed and my first thought in the morning. By all normal standards, it's too fast; I shouldn't be having these kinds of feelings for her, but she's so alluring, I'm helpless to resist her pull.

Guilt still niggles. I still very much love Valorie, and I always will. But at the same time, I'm starting to open myself up to the idea that having feelings for someone else doesn't detract from what I had with her. No one will ever replace Valorie, and I wouldn't want them to. But I'm slowly starting to see there's still a possibility of happiness and love in my future.

I'm not saying I love Mallory, just that I'm open to the idea that one day I could. The only thing really holding me back is the fact that they're sisters—fucking twins—but at the same time, maybe that's why things with Mallory seem so right? Maybe she's the universe's way of giving me back a little bit of what I lost.

Giselle greets me brightly when I walk into Bayside to grab our order. I didn't even check what was on the menu, just asked for two chef's specials and called it a day. I've yet to try anything from here that wasn't phenomenal, and based on the tantalizing smells wafting up from my to-go bag, I have every confidence that this will be just as delicious.

Mallory texts me, telling me to let myself in, which I do. I call out for her when I step inside.

"I'll be right down!" she hollers back from her loft.

I walk the food back to the kitchen and begin plating it. My stomach rumbles in anticipation at the sight of the juicy grilled chicken atop sweet potato hash with broccolini on the side. I'll never forget the time I mistakenly called it broccoli—and I thought Jenny's eyes were going to pop out of her head. Needless to say, Nate and I both are now well versed in the differences between broccolini and broccoli. The smell of the Conecuh sausage in the hash has my mouth watering.

But when Mallory walks into the room dressed down in a pair of stretchy, skin-tight yoga shorts and an oversized sweatshirt, I'm hit with an entirely different kind of hunger.

"You ready to eat?"

Her stomach lets out a cute little rumble, and she blushes. "Clearly. It smells divine."

As we dig into our food, I'm not sure which I appreciate more, the flavors bursting across my tongue or the little mewls of delight Mallory makes with every bite.

Once we've both all but licked our plates clean, we move to the couch. "Are you ready for this?" I ask her. "Hell, am I ready for this?"

She bats her lashes innocently. "I don't know, are you?"

I puff out my chest, Captain America style. "Cricket, I was born ready."

We both retrieve our shopping bags and plop down onto her couch. "You go first, Duke."

"All right." I pass her my bag, watching with rapt attention and bated breath as she slides the books from inside.

"Fair warning, I cheated and bought two. In my defense, only one is for you."

"Hmm," is all she says. When she pulls out the first book, her eyes cloud with confusion. "*Watchmen?* I think…there's a movie, right?"

"There is, but I promise the graphic novel is so much better."

"I'll let you know what I think." She moves to the second book, and this time her eyes gleam with joy. "You…you bought a book for my students?"

"Yeah. I heard Nate read this one to Tatum once, and by the end, we were all crying from laughing."

Mallory runs her fingers over the dust jacket. "*The Book With No Pictures,* huh?" She opens it and reads the first few pages, her lips already tipping up in a smile.

"Duke, they're gonna love this." She flings herself toward me, face-planting in my chest as she wraps her arms around my middle. It's probably the most ungraceful hug of all time, and yet somehow, it's also one of the best.

She pulls away, moving back to her seat, and I instantaneously miss the feel and heat of her body pressed to mine. "Your turn!"

My brows dent in when I see the book Mallory selected. "Doppel…banger? The hell is this?" My eyes take in the dude on the cover, with his hands behind his head and his button-down gaping open to expose his chiseled abs. The longer I stare at the cover, the more confused I become. "'Bang enough frogs and one's bound to become a prince…right?' Cricket, baby, what is this?"

Her eyes light up with pure pleasure—most likely at my expense. "Hear me out. I know, you're a big strong man and romance probably isn't your genre of choice, but it's a romantic comedy, and I guarantee you will pee yourself from laughing so hard. It's about a single dad of two daughters and the over-the-top, outspoken, sassy woman he falls for. I promise, it's hilarious. Plus, the sex is hot." She shrugs like she didn't just tell me she enjoys reading about hot sex.

I shift the book to cover my lap, because dammit, now all I'm thinking of is hot sex with her. Right here on this couch. With me kicked back like the dude on the cover while she rides me with her head tipped back and her hair wild as hell. With all the lights on, so I don't miss a damn thing.

I must stay lost in my fantasy a little too long, because seemingly out of nowhere, Mallory whacks my shoulder. "Duke! Earth to Duke!"

"Huh? Yeah? What?"

Mallory laughs at my confusion, the sound like a balm to my battered soul. "Didn't you want to pick the movie?"

"Oh, yeah." She passes me the remote, and I scroll through Netflix's available titles before settling on *The Ballad of Buster Scruggs*. We both go into it blind, and while it's one hundred percent one of the strangest movies I've ever seen, it's also stupidly funny, and if Mallory's laughter is anything to go by, she agrees.

By the time the credits roll, I'm once again laid out on this short-ass couch, but this time Mallory's snuggled into me with her back to my front and her head resting on my outstretched arm. For as uncomfortable as this couch was when I slept on it the other night, I find that with her nestled into me, I'd be perfectly content to never leave.

Except we both have to be at our jobs bright and early, and I definitely didn't think to pack a bag. But a little longer won't hurt, right? Just a few more minutes…

I WAKE WITH A START, wondering where I am and who's holding me. As soon as my eyes adjust, I realize I'm still on my couch with Duke. He's sleeping soundly behind me, though I don't know how with the way my hair is practically smothering him.

As gently as I can, I roll myself out of his embrace and get up from the couch. I'm not quite sure where I left my phone, so I pad to the kitchen to check the time. I'm shocked to see it's five-fifteen—only forty-five minutes until my alarm is set to go off.

I'm not sure what time Duke needs to be up, and there's definitely no point in me going back to sleep, I start a pot of coffee and hit the shower, leaving the door open a smidge so that I'll hear if he wakes up.

As the hot water rains down over my body, I can't help but wish I was in Duke's shower with all of the bells and whistles. I lather up my hair, washing it twice to combat the three days of dry shampoo I was rocking before applying a conditioning mask. I really need a color appointment, but I've been putting it off; finding a new hairstylist is hands down one of the worst parts of moving.

I fly through the rest of my routine, wanting to finish

before Duke wakes. Except, when I step out of the bathroom wrapped in only my towel, there's six-feet-plus of man muscle leaned back against the sliding glass door, coffee in hand, looking at me like he wants nothing more than to show me just how much more enjoyable showers for two are.

"Hi." I greet him shyly, acutely aware of the fact that I'm completely naked beneath this rectangle of terrycloth.

His eyes eat me up. "Damn, Cricket. You're so beautiful."

I avert my gaze; I've been called a lot of things in my life, but beautiful has never been one of them.

Duke places his still-steaming coffee down on the little hammered bronze side table I have and steps toward me, a predatory look in his mossy green eyes. He advances, completely uncaring that I'm still slightly damp from my shower, until we stand flush. He spears his fingers into my tangled, wet hair, forcing me to look up at him. "I need you to listen to me, okay?"

"Okay."

"You are so damn beautiful. Inside and out. You're stunning, Mallory. You're one of those few people whose insides are just as pretty as their outsides. You're so fucking smart. You have this drive and passion that radiates out of you. You have so much heart that your kindness overflows. Your laugh is so infectious that everyone in hearing distance can't help but smile. Your body—*mmm*—don't even get me started. Your eyes are like smelted gold, precious and shining. And your lips, Cricket, they're the most inviting, kissable lips I've ever seen. I daydream about claiming them far more often than I'd like to admit."

My heart beats so furiously in my chest I swear it knocks against my rib cage. The way he's looking at me, his face sincere and honest, tells me he meant every word.

I push up on to my tiptoes and wrap my arms around his neck. "Then do it," I whisper just before he seals his lips to mine.

Duke kisses me completely and totally senseless until his phone chirps in his pocket. He breaks away with great reluctance. "That's my alarm." He speaks the words against my lips before claiming them once more. His kiss is bruising, full of want and need and longing. His phone goes off again and he groans, stepping back from me. "Let me see you again tonight?"

"Yes."

"I'll text you after work." He presses one last kiss to my forehead before he turns and walks out the front door.

As I watch him go, I'm struck with a sudden sense of...*rightness*...like we're both exactly where we're supposed to be.

STARTING my day well-rested truly is something else. It's like as if the hazy perma-fog that's been following me since Val's death has finally lifted, allowing me rest, but only when I'm with Mallory. There's something about her that calls to me, that calms the storm raging inside me. There's something about the feel of her body wrapped in mine that allows me to sleep peacefully.

Work is a whole lot of the same. A few traffic stops, a call for some punk-ass teens that were loitering at the corner store when they should've been in school, but even still, I couldn't imagine myself ever doing anything else.

"I brought you some roast," Nate tells me as I drive us back to the station for lunch.

"All the fixings?"

Nate taps the dash twice. "You know it, brother."

"Nice! Wait. Who made it, your mama or Jenny?"

He laughs, but he knows exactly why I'm asking. While Jenny's roast is a solid ten out of ten, Mrs. Reynolds' is a twenty. I don't know what she does that makes it so damn good. Hell, the way I crave the stuff, she probably seasons it with crack.

"Mom made it."

"Hell yes." I throw the car into park, cut the engine, and hop out. "Come on, let's go. Hustle, boy!"

Nate smirks. "I like this side of you."

I squint at him. "What's that supposed to mean?"

He shrugs. "I know this sounds..." He trails off, waving his hand dismissively. "You just seem happier, more upbeat. Just more...here. I like it."

I push open the glass entry door, holding it for him. "Uh, thanks, I guess," I mutter as he passes. We both stop and greet Mary, the department receptionist, on our way back to the break room.

Nate heats our food and slaps out a portion for me. We eat in relative silence, his earlier words replaying as I chow down. "You meant what you said out there just now?"

He nods as he finishes chewing his bite. "Yeah. Something's different in you. It's like...your light's back on or some shit."

"I feel different." I gulp down a few sips of water. "Better. I feel better."

"It's got something to do with Mallory?" He's fishing; Nate Reynolds can out-gossip a granny.

"Yeah, it does. She...soothes me."

"Good, man, that's real good."

"You don't think it's wrong?"

"It's all relative, Duke. Sometimes what's wrong for one person is right for another. If y'all make each other happy and are willing to wade through a little bullshit, then who is to tell you any different? Sure, it's an unusual situation, but that's life, brother. It's messy and complicated and with jagged pieces that cut. Not everything fits into nice little boxes. Sometimes we can't help who we love; you're both consenting adults. I say go for it. Plus, it's not like y'all being together hurts anyone."

I laugh, but it's lacking all humor. "Nancy would lose her mind."

"Fuck Nancy!" Nate punches a fist into the air. "I've been wanting to say that shit for so long. I know she's struggled since losing Val, but seriously, Duke, don't allow her a say in this. If it were up to her, she'd have you alone and miserable, pining after a ghost for all of eternity right alongside her. She's the kind of woman who takes twenty miles on an inch. Straight up, there are only two people who should have a say in a relationship, and that's the two in it."

"You're right. Damn, you're right."

He winks, balling up his water bottle and shooting it toward the trashcan where it sails in. "Usually am." *Jackass.*

———

I text Mallory at the end of my shift as promised, all too eager to see her. I don't even care what we do tonight; we could sit and watch paint dry for all I care. I just want to spend time with her.

ME

Still wanna get together tonight?

MALLORY

Absolutely. Got any ideas?

My mind swan dives right into the gutter. *Why yes, Cricket, I have plenty of ideas.*

ME

I'm open to anything.

MALLORY

Would you be open to touring a gym with me so I don't have to go alone?

ME

Sure. Which?

MALLORY

The one on the corner of Main.

ME

I work out there. I'll pick you up at 5:30?

MALLORY

Squee! See you then!

While showing Mallory my gym is definitely not the third date I envisioned, I'm down to spend time with her any way I can. Not to mention, the thought of her sweaty, dressed in spandex? *Yes. Please.*

———

I pick Mallory up at exactly five-thirty on the dot, and like the last time I picked her up, she's on her front porch waiting on me. What really makes me smile, though, is the fact that she's cozied up in her lone Adirondack chair, reading the copy of *Watchmen* I bought her. In fact, she's so absorbed into it, she hasn't even noticed me, which is some feat with the way my truck growls. My old metal beast lacks automatic windows, so I settle on tapping the horn. She jumps about ten feet in the air when I do, and I'm still laughing my ass off when she yanks open the passenger door and climbs up into the truck.

"You asshole!" she squeals, but she's laughing, too. "You scared the shit out of me, and you almost made me lose my place."

"Does that mean you're liking it?"

"Yeah, I am. I didn't think I would, to be honest, but it's really good." She secures her seat belt, knowing I won't even put the truck into gear until she does. "What about you? How are you liking Jeff and Gina?"

I duck my head. "Are you gonna be mad if I tell you I haven't started it yet?"

"Yes!" she shrieks. "You have to read it! A deal's a deal. Please?" Right there, it's that single word that breaks me.

"I'll start it tonight."

"Promise?" she asks as I park outside of the gym. "No, wait. Pinky promise?"

"What are we, five?" I laugh.

"Might as well be. I mean, I spend five days a week with five-year-olds; their antics are bound to rub off on me." She balls her left hand into a fist with her pinky finger sticking out. "C'mon, pinky promise."

I link my little finger with hers. "Yeah, yeah. Let's go check out the gym."

Inside, we're greeted by a male receptionist I've never seen before. His too-light-to-be-natural blond hair is slicked back away from his face; he's dressed in a pair of workout shorts and a compression top so tight I'm pretty sure I can make out his individual strands of chest hair. "Welcome to Bay Ridge Fitness. How can I help you today?" The guy only has eyes for Mallory, speaking to her—and only her—as if I'm not standing right beside her with my hand on her damn back.

She offers him a small smile. "Hi, I was hoping to learn a little bit about your membership options and maybe get a tour."

Mr. Receptionist places both of his palms on the desk and leans forward, invading Mallory's space. "I'd be more than happy to give you a personal tour." The way his eyes slide over her body tells me his tour would most likely end in either the locker room or an empty office.

Luckily my girl doesn't take the bait. "Oh, that's so sweet of you to offer. But I brought my boyfriend here with me." She reaches for my hand and tugs me forward. "He's already a member and said he'd be happy to show me around."

As if he's just noticing me, Mr. Receptionist's eyes flick my way. "Great." His entire demeanor changes now that he knows he doesn't have a chance in hell with Mallory. He's all business now. "We have three plans: bronze, silver, and gold." He covers the ins and outs of each tier before signing her in as a guest and leaving us to our own devices.

I walk her through the gym, pointing out things I think she'll appreciate—like the multiple water coolers and towel stations. The tour is relatively quick; I mean, a gym is a gym, right? But Mallory seems to like it, so she signs up for the base level membership.

"Wanna grab something to eat?" I ask as we walk back to my truck.

"God, yes," she moans, the sound shooting straight to my dick.

We hit up a drive-thru, eating our food straight from the bag as we drive back to her house, laughing and cutting up the whole way.

When I pull into her driveway, she turns to me and asks, "You wanna come in?"

Fuck yeah. Instead of a verbal reply, I hop out of the truck and start up the front steps. "C'mon, Cricket!"

She breaks into a run behind me, scrambling up the stairs. The toe of her shoe catches on the top step, sending her flying my way. I reach for her just in time, pulling her into me. With our bodies flush, Mallory's breathing hard—though if it's from her fall or our proximity, I'm not sure. What I do know is with the way she's clinging to me, her big eyes pleading, I have to kiss her. *I have to.*

Gently, I lean down and capture her lips with mine, sucking and nibbling, until she's writhing in my arms. "Duke, I need more."

"I'll give you what you need, Cricket. Open the door, baby."

I release her, and she has the door unlocked in the blink of an eye. Once we're in the house, I take a seat on the couch. "C'mere," I murmur lowly, crooking my index finger her way, commanding her to close the distance between us. Mallory nibbles her lower lip in an alluring mix of innocence and sin. She moves to sit beside me, but that won't do. "Nah, right here." I grip her thigh, pulling her down onto my lap so she's straddling me.

Aside from the sound of our breathing, the room is completely silent as her soft hands come up and cup my cheeks, her fingers brushing over my stubble. Mallory gives me a soft, tender look—one that looks a whole lot like love—before brushing her lips against mine.

As her kiss turns from tentative to exploring, I can't help but marvel over how now that we've worked out our shit, everything with Mallory feels effortless in a way I never had with Valorie. I know I'm a shit for even thinking it, but there's something about this woman that fucking sets me on fire.

All thoughts of love, lust, whether what we're doing is wrong or right—of everything except the here and now—flee my mind when her tongue tangles with mine once again. *Fuuuuuck.* I can't remember anything that's ever felt as good as the feeling of her on me. This may not be our first kiss, but somehow, this one seems different, like we're on the verge of crossing some invisible line we've been toeing.

Our kiss becomes frantic and feverish as she rolls her hips, rubbing herself against my hardness until we're both panting. "You still need more?" I ask, nipping at her juicy bottom lip.

She moans low, this hungry, throaty sound as she presses her hips into mine again, rolling them faster in search of friction. I spear my fingers into her hair, gathering it into one hand. With her strands tightly grasped in my fist, I pull her head back, baring her neck to me. I lick, kiss, and bite my way down the smooth slope of her neck as I work my other hand beneath her shirt.

"Yes, please." Her voice is tight with want as I tweak her nipples over the lace of her bra, wishing like hell it was off and on the floor. As if she can read my mind, Mallory pulls away from me and whips her shirt over her head. I waste no time ridding her of the offending lace, dipping down to lick and suck at her rosy buds, one after the other.

I'm about ready to throw her fine ass down onto the couch and show her just how good I can make her feel, but suddenly she shoves away from me. "Take off your shirt," she rasps, sounding like molten sex.

Her cheeks are rosy from my stubble, and her lips are swollen from my kisses; she looks like a goddess. I'm all too happy to oblige and tug my shirt overhead, depositing it somewhere on the floor. With both hands to my chest, she pushes me into a reclining position and pops the button on my jeans. "I want you. I...I want you." Bold as fuck, she reaches for me, wrapping both of her hands around my hardness.

A groan fights its way past my lips, and my eyes damn near roll back into my skull as her small, warm hands work my dick like she was put on this fucking earth to bring me pleasure.

Her pace increases, and my hips buck, causing me to thrust up into her hands...and all I can think is if her palms feel like heaven then sex with her must be nirvana. God, I'm close, *so close*—and then she leans down, engulfing my crown with her pillow-soft lips, and I'm a goner. Before she can even really suck—before I can warn her—I'm coming, shooting my release straight down her throat.

She pulls back, releasing me with a wet *pop*. Her throat works as she swallows. I sit back dazedly. My first post-Val orgasm that wasn't delivered by my right hand. A riot of emotion swells and crests inside me, slamming against my chest like waves breaking on the rocks. Love, lust, desire, reluctance, acceptance, confusion...but strangely enough, guilt isn't present.

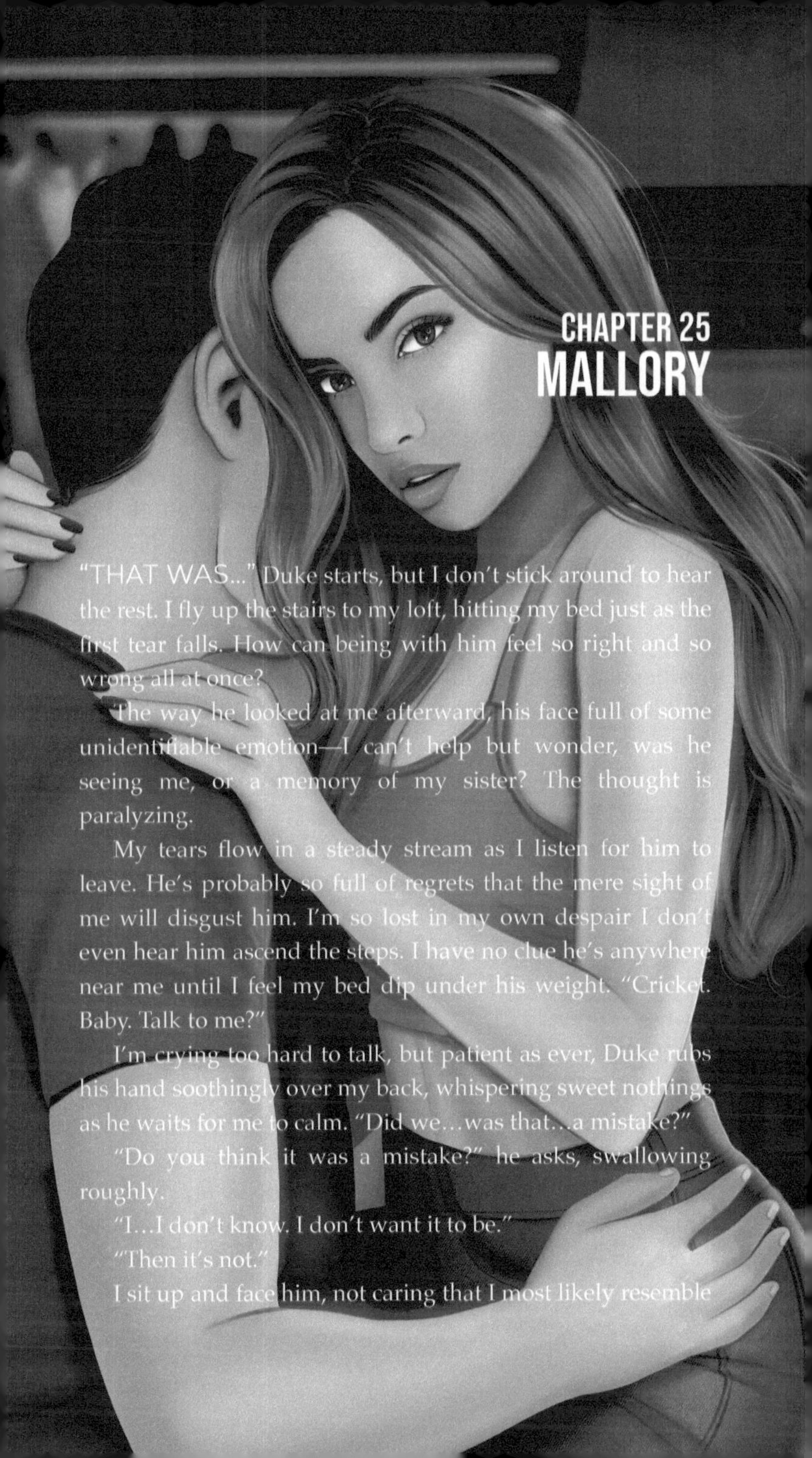

"THAT WAS…" Duke starts, but I don't stick around to hear the rest. I fly up the stairs to my loft, hitting my bed just as the first tear falls. How can being with him feel so right and so wrong all at once?

The way he looked at me afterward, his face full of some unidentifiable emotion—I can't help but wonder, was he seeing me, or a memory of my sister? The thought is paralyzing.

My tears flow in a steady stream as I listen for him to leave. He's probably so full of regrets that the mere sight of me will disgust him. I'm so lost in my own despair I don't even hear him ascend the steps. I have no clue he's anywhere near me until I feel my bed dip under his weight. "Cricket. Baby. Talk to me?"

I'm crying too hard to talk, but patient as ever, Duke rubs his hand soothingly over my back, whispering sweet nothings as he waits for me to calm. "Did we…was that…a mistake?"

"Do you think it was a mistake?" he asks, swallowing roughly.

"I…I don't know. I don't want it to be."

"Then it's not."

I sit up and face him, not caring that I most likely resemble a deranged raccoon, what with my hair a mess from his hands and my eye makeup smeared from crying. Without an ounce of hesitation, Duke pulls me into his lap. "That easy?" I ask, nestling my head into his chest, readily accepting the comfort he's freely offering.

"Mallory, I can tell you right now, there won't be anything easy about us. It's gonna be a tooth-and-nail fight, and even then, some people may think it's wrong. But listen to me when I say I want you. *I want us.* I know this is new and scary and maybe even a little forbidden, but the way you make me feel…I've never felt anything truer in my life."

His words pierce me. Surely, he can't mean all of that, right? "But what about…" I trail off, allowing him to fill in the rest.

"Val? What about Val?" he asks, running his thumbs under my eyes, brushing away the last of my tears and melting makeup. "I think…I think she'd want both of us to find happiness. I think fate brought you and I together, and I think we'd be foolish not to at least give it a try."

"But what if it doesn't work out? What if we sizzle and burn out? What then?"

"Cricket, baby." He presses his lips to my forehead. "We won't know if we don't try. Take a chance with me?"

He sounds so earnest, so convincing, I already know I'm going to agree. Heck, he could probably lead me off the side of a cliff and I'd follow willingly. "Okay, Duke. I'll take a chance with you."

His lips tip up. "Really? You mean it?"

"Yeah, I do." Duke lunges for me, tackling me back to the mattress. My eyes fall closed as my head hits the bed, my lips tingling in anticipation of his kiss, but it never comes.

Instead, he trails his trembling fingers down my cheek, his touch reverent. "Thank you. I know neither of us knows what the future holds, but I'm exactly where I want to be in this moment."

I reach up and cover his hand with mine. "Me, too." He pulls back just enough to look me in the eye, pausing to search my gaze. After a beat, he must finally see what he's looking for because in one fell swoop, his lips are pressed to mine, sealing this new thing between us with a kiss.

A kiss that quickly gives way to roaming hands and panting breaths, until, one piece at a time, the clothing separating us disappears. By the time Duke has me naked beneath him, I'm a sweating, writhing mess, overwrought with need.

"You're so damn beautiful." Duke stares down at me in awe, his eyes trailing my body like a caress. "Let me make you feel good."

"God, yes, please," I moan wantonly, his every look, word, and touch driving me wild. Even before, when we were at odds, Duke had this unfathomable hold over me; my body craved his touch long before my mind wanted his company.

He draws his index finger down the bridge of my nose, traces my lips, skims over my jaw and blazes a path down the center of my chest. His finger dances around my navel before finding my center. He teases me, gliding his finger up and down, up and down, taunting me with the promise of my release.

I'm desperate for him, dizzy with desire. My breaths are shallow, and my heart beats furiously behind my breastbone. His fingers brush over my clit causing my back to arch and my threadbare patience to snap. "Please, Duke. Oh, God, please."

We lock eyes, and he smiles wickedly. "I've got you, Cricket." He kisses his way down my body, his lips following the same path his finger took only minutes ago. I tense when his lips meet my center—a place no man has put his mouth—but his talented tongue chases all of my doubts and insecurities away, leaving nothing but pure, undiluted pleasure in return. He licks and sucks and nips at my swollen flesh with a precision I never knew was possible, as if he can anticipate my body's needs before I even know them.

I'm shaking and sweating and swearing to gods I've never even heard of, I'm so desperate to tip over the edge of the cliff I'm teetering on. I'm babbling and begging; hell, I may even be crying. But through it all, Duke's ministrations never once stop or let up. No, he feasts on me like a man possessed until I finally topple over. I cry out his name as blinding light flashes behind my lids and electricity courses through my veins; a pleasure unlike anything I've ever known before lights me up from the inside out.

"Beautiful. That was so damn beautiful," Duke coos in my ear as he brushes my damp hair away from my sweat-soaked face.

"Will…will you stay the night?" I ask, hating the thought of him being anywhere but here after what we just shared.

"Of course, Cricket. There's nowhere else I'd rather be." He peppers soft kisses all over my body before reaching my lips. "Let's rinse off, and then if you're up for it, we can watch a little TV." I start to agree but a huge yawn eclipses my words. "Or we can sleep. I'm good with either."

EVER SINCE DUKE and I made things official a week ago, I've been floating by on cloud nine. I feel calm and settled, so much so that even when one of my children has a meltdown the size of Texas, my feathers remained unruffled.

To make things even better, Jenny invited me to join her and Natalie for a nail day—something I haven't done at all since moving here, but used to do monthly with Ash.

For as much as I was dreading moving here, it's safe to say things are looking up. I could easily see myself calling Bay Ridge my home. And I haven't run into my parents at all. I guess those fifteen minutes between here and Orchard Grove make a world of difference. I know I'll have to face her one day, if only for my own healing, but with any luck, that day won't be anytime soon.

I arrive at the nail salon a few minutes early and head in to pick my color. Back in Cottonwood, I always either did a fun design—in Knight U's colors during college—or something the kids in my classroom would find fun. Today though, I'm doing this for me; I'm picking a color I like, simply because it makes me smile.

By the time Jenny and Natalie stroll in, I've narrowed it down to two choices; a shimmery teal or a pearlescent opal color. "Hey, girl," Jenny says, hugging me hello. "Hopefully we didn't keep you waiting too long."

"I was early," I say, a little embarrassed by my eagerness.

"Which color?" Natalie asks, nodding toward the two glass bottles clutched in my hands.

"I don't know. I love them both for different reasons; the teal because it's my favorite color and I like the shimmer—the kids in my class will, too. I'm not really sure why I like the other so much, but…oh my God, I am really overthinking this!"

The three of us dissolve into giggles.

"Let me see them," Jenny says, extending both of her hands my way, palms up.

I hand over both bottles and she shakes them both, inspecting the colors. "This one kind of looks like an opal. Did you know opal is considered a precious gemstone by several cultures? Like, in Roman times it was carried as a good luck talisman and believed to bring its owner good fortune. And let's be real, we can all always use a little good fortune."

When Natalie and I both just gawk at her, Jenny simply shrugs. "What? I watched a documentary on it the other day."

"Why don't you get both?" Natalie asks. "One on your nails and one on your toes."

"Oh, good plan. I see where Tatum gets her smarts from."

Natalie preens. "Can I get a recording of you saying that? You know, to play for Alden…nightly."

Both women select their colors, and we claim three chairs side-by-side, each of us sighing in delight as we sink our feet into the hot, bubbling water.

As the three of us chat about mindless topics, moving from one to the next with ease, I can't help but revel in the sense of contentment seeping into my bones. I spent so much time convincing myself that I was better off alone that I didn't truly realize what I was missing until Ashley and these two ladies beside me came along.

"Oh, hey, back to the opal, how are things with Duke?"

"Huh? What? What does my nail color have to do with him?"

Jenny smiles a small private grin as if she knows something we don't and finds it humorous. "Opal is the birthstone for October. Duke was born in October. Ergo, did the two of you ever work things out?"

My cheeks flame. While Duke and I are definitely together, we haven't really discussed whether or not we're telling people about us. Or maybe I'm just making a mountain out of a molehill. Either way, I don't want to inadvertently spill the beans—especially not without talking to him first.

"Oh, um. Well. What do you mean?"

Jenny looks at me as though I'm plumb crazy. "Y'all were already like a grease fire and then at mine and Nate's engagement party…girl. It was like someone poured water trying to put y'all out."

Natalie smirks. "And everyone knows what happens when you throw water on a grease fire."

I try to bury my head in my hands, but the little gel-filled baggies the nail tech put on them impedes my movement. *Lovely. Did I say I love manicures? I lied. I hate them.*

"Well? C'mon, girl. Talk."

I try to act cool and unaffected. "We're fine."

"Fine?" Natalie asks, exchanging looks with Jenny. "What's fine mean? Fine like I say to Alden when I'm pissy but don't want to fight or fine like…" She trails off, waiting on me to fill in her blank.

"Fine like fine. A work in progress," I say, and it's not a lie. Duke and I *are* doing just fine and we *are* a work in progress. It's like he said, our relationship is going to be one with bumps and curves along the way, but if we work together, I think we really stand a chance of fostering something magical between the two of us.

"Damn," Jenny sighs dramatically. "I was hoping you meant fine like on-your-way- to-happily-ever-after fine."

I scrunch my nose, debating internally for all of two seconds before asking, "You mean neither of y'all think it would be weird for us to be together? You know, hypothetically."

"You mean because of your sister?" Natalie asks, her voice even, with not a trace of judgment to be found. I nod, and she continues. "Listen, it doesn't matter what you do, people are going to have an opinion, and they're going to criticize. It doesn't matter if it's your brows or who you love, people think they're entitled to voice their thoughts on the matter. The trick is discerning which voices are speaking in your best interest and blocking out the rest.

"If getting pregnant at seventeen taught me anything it's that the people who truly love you and want the best for you won't yell their opinion in your face. Instead they'll speak a gentle truth."

Jenny shifts her eyes from side-to-side, waggling her brows. "What my bestie here is trying to say is *you do you, girl.* Plus, way-way back, if a woman's husband died, oftentimes his brother would step in and marry her to—"

I crack up. "No. Just no. Stop! You're not helping your case here. No."

Jenny looks to Natalie for back up. Luckily, she sides with me. "Yeah, no way, babe. You took that to creep-tastic levels. Mallory and Duke are nothing like that. IF they end up together, it'll be born out of love, not necessity."

With my eyes cast down toward my lap, I smile. I'd like to think Natalie's right, that our relationship is born out of love and that we'll beat the odds and stand the test of time. But sometimes my old insecurities rear up, planting poisonous thoughts—ones I keep buried down deep, in fear that speaking them will somehow give them life and make them true.

———

Once I get home from the nail salon, I shoot Duke a text, asking him what he's up to.

DUKE

Just finished cutting the grass, about to shower.

ME

So, what I'm hearing is you're all sweaty and possibly naked?

When his reply isn't instant, I start to second-guess myself. When the three little *typing* bubbles bounce and stop a few times, my second-guessing turns to straight-up doubt. *He probably thinks I...*his reply pings through, ending the self-sabotaging thoughts.

DUKE

Damn it. Now you've got me hard.

ME

I'd say I'm sorry, but...

DUKE

But what?

ME

But I'm not sorry. I like knowing that I turn you on. It makes me feel...powerful.

DUKE

Cricket, baby. You're a goddamn force to be reckoned with. Strong and beautiful. Smart and kind. A full-package deal.

ME

Look at you, sweet-talker.

DUKE

Why don't you do just that?

ME

Do what?

DUKE

Come over here and look at me.

ME

What if I don't want to just look? What if I want to touch, too?

DUKE

Fifteen minutes and I'm starting without you.

ME

On my way.

As tempting as it is to press the pedal to the metal and race to Duke's house, I drive the speed limit the entire way, making the trip in sixteen minutes flat. I ring the bell and let myself in. "Duke," I call out, only getting a grunt in reply.

I head straight back to his bedroom, expecting to find him freshly showered and fully-clothed with a teasing smirk on his handsome face. Instead, I find him in the bathroom, leaned back against the counter, palming his thick erection as the bathroom fills with steam from the running shower.

"Nice of you to join me," he says, sounding as casual as can be, like he's not freaking touching himself right in front of me. *Who is this man and what has he done with Duke?*

His boldness short-circuits my brain. "Um. Whoa. Hi." I struggle to keep my gaze locked with his, especially with how the muscles in his arm flex with each pull.

Duke rakes his teeth over his lower lip. "So, what's it gonna be? You gonna watch or you gonna touch?"

This man, he redefines sexy—no, forget that, he is the walking, talking, living, breathing embodiment of the word. "I…" My response fizzles on my lips as I watch his hand make another slow stroke, twisting at the tip.

He laughs deep and low and throaty, the sound shooting straight to my core as he maneuvers past me. I watch dumbfounded as he steps into the shower. *Is this really happening?* He groans as the steaming water pours over him. "The water feels real good, Cricket baby, but I bet you feel better. Why don't you come in and let me find out? I promise you'll like it."

Helpless to resist him, I strip and join him in the shower where he makes good on his promise with that expertly talented tongue of his.

After our shower, Duke tries talking me into staying the night with him. "C'mon, you know you wanna." He's a sight to behold dressed in nothing more than a pair of tight black boxer briefs as he towels off his still-dripping hair. Meanwhile, I'm still wrapped up in one of his fluffy towels.

He's right, too, I definitely want to stay. However, I know what will happen if I do, and I'm not prepared—mentally or physically—for what sex with him will do to me. Heck, it was hard enough to resist him in the shower after he brought me to two screaming orgasms, but I know it's for the best. When Duke and I finally sleep together, I want to know his feelings are for me and not confusion from missing my twin.

"I've got to get up early-early and weed the flowerbed," I say as an excuse.

"You know I'll come over and do that for you, right?"

I pop a brow at him. "And you know I'm perfectly capable of doing it on my own, right?"

He grins. "Yeah, I know. Doesn't mean I wouldn't do it anyway."

I lift my shoulder in a half shrug. "It is what it is. If I don't tend to it soon, the weeds will overtake the flowers."

"Stay anyway. I'll wake you up early."

"I don't want you to have to do that."

"I don't mind."

"Seriously, it's fine—"

"Cut the crap, Mallory. You obviously don't wanna stay; what gives?" He leans back against the doorframe, assessing me with his cool, penetrating gaze.

Grasping at straws, I blurt out, "I don't wanna sleep with you." My cheeks instantly burn with humiliation as I wish I could take back my words—too bad life doesn't work like that.

I'm fully expecting him to be annoyed with me, maybe even hurt, so his laughter takes me by surprise. "Could've fooled me with the way you were screaming my name not even ten minutes ago."

Gooseflesh covers my skin as his words wash over me. "I...that's not what I meant."

Duke crosses the room to me and runs his calloused hands over my shoulders and down my arms. "I know what you meant, baby; I'm only teasing you. You're not ready for sex and that's fine. I'm more than willing to wait. I just want you here, next to me, in my space." He presses his lips to my forehead in a soft kiss. "Will you please stay?"

How's a girl supposed to say no to that? "Yeah, Duke, I'll stay."

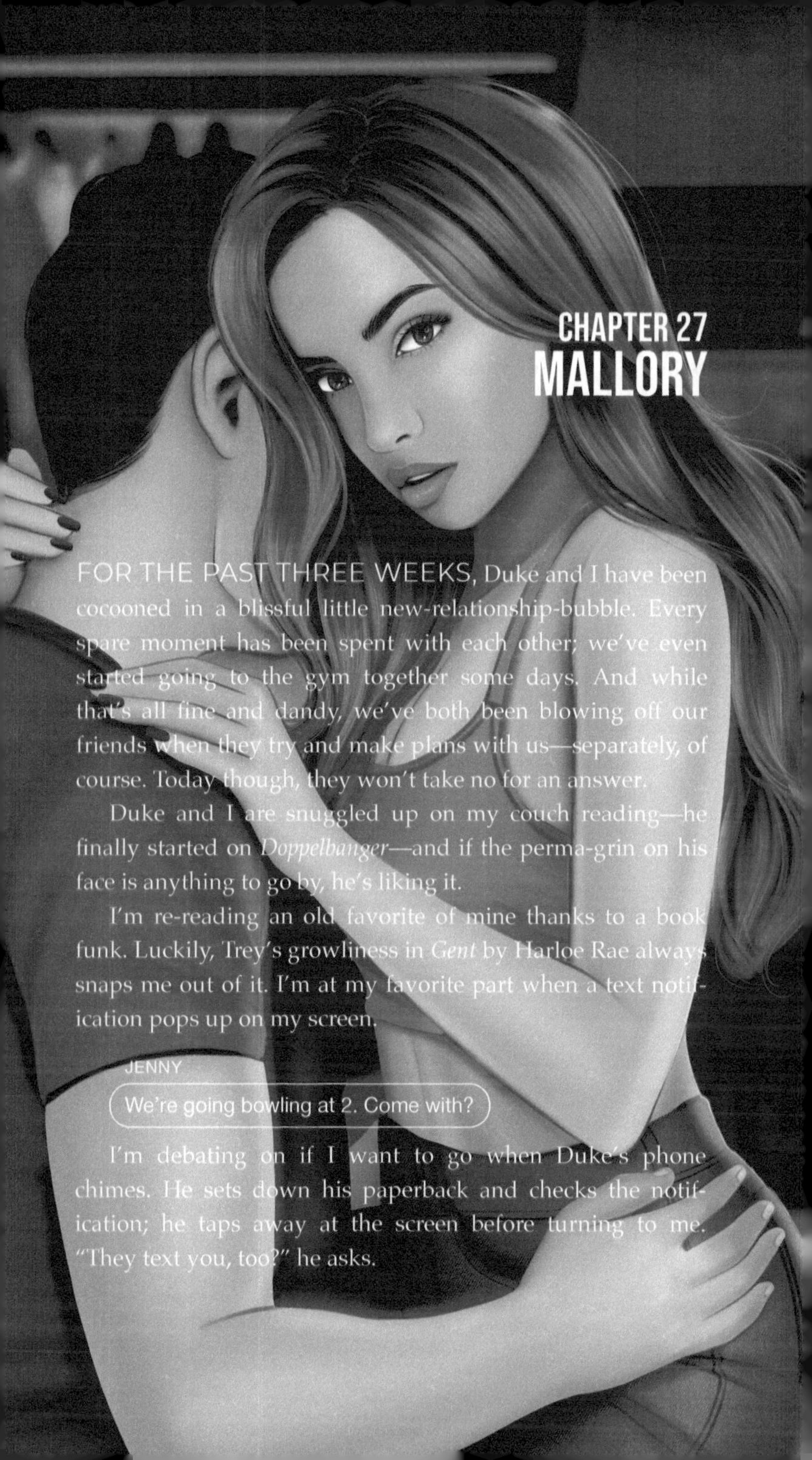

FOR THE PAST THREE WEEKS, Duke and I have been cocooned in a blissful little new-relationship-bubble. Every spare moment has been spent with each other; we've even started going to the gym together some days. And while that's all fine and dandy, we've both been blowing off our friends when they try and make plans with us—separately, of course. Today though, they won't take no for an answer.

Duke and I are snuggled up on my couch reading—he finally started on *Doppelbanger*—and if the perma-grin on his face is anything to go by, he's liking it.

I'm re-reading an old favorite of mine thanks to a book funk. Luckily, Trey's growliness in *Gent* by Harloe Rae always snaps me out of it. I'm at my favorite part when a text notification pops up on my screen.

JENNY

We're going bowling at 2. Come with?

I'm debating on if I want to go when Duke's phone chimes. He sets down his paperback and checks the notification; he taps away at the screen before turning to me. "They text you, too?" he asks.

"Jenny invited me bowling."

Duke nods. "You wanna go?"

I beam, ecstatic that he's actually asking me to join him out with our friends. Our time alone these past few weeks has been nothing short of wonderful, but I'm more than ready to take this thing public. As of right now, I'm pretty sure only Ashley knows—and that's only because she tricked me into telling her one night last week on a video chat. She squealed and I-told-you-so'd for a solid five minutes…the little smartass.

I try and play it cool though. "Um, if you do."

He falls silent for a quick minute, cracking his neck. "Yeah, let's go. We can ride together."

Internally, I squeal with excitement. Externally, I settle for a simple, "Sounds good," before texting Jenny back that I'll see her there. She sends back a million different emojis expressing her excitement.

JENNY

Good! It's been forever since I've seen your face!

ME

Has it?

JENNY

YES! Almost a month, you heifer! It's almost like you have a secret boyfriend you're hiding away with.

I sputter out a cough, dropping my phone. "You okay?" Duke asks, but I quickly recover, assuring him I'm fine.

ME

See you soon!

JENNY

> Suuuuuuure. Try and avoid me. I'll get you to
> spill all of your secrets by the third frame.

We both resume reading until I have to stop in order to get ready. Duke follows behind me up the stairs, book in hand. He plops down onto my bed and buries his nose between the pages while I select an outfit—because the ratty shorts and bralette I'm rocking won't cut it.

I dress in a pair of cut-off black denim short-shorts and an over-sized threadbare camo t-shirt that I knot in the front, exposing a sliver of my abdomen. I toss my hair up into a messy-bun, slip my feet into some cute woven sandals, and toss a pair of socks into my bag.

I check my reflection and ask Duke what he thinks. He cracks up, and I whirl around to face him ready to ask exactly what about my appearance is so funny. Only he's not laughing at me; nope, he's full-on belly laughing at the book I bought him.

"What part?" I ask.

He wipes tears from beneath his eyes. "The dolphin," is all he says and I crack up, too, knowing exactly which part he's referring to. He slides his bookmark between the pages and closes the book, his eyes on me. "Damn, Cricket. You look amazing."

I give a little mock-curtsey. "Why thank you, kind sir."

Duke springs up from the bed, draws me into his arms, and kisses me until my bones turn to jelly. He pulls away; I collapse into his chest, unsteady on my feet, and he grins. "Sure you don't wanna stay here and finish what I'm trying to start?"

I smack playfully at his chest. "Your pin and balls aren't the ones I'm looking to play with today."

He laughs and it does something magical to me. "And

that's not the kind of *strike* I was looking for." He presses one last kiss to my lips. "C'mon, I'll drive."

Duke holds my hand the entire drive to the bowling alley, and like always, the small touch sends my pulse into overdrive. He pulls into a parking spot near the back of the lot and hops out, coming around to open my door for me. He guides me toward the entrance with a hand pressed to the small of my back.

Ever a gentleman, he rushes forward to hold the door open for me and I pass through, expecting him to bring his hand back but he doesn't. At the counter, we grab our bowling shoes and head over to the lane Jenny and Nate have reserved.

"You're here!" Jenny exclaims, hugging me tightly. "You're really here!"

Laughing, I shake out of her embrace. "Live and in the flesh, you little nutter. Dramatic much?"

Jenny sighs dramatically. "Uh, no. It's been too long. Wanna tell me what's kept you so busy?" She waggles her brows and nods toward Duke. "Could it have anything to do with the handsome fellow you arrived with?"

I whirl around to face Duke. "Can't a friend give another friend a lift?" he asks, he's begging me to understand, but I don't. I really freaking don't.

Jenny's not buying it though. "Since when are y'all friends?"

Duke shrugs. "We worked it out."

I swallow down the scoff that begs to burst forth. *So much for telling our friends.* Determined not to let Duke's weirdness get to me, I fish my socks out of my purse and lace up my bowling shoes.

Natalie and Alden join us, and Jenny sets up the scorecard announcing we're playing couples. That gets Duke's attention. "But—" He starts to protest, but Jenny shushes him.

"You can team up with Mally." She cuts her eyes my

way, studying my reaction. I carefully school my features, hoping she can't read the way my heart's breaking in my chest.

Duke doesn't say anything else; he simply moves over to sit next to me. Natalie and Alden go first, followed by Jenny and Nate, with Duke and me bringing up the rear. I bowl a strike on my first try and instinctually go to hug him, but he brushes me off with an awkward high-five.

The game drags on with Jenny peppering me with questions between turns. "Why did you really ride over with Duke?" "Is he why you've been so busy lately?" "If y'all are friends, why is he acting so weird?" I do my best to ignore her, either outright or through a subject change, mostly because I don't know what to say.

Jenny's on a mission though and refuses to give up. "What's really going on?" she asks. I grab my ball from the return in preparation for my turn. I shrug, not trusting my own voice.

On my first turn, I knock down all but two pins, leaving a split. Miraculously, I knock down the remaining two, ending my turn with a spare. I join in on the cheering, despite my sour mood, lifting my arms over my head in a little dance as I spin to face everyone. My eyes lock onto Duke moving toward me and stupidly I think he's going to claim me in front of his friends, so I rush to meet him, rising on my tiptoes to kiss his cheek.

Much to my mortification, he steps back out of my reach and busies himself with grabbing his ball, refusing to look me in the face. My eyes fill with tears and my cheeks flame.

I nod to myself. "Okay. Okay. I...I um." I swallow roughly trying my hardest not to let the tears fall, but it's useless. "I think I'm just gonna go." I dash out the door, still in my bowling shoes. I've never felt like a bigger idiot than I do now. I thought we were nurturing something, that what we had was real. Now though...now I realize I was nothing more than a cheap stand-in for the girl he lost and the knowledge guts me.

I run through the parking lot, uncaring of how crazed I probably look. I keep running until I reach a little corner store a block away, where I order an Uber from my phone. Thankfully there's one five minutes away.

As I wait, I do my best to harden my heart. I may have been the only one invested in our relationship, but I swear here and now, I'll never be so easily fooled again.

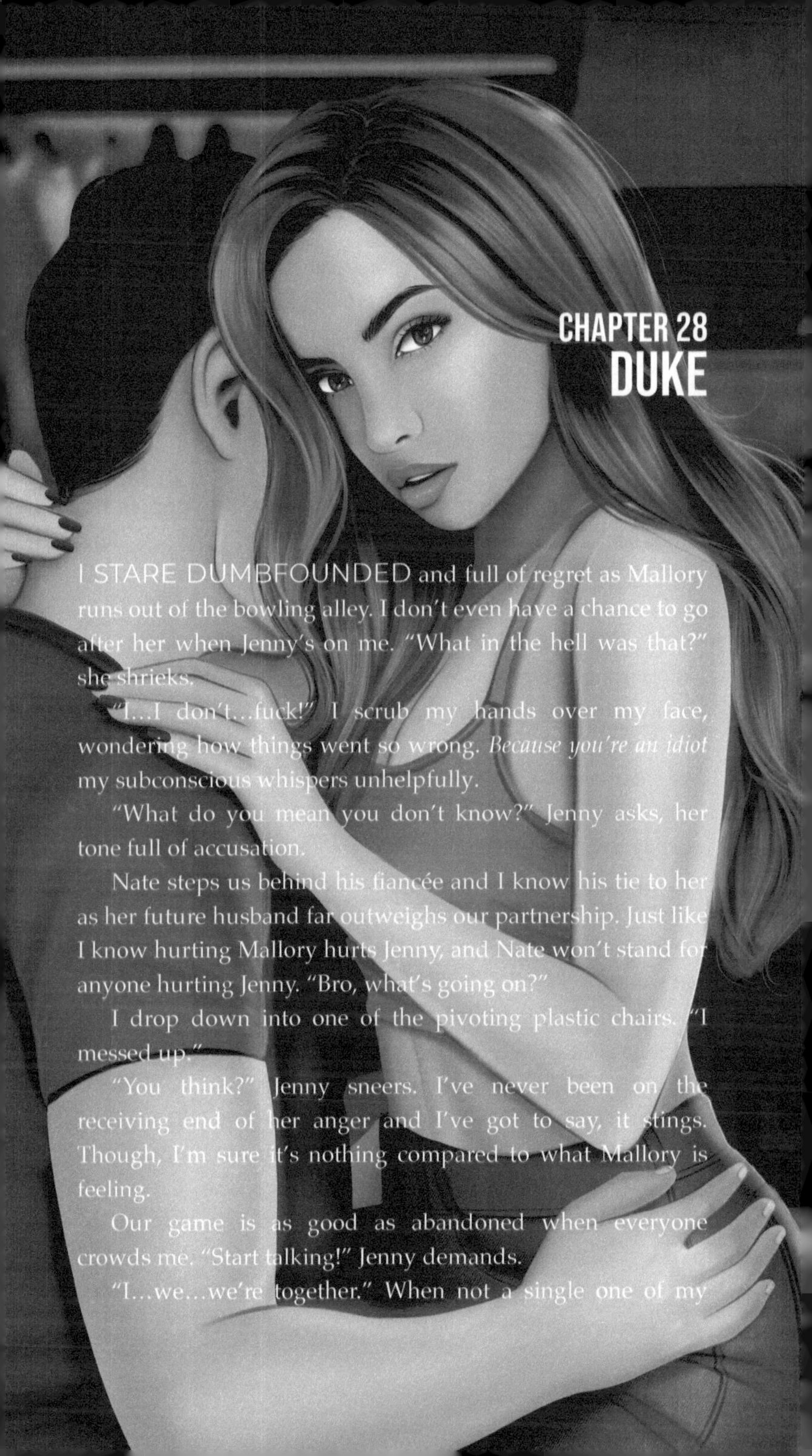

I STARE DUMBFOUNDED and full of regret as Mallory runs out of the bowling alley. I don't even have a chance to go after her when Jenny's on me. "What in the hell was that?" she shrieks.

"I…I don't…fuck!" I scrub my hands over my face, wondering how things went so wrong. *Because you're an idiot* my subconscious whispers unhelpfully.

"What do you mean you don't know?" Jenny asks, her tone full of accusation.

Nate steps us behind his fiancée and I know his tie to her as her future husband far outweighs our partnership. Just like I know hurting Mallory hurts Jenny, and Nate won't stand for anyone hurting Jenny. "Bro, what's going on?"

I drop down into one of the pivoting plastic chairs. "I messed up."

"You think?" Jenny sneers. I've never been on the receiving end of her anger and I've got to say, it stings. Though, I'm sure it's nothing compared to what Mallory is feeling.

Our game is as good as abandoned when everyone crowds me. "Start talking!" Jenny demands.

"I…we…we're together." When not a single one of my

friends seems even remotely shocked or outraged, I add, "But y'all already knew that, huh?"

Nate shakes his head at me. "I mean, we didn't know for sure."

"But you just confirmed it," his sister adds.

"Really though," Natalie starts again, "the two of you drop off the face of the earth and didn't expect any of us to put two and two together?"

"The real question is why y'all hid it from us?" Jenny taps her foot impatiently, not caring one bit that she's put me on the spot.

"Because!" I explode. "How in the hell am I supposed to announce I'm dating Valorie's twin sister? I mean, how fucking wrong is that?"

I drop my head into my hands, feeling like utter crap.

"It's not wrong," Jenny whispers. "Wanting her, loving her isn't wrong." Her voice grows louder and louder as she continues. "Wrong is making that poor girl fall for you only to diss her in front of your friends. Wrong is making Mally feel like a dirty secret. Wrong is—"

"I fucking get it!" I roar, jumping up from the chair. It quickly swivels without my weight in it, the arm knocking me hard in the back of my knee. *Shit, that hurt!*

This time it's Alden who speaks up, which really catches me off guard. "Obviously you don't, man, or you'd already be out the door after her."

His words hit me like a bag of bricks to the face and without another word, I take off, stopping only to exchange my shoes. Unfortunately, the pimply-faced kid behind the counter won't return Mallory's since she left still wearing theirs. Whatever. Her shoes are the least of my problems. At this rate, I'll be lucky if she's even speaking to me.

I sprint out the door, my eyes frantically scanning the parking lot for Mallory. She couldn't have gotten that far. She had less than a five-minute head start, so where in the hell could she be? My head moves on a swivel, looking out for any sign of her. But she's nowhere to be found.

How in the hell could I be so stupid? I was so damn caught up in what our friends would think that I completely disregarded Mallory's feelings—and let's be real, hers are the most important of all.

I skip right over trying to call her; there's no way she'll answer. Instead, I haul ass to my truck, crank the engine, and take off for her house, praying like hell she's there.

The short drive feels like a lifetime, like eons and eons have passed. I barely have the truck in park and I'm flying out of it and up her front steps. I pound on her front door, because fuck being polite when my entire future's at stake.

I'm half expecting her to ignore my sorry ass, I know I would if the tides were turned. I'm about to knock again when the door swings open, bringing me face-to-face with Mallory. Her eyes are puffy from crying, the tip of her nose and cheeks red. She looks small and fragile and I feel shittier than ever.

"Can I come in?" I ask, already knowing what her answer will be.

Even still, when she shakes her head and slips out onto the porch, it stings. "I...I don't think there's anything to say, Duke."

"There is," I insist.

Mallory offers a pained smile. "You should go home."

"No. Not until we talk. Or at least until you let me talk."

"Why?" she wails, a fresh round of tears starting. "Why? So you can drive the knife in a little farther? Are you worried you didn't make your feelings clear enough? Wanna hurt me a little more? *Oh, poor stupid pathetic Mallory...she actually thinks—*"

I slam my lips against hers, backing her into the front door trying to push all of my truths into this kiss, as if it can somehow shove all of her doubts away.

Only it doesn't work and instead she's shoving me away. "What in God's name is wrong with you? You spend a damn month making me fall for you, leading me on and on and on only to give me the cold shoulder in front of your friends! A night YOU wanted to go to! Don't you get how cruel that was, how cruel you are? I gave you my deepest, darkest secrets and you...you..." Her words devolve into heaving sobs.

Seeing an opening, I pick up where she left off. "I hurt you, Mallory. But I never led you on, not once. Everything between us was as real as the wooden planks beneath our feet. You're so amazing and I am so goddamn lucky to have you. I...I, we've been in this isolated bubble and when we got in front of everyone, I just...froze.

"I know that doesn't make it right. You deserve better than me, but please, *please* give me another chance. Please, Cricket baby, let me make this up to you. I was stupid and scared and wrong. So. Damn. Wrong. I was so concerned with what they'd think about us being together that I let it dictate how I treated you. I'm sorry. So sorry." Mallory starts to shake her head, but I press on. "I know. I know, I could apologize one-hundred times over and it still wouldn't be enough. I just want a chance to try and make this up to you; to do it right."

My chest is heaving and my heart racing by the time I finish. Mallory's tears have dried, but she still looks utterly crestfallen. "Actions speak louder than words, Duke, and your actions really, really hurt me." She gives me one last watery smile before slipping back into her house, closing and locking the door with me still on the porch.

'Actions speak louder than words, Duke.' Her parting words play over and over again in my mind. Mallory wants actions? I'll give her actions. I'll show her every way I can exactly how much she means to me. I'll fight day in and day out to prove to her that my feelings for her are real. I won't stop until she forgives me, even if it takes an eternity.

AFTER MY FRONT porch showdown with Duke, I put my phone on silent and hide away in my bedroom, cocooned in the safety of my comforter. Eventually, after many more tears, I fall into a fitful sleep where dreams of our time together flicker beneath my lids, taunting me with visions of what could have been.

His words visit me as well, tearing my heart in two. I don't know what to believe. Was it all for show…some elaborate prank to get back at me for God only knows what? Or was it real…did he truly care about me and simply freeze when in the spotlight?

The following morning, I wake with a pounding headache; but that's what hours of crying will get you. Here's to hoping I don't look as bad as I feel. I kick off the covers and trudge downstairs, hoping a little caffeine will go a long way today. The only upside to my current situation is it's the weekend, meaning I don't have to face fifteen five-year-olds with a broken heart.

With my coffee brewing, I head to the bathroom to shower. A quick glance in the mirror blows my earlier hopes to smithereens; I look worse than I feel. My hair's a rat's nest, my eyes are bloodshot and puffy, my nose is red, and my cheeks are splotchy. Legit, I look like the before picture for some kind of skincare regimen—if only I could scrub and moisturize this heartbreak away.

Even though I know it's not possible, I turn the water to scalding and attack my skin with my loofah to try to wash away the feelings until it's red and raw and aching...like my heart.

I'm aware I'm being overly dramatic, but this hurts, dammit. My heart feels like it's been run through a blender, like that old Eve 6 song. *Jesus. I need some perspective and fast. Losing Duke isn't the end of the world regardless of how it feels right now. I've survived worse.* But maybe that's why this hurts so bad—for the first time in my life I wasn't merely surviving; I was thriving.

I shut off the water and wrap myself in a towel, refilling my coffee before plodding back up to my loft. I dress in a pair of loose-fitting shorts and one of Duke's shirts— pathetic, I know—and pick up my phone. I don't bother checking any of the notifications blinking at me, calling Ashley instead.

"Yellow?" she greets like the weirdo she is.

"Hey, Ash."

"What's wrong?" she asks, her best friend Spidey senses kicking into full alert.

I sniffle, hating myself just a little for being so weak for him. "Duke."

"Tell Mama Ashley all about it."

"You don't have kids."

"Irrelevant. Now spill."

I tell her everything, from start to finish. "I...I just feel so stupid, Ash."

"You're not stupid, Mally."

"He played me. Like a dang fiddle."

My best friend makes a noise in the back of her throat.

"Did he though? No, listen. You told me he said he just sort of froze and I think he's telling the truth."

"Whose side are you on?" I cry, sounding like one of my kindergarteners when they don't get their way.

"Yours, always. Which is why I want you to listen to me. As much as you don't want to hear this, Duke had a point. Even though they've never met Valorie, they all know he was with her and they all know you're her twin. People love to judge and the thought of having to choose between them or you or to even have to explain himself or defend his relationship with you probably freaked him out to the point of shutting down. Does that make it right? No. But, from what you've said, I think he realizes he messed up and feels bad. I think if you let him, he'll prove over and over just how much you mean to him."

My eyes fill with tears again—I swear, I'm starting to think I'm defective. I didn't even cry this much when I lived with my parents. "You really think so?"

"Yeah, I do. But, don't take either of our words for it. Let him *show* you."

"But what if he doesn't?" I ask, the thought filling me with dread.

"Then fuck him."

I smile for the first time since the whole bowling alley fiasco went down yesterday. "Thanks, Ash. Love you big."

"Love you bigger; let me know how it goes." She ends the call and I melt back into my bed. I may be caffeinated and showered, but I'm still not quite ready to face the day.

Apparently, the universe has other plans for me though, because right as I get comfy there's a knock at my door. Figuring it's Duke, I holler, "Go away, Duke!"

The sound of a key in my lock has me bolting upright. I tense as the door opens. "It's not Duke, it's your landlord dearest here for a broken heart check. It's in your lease, subsection three or something."

As much as I don't want to, I smile. I'm still not used to having anyone other than Ash. The question is…is she here for me or for him?

"C'mon, Mally, we've brought you something."

"We who?" I ask, instantly on edge.

The sound of little feet racing up the stairs followed by a blur of brown curls racing my way is my only answer. "Ms. Mally!" Tatum launches herself at me like a little spider monkey. "Look! I'm here!"

"Tatum Warner! Get your tail downstairs!" Natalie yells.

Tatum huffs out an over the top sigh. "Yes, ma'am." She scrambles off my bed, tugging on my hand. "You, too. Aunt Jenny brought all kinds of stuff. She said you needed a happy."

I smile at her sweet innocence. "You being here already has me happy."

"For reals?" Tatum studies me. "You don't look happy."

Thanks a lot, kid. "Oh, yeah? And how do I look?"

"Like Amelia looked after Hayes kicked over her blocks last week."

I try and swallow but my throat feels like sandpaper. Kids see so much more than we give them credit for. "Head on down, sweetheart. I'll be right there, okay?"

Tatum gives me one more slow lookover before flying back down the stairs. I quickly shuck off Duke's shirt, trading it for a tank top with an oversized cardigan. I give myself a few more seconds of peace before joining everyone downstairs.

"So, y'all are here," I state as I step into the kitchen.

"We are," Jenny replies. "And we brought reinforcements."

Shaking my head to clear my racing brain, I ask, "What does that even mean?"

Natalie and Jenny exchange a look, silently communicating with one another, until wordlessly Natalie starts emptying out the grocery bags on the counter. I take stock of the contents, noting the familiar ingredients: a tub of vanilla ice cream and one of butter pecan, a jar of caramel sauce, Magic Shell topping, chocolate sprinkles, and whipped cream.

"Wha—how?" I ask, feeling crazy emotional as Natalie starts assembling the sundaes in precisely the right order.

Jenny opens her mouth to speak but Tatum beats her to it. "Mr. Duke said you had the sads because he was a dumbass —you can't get mad, Mama, that's exactly what he saided— and told Aunt Jenny this would help."

Jenny and I barely suppress our laughter while Natalie fights back a grin as she scolds her daughter all the while spooning sprinkles into each bowl. I guess what they say about motherhood and multi-tasking is true.

The four of us each grab a bowl and move to the living room. I lose myself in the flavors and the memory of making this for Duke. *Great. Now even this makes me think of him.*

Jenny finishes first since her serving is much smaller than everyone else's due in part to her being a type one diabetic. "So. I was right; you did have a secret boyfriend."

My shoulders sag and I push away my bowl with two bites still remaining. "Had. Past tense."

Natalie reaches over and squeezes my shoulder. "Don't count him out just yet."

"Look, I know y'all are close with him and…wait! How did y'all know about Ashley's Has the Sad's Sundae?"

Tatum rolls her eyes, the sass this kid has could easily rival a teenager. "I already told you, Mr. Duke sent us."

"Really? He…" Words fail me as the implications of Tatum's words become clear. Not only did Duke remember what this sugary concoction was for, he sent our friends over here for my benefit. He sent them here to comfort me. Because he knew he messed up.

"Girl, he's got it bad for you." Jenny smirks, looking all

too smug. "I called it, in case you forgot; at my engagement party, I told you he wanted you and as per usual, I was right."

Natalie snorts. "How does my brother handle you?"

Jenny wags her brows and Natalie gags. "Oh, God. Forget I asked!"

Tatum stares at both of them like they're insane; I'm starting to wonder if the kid might just be on to something.

I bury my face in my hands. "What do I do?"

"You decide if he's worth it and if he is, you give him another shot," Natalie says at the same time Jenny shouts, "Make him grovel!" *Yep, totally crazy because Duke Kincaid is not the kind of man who grovels.*

"Wanna know what I think, Ms. Mally?" Tatum asks, coming to sit beside me.

While I'm not sure what kind of advice a five-year-old with no knowledge of the situation can offer, I humor her. "Sure, lay it on me."

"I don't wanna lay on you. I wanna give you advice." Tatum sounds absolutely exasperated.

The urge to chuckle at her pure cuteness is overwhelming, but I manage to rein it in. "Right. Sorry. Continue."

Tatum heaves out a sigh, steepling her fingers beneath her chin in a way that is all her daddy. "Remember Amelia's blocks?"

How could I forget? "Yup. She was really sad when Hayes kicked them over. Mad, too."

The little girl's eyes brighten and she bounces in her seat. "Exactly! It's just like that. Mr. Duke knocked over your block heart and made you sad and mad. But remember what you told Amelia, Ms. Mally? You tolded her it was okay because she could rebuild them into something even better! You can do that, too! You can rebuild your heart with Mr. Duke into something better!"

By the time she's finished, Tatum has rendered her mother,

Jenny, and myself speechless. The more I think about it, the more it makes sense. Duke did kick over my feelings like a tower of blocks, but that doesn't mean all hope is lost. It doesn't mean we can't rebuild.

MONDAY MORNING DAWNS and while my heart still feels heavy, it's less so. My eyes are also less puffy and my cheeks less red. And in keeping with the less theme, I'm hoping today is less awful than the last two.

I still haven't checked any of Duke's messages or returned his calls, which makes me a total wimp. But I'm so dang scared of the hold he has over my heart that not knowing almost seems easier. *Nut up, buttercup*—that's what Ashley would tell me, and I will…after say ten or so cups of coffee.

I cave after only two.

DUKE

Mallory, where are you?

DUKE

Please answer your phone.

DUKE

Cricket, baby, please. I know I messed up, but we need to talk.

DUKE

Thank you for answering the door and for letting me apologize face to face. I know my words aren't enough. I'll find a way to make this up to you. Swear it.

DUKE

You're so damn beautiful. I hate knowing I made you cry.

DUKE

I miss you, Cricket.

DUKE

You wanna know why I call you that? Text me back and I'll tell you.

Sneaky bastard. While I've never outright asked, I've always wondered. I down the rest of my coffee and reply before I lose my nerve.

ME

Why?

His reply is instantaneous.

DUKE

Did you know crickets are a sign of good luck...that they symbolize happiness?

ME

Nope, definitely didn't know that. Also not buying that as the reasoning behind it. So...

DUKE

You're right. No BS...at first it was because you were like one...always there, chirping away, and driving me nuts.

ME

Charming...

DUKE

But now, my happiness is so tied up in you, I'd do damn near anything to see you smile. I know I messed up, baby, but please let me prove to you how serious I am about us. Please?

ME

I forgive you, Duke. But I'm not sure I trust you.

DUKE

I can work with that. I can def work with that.

I don't respond to his last text; I have exactly ten minutes to get to the school and no time to waste if I want to beat the carline traffic. I do my best to push him from my mind; my kids deserve my full attention and I have fun plans for our class today.

However, a little before lunchtime, there's a knock on my door. "Hang on, guys, let me see who's here." A chorus of groans and grumbles rise and I clap my hands, getting their attention. "Clap twice if you can hear me." Only a few students clap and the door knocker knocks again. "Clap four times if you can hear me." The entire class claps. "Thank you. Please wait patiently and I promise we will finish our story."

This time, they stay quiet, allowing me to tend to our visitor. I'm expecting a parent joining us for lunch or another teacher, not a random police officer holding a stunning succulent garden in a sleek weathered slate pot. "Mallory Parsons?" he asks, sounding all kinds of official.

"Um, yes...sir."

"These are for you." He passes me the pot and I accept, not knowing what else to do. "Officer Kincaid says for me to tell you that the best is yet to come." He pivots on the balls of his feet and heads toward the exit, leaving me with a ton of questions. *The best is yet to come...what does that even mean?*

I finagle the attached note out of its little holder and read it before stepping back into my classroom.

Cricket,
My life succs without you.
Succs...get it?
Yours, Duke

I'm smiling like a love-struck fool, precariously balancing my succulents as I step back into the room and pull the door shut behind me. Tatum, being the precocious child she is, immediately calls out my floral delivery. "Oooh, Ms. Mal— Parsons! Did Mr. Duke send you those?"

Until now, my knowing her parents socially has never been an issue, but the second those words leave her lips, a barrage of questions from her classmates follow.

"Who's Mr. Duke?" "Is he your boyfriend?" "Do you love him?" "Are you gonna marry him?" "Mr. Duke and Ms. Parsons sitting in a tree..."

They're so excited over the potential of having the inside scoop on my love life that it takes me clapping out numbers four times to get their attention. "Children. If you can hear me, clap three times."

They clap back, but Tatum speaks out. "Please just tell us who they're from? Please?"

This kid is relentlessly cute; it's a wonder her parents can ever tell her no with her big, puppy dog eyes. "They're from my friend. He's a police officer."

Tatum smirks and turns to the girl next to her. "Told you. Mr. Duke's a cop with my uncle Nate."

I field a few more questions from my more persistent children, resigned to finishing our story after lunch.

The rest of the school day runs smoothly with no hiccups and when I get home, I'm ready to stuff my face and veg out on the couch. Only before I can do that, I need to thank Duke for my lovely succulents. They look right at home on my coffee table.

ME

Thank you.

DUKE

You're welcome. What are you up to?

I'm not sure I'm ready to casually chat with him, but his question seems harmless enough.

ME

Trying to figure out dinner. You?

DUKE

Same. I'm thinking Chinese.

ME

Omg. I could get down on some lo mein.

Duke goes silent again after that, but I'm too absorbed in my show to really notice. He's got me on a huge true crime kick and *Murder Mountain* is freaking fascinating. I'm binging happily when a knock sounds at my door. I pause my show and pad over to the door, checking the peephole.

There on the other side of the door is a gangly kid sporting a hat with the logo of a local food-delivery company. *What the…?* I open the door and say, "I didn't place an order."

"I've got an order of chicken lo mein and two eggrolls for a Mallory Parsons. Is that you?"

That sneaking sneak. He sent dinner over—innocent conversation, my ass.

"Oh, um, yes, that's me. Thanks." The kid passes me my food. "Oh! Let me grab some cash to tip you."

He holds his hands up in front of him. "It's already been taken care of. You have a nice night."

Here I am for the second time in one day texting Duke to say thanks.

ME

You trickster. Thank you though. I was going to settle for a T.V. dinner.

DUKE

That would have succed. Heh.

ME

Yeah, yeah. You're cute and clever.

DUKE

Oh, so you think I'm cute? Tell me more...

ME

Goodnight, Duke.

DUKE

Goodnight? It's not even six.

ME

Goodnight.

I could easily keep texting him, but with every gesture and every message, I can feel my heart thawing toward him. And while I meant it when I said I forgave him, I'm not quite sure I'm ready for anything more...yet.

ON TUESDAY, my morning starts with a breakfast delivery—eggs, bacon, and toast; the Duke special. During naptime, he has a coffee sent to my classroom from Oh, Sugar. And for dinner, he has the most amazing steak ever delivered from Bayside Café. I'm two bites in when my phone rings with his name popping up on the screen.

I swallow my bite and answer. "I'm guessing I have you to thank for this delicious meal?"

"Sure do. And guess what else?"

Nerves zing over my skin. "What?"

"I got the same thing, so I figured we could eat together… over the phone," he groans. "Fuck. That sounded way cooler in my head."

My lips part as a smile overtakes my face. "I…I think it's sweet."

"Really?"

"Yeah, Duke, just like everything else you've been doing this week."

"Sweet enough to earn me a real date?"

I'm so tempted to say yes; it's on the tip of my tongue. I'd say he's shown he cares. I'm going to do it. "Yes."

Duke lets out a gleeful holler and then clears his throat, trying to play it off. "Cool, cool. How about Friday night?"

"Sure, Duke. Friday sounds good."

"I'll pick you up at six?"

"Yeah, that works for me."

"Good. I miss you, Cricket baby. A lot." His voice clogs with emotion.

"I miss you, too," I whisper before ending the call.

Wednesday and Thursday pass in a flurry of sweet texts and anticipation. We also talk on the phone each night until I fall asleep to the sound of his voice. To an outsider, all of this probably sounds insanely immature. But to a girl who never had anything like this in high school—or college, because my ex sucked—it's perfect, a dream come true.

I take extra care getting ready Friday morning because knowing my luck, I'll somehow not have time to freshen up after school and I want to look my best after not seeing Duke for almost an entire week.

It was really jarring to go from seeing him almost daily to not at all. Clearly, I'm not a cold-turkey kind of girl and I really, *really* want tonight to go well.

Without knowing where he's taking me, I opt for olive colored jeans, a loose-fitting white top, and a floral-patterned kimono. I keep my hair simple, styled into a messy braided bun and my makeup natural; the last thing I need is fifteen small children pestering me about why I look so fancy.

The first half of the day passes like molasses, especially with no wake-up text or anything from Duke. But I brush it off, not wanting to look needy. However, when lunchtime nears and I still haven't heard from him, I discreetly shoot him a text; it goes unanswered.

At ten-forty-five, we line up and head to the cafeteria. As we approach the doors, the sight of Duke decked out in his uniform stops me in my tracks. "Hey there," he greets with a wink.

"Uh. Um…hi," I reply lamely. But, in my defense, what on earth is he doing here?

"You hungry?" he asks and I nod. "What about y'all? Are you guys hungry?"

"YES!" my children all shout, blatantly ignoring the no-talking-while-in-line rule. I can't really blame them though.

"Do y'all like pizza?" Again, he's met with happy yells. "Okay, good, and cupcakes…do y'all like cupcakes?"

My kids are no longer human, howling like hyenas with excitement. And while I'm every bit as over the moon as they are, other teachers are giving me the look—the one that says *thank God my class doesn't act like that.*

"Class. Clap once if you can hear me." No one claps. "Class! Clap three times if you can hear me." Duke grins and claps right along with them. "Great. Please proceed single file to our table."

I count off the kids as they walk past me and Duke falls in beside me as I bring up the end of the line. "You know, you're kind of hot when you get all authoritative," he says out of the side of his mouth.

"Oh, yeah? You're into being talked to like a child?"

He stops me with a hand to my wrist. "Baby, I'm into you talking to me period, however I can get it."

My cheeks flame. "What are you even doing here?"

"Couldn't wait until tonight. Now, c'mon, I got two large piping hot pizzas and two dozen cupcakes."

Tatum monopolizes most of Duke's time during our lunch period, which is fine by me. She's so freaking cute as she brags over him. I also catch a few other faculty members checking him out, which leaves me wondering how I'm lucky enough to call him mine. That thought gives way to guilt, though because if not for Val dying…he wouldn't be. Plain and simple.

I shake off my macabre thoughts, determined to enjoy the food he brought as well as his company. I have to believe my sister would want us to find happiness—even if that means being happy together.

The rest of the day passes in a blur and before I know it, six o'clock is here and Duke's knocking on my door, a box of chocolates in hand and a gleam in his eyes that skyrockets my heart rate.

"Ready for our date?" he asks as I step out onto the porch, his hand brushing my mine as I move past him. The barely-there touch ignites a maelstrom of emotions inside me.

Ready or not, here we go.

TO SAY I'm nervous would be an understatement. I'm low-key worried I'm making a monumental mistake taking Mallory back to the scene of the crime, so to speak. But at the same time, us getting a redo feels right.

When Jenny invited us out and I agreed, she lit up like a bonfire. And I'm the asshole that dimmed her flame. Now I'm more determined than ever to breathe life back into it—and everyone knows oxygen only fans the flames.

"Where are we going?" Mallory fidgets in her seat, glancing around as if a neon sign with our destination will pop up if she looks hard enough.

"There's no fun in telling you; it'd spoil the surprise."

She bats her long lashes at me, tempting me to spill my secrets, but I hold strong, hoping like hell this doesn't blow up in my face. "Ugh. Fine. Spoilsport."

I'm tense as I turn into the bowling alley parking lot, my grip on the wheel white-knuckle strong. "Duke..." Mallory whimpers from the passenger seat.

"Do you trust me, Cricket?" She nods silently as she fidgets in her seat. "Good. I've got you. I'm gonna make this right."

I park my truck and cut the engine before coming around

to open her door. Like the last time we were here, I guide her toward the building with a hand to her back. Unlike last time, Mallory is practically shaking with her nervous energy. I hate knowing I'm the cause of her distrust; I hate knowing I hurt her.

At the door, Mallory hesitates, turning to face me. "Please don't make me regret this."

I hold her golden gaze before pressing a chaste kiss to her lips. "No regrets, Cricket baby. Not between us—never between us."

Mallory steels her spine, standing straight with her head held high—it's truly a thing of beauty to watch her strengthen her resolve. It's even sweeter knowing she's walking through these doors with me.

Inside, Jenny, Nate, Natalie, and Alden are holding down our lane. Mallory sees them and casts a worried glance back my way. Desperate to soothe her, I step to her side and grasp her hand with mine, twining our fingers together, claiming her for our friends to see.

She sucks in a nervous breath and I lean down to whisper in her ear, "There's no more hiding, Cricket. You're mine and I want everyone to know."

The next few hours are split between ten frames, three plates of nachos, just as many pitchers of beer, and countless smiles. There's something freeing about being able to touch and hug and kiss Mallory whenever I feel like.

Once the last pin is knocked down, Jenny tallies the scores, gleefully announcing that she and Nate won. "Nat, you and Alden came in second place; which means last place goes to Duke and Mallory." Her lips tip up in a good-natured smile. "How's it feel to lose, sucker?"

With an indulgent smile, I wrap an arm around Mallory's middle and tug her to me. "Feels a lot like winning," I reply to Jenny before capturing Mallory's lips in a too-hot-for-public kiss.

———

Summer gives way to fall as Mallory and I continue to nurture this flame between us. The more I get to know her, the more I realize just how different she truly is from her sister. I'm talking night and day. Where Valorie was rigid and a numbers girl, Mallory is a little more carefree and impulsive; and I don't mean either of those in a bad way. When I was young, Valorie was exactly what I needed to mellow me out and keep me on the straight and narrow.

But now...it's as though Mallory is tailor-made for me. She constantly pushes me to step outside of my box; whether it's something small like reading a romance novel or something huge like finally purchasing furniture for my house, she keeps me on my toes and I love it.

Currently, we're snuggled up on my brand-new massive leather sectional with a chunky cable knit blanket that Mallory insisted would look great in my house covering us. "Are you sure you wanna sell the stuff you and Val bought? You know I wouldn't mind if you used it, right?"

She's so damn perfect. Most women won't let you keep a sweater your ex bought, but here she is offering to use the furnishings her own twin picked day in and day out. "Cricket, I'm sure. Plus we already bought this beast," I say, patting the cushion next to me.

She rolls her beautiful eyes at me. "Duke. The only thing you've bought so far is this couch—"

"And this blanket," I say, interrupting her, tugging it tighter around us.

"And this blanket." She laughs lightly before turning serious. "You still have so much in storage—a dining table, dressers, rugs, and more. I...I understand if looking at the things you bought with her is too painful, but please don't sell it all if I'm the reason. I know Val will always be a part of you and I would never want to take that away."

I stare at her, dumbfounded by her words, her thoughtfulness, her…Mallory-ness. "I'll think about it, okay?"

She smiles and my heart beats a little harder in my chest. *Will there ever come a day where she doesn't affect me like this? I sure as hell hope not.* "Sure. But while you're thinking about it, can you think about helping me out with my booth for the fall festival?"

I tug her onto my lap, lunging for her and capturing her lips with mine in a mind-bending kiss. I lick into her mouth, my tongue mingling with hers before pulling away. Foreheads pressed together, I run the tips of my fingers over her cheek. "Now that I don't have to think about it; of course, I'll help. The department usually sends some guys, I'll make sure and get my name on the list tomorrow. Nate's, too."

Her honey eyes go molten as she looks at me with so much affection. "You're such a good man. So good to me. What did I do to deserve you?"

I give her a boyish smile. "You're you, Cricket baby. You're you."

TRUE TO HIS WORD, Duke signed both Nate and himself—along with two other officers—to represent the Bay Ridge PD at the school's fall festival. Duke and I arrive early to set up my booth—I totally lucked out with being assigned the pumpkin painting booth.

It only takes us fifteen minutes to set up. We have one rectangular table loaded down with miniature craft pumpkins, paper plates, and an assortment of non-toxic water-based paints and more paintbrushes and sponges than I've ever seen. We set up a second table, dividing it down the center; the left side for painting and the right for drying.

"Looks good, Cricket," Duke says, surveying our work.

"Thanks to you." I rise up and kiss his cheek, loving the feel of his scruff beneath my lips. "You ready to spend your day corralling kids with me?"

His eyes flash with some unknown emotion. "Baby," he growls out, the husky tone shooting straight to my center. "I'm—"

Whatever he was going to tell me is washed away by Tatum's arrival. "Ms. Parsons! Mr. Duke! I want to paint a pumpkin. Can I? Please?"

Duke scans the festival area. "Where are your parents?"

Tatum shrugs. "They were talking to Uncle Nate, but I saw y'all and—"

"Tatum!" Natalie's panicked voice rings out.

"She's over here, Nat," I call back before turning to face Tatum. I crouch down so we're eye-to-eye. "I thought we talked about this; about not running off? Remember?"

The little girl's shoulders slump and I feel bad—but only a little, because her safety and well-being is more important. "Yes, ma'am, I remember."

Natalie pulls her daughter aside for a few minutes, most likely to reinforce what I said, before returning to the booth. "Let's paint Daddy a pumpkin?"

A sullen Tatum instantly brightens. "Can we make it look like Branch?"

"We can try." Natalie winks at her daughter and begins mixing paints in search of the perfect grayish-blue.

By the time the festival wraps up, Duke and I are both exhausted. "That was..." He trails off for a second, searching for the right word. "...Intense."

"But in a good way?" I ask, hopefully. I love kids—obviously—and want a big family. If Duke didn't feel the same, it might crush me. I guess we still have a lot to talk about.

"Definitely. Some of those kids were a trip. And don't get me started on the way Tatum bossed all of her friends around like a little drill sergeant."

"More like a commanding officer." I wink at him and he smiles.

Duke bends down and retrieves something from beneath the table. "So, I managed to save two pumpkins. Wanna paint one?"

My body tingles at his thoughtfulness. "Yes! And we can trade when we're done?"

"Perfect."

We both set to work painting our pumpkins. I go for a simple concept that will match his house, painting the entirety of the sphere a soft cream color, accenting it with a wide gray buffalo-check and the letter K—for Kincaid—on the front in teal. Yeah, yeah, I snuck my favorite color in… sue me.

Duke, on the other hand, goes all out, painting the pumpkin white and covering it in an assortment of candy-colored hearts with the words *No regrets, always* in gold. My eyes mist with tears when he presents it to me and I fling myself at him, wrapping my arms around his neck and my legs around his waist as I kiss him senseless. "I love you," I whisper the words against his lips, meaning them with every fiber of my being.

He tenses under my touch momentarily before reclaiming my lips with his. He pours his unspoken reply into his kiss, drowning me in a tidal wave of emotion. Sure, he didn't speak the words back to me, but I can feel it—he loves me, too, and I'm okay to wait him out on this. After all, the best things in life are worth waiting for.

AS THE WEATHER GROWS COLDER, my relationship with Duke grows stronger. Over the past few weeks, he still hasn't told me he loves me back, but he shows me daily and that means way more. I meant it when I told him actions over words and Duke leaves no room for doubt with his.

"It finally feels like things are falling into place," I tell Ash as we video chat.

She's quiet as she polishes her little toe. "It's fate. I told you this is where you belonged."

I smother a laugh. "Yup, you called it."

"But…" she hedges, knowing me too dang well.

"But? But nothing."

"Lies!" She holds up her fingers making a cross. "Speak truth, evil-doer!"

"My God, you're weird. Right, but weird."

She smirks. "Let's focus on the *right* part. What am I right about?"

Heaving out a sigh worthy of a teenaged blockbuster, I throw myself back onto my bed. "I want to go visit Val." She remains silent, knowing there's more. "And I…I think maybe I should go see my parents."

"Closure." It's a statement, not a question.

"Yeah, something like that. It's just…I feel like they still have so much power over me and avoiding them is the coward's way out. I want to be strong. I want to show them—and me—that they didn't break me, that I'm whole and healthy and happy and there's nothing they can do to take that from me. Is that dumb?"

Ashley tsks me. "Your feelings are never dumb. You do you, Mally. Show your mean-ass mama what a badass daughter she has—show her you thrived despite her constantly trying to cut you down. Show. Her." She screws the brush back into the polish bottle. "Plus, I think going to see your sister will be good for you, too—cathartic."

"Yeah. I've wanted to go for a while now, but…it feels weird. Like, I know she's dead, but I still want to talk to her, to tell her about Duke and me."

"Everyone heals and grieves differently; there is no right or wrong way. I happen to think it's hella cool you want to go chat with her."

"Really? You don't think I sound crazy?"

Ashley levels me with a serious stare. "No more crazy than any other person coping with the loss of a loved one. Obviously, your situation is a little different than most, but I think it's honorable. I believe souls linger after death, and you talking to her…I bet it will give her peace just as much as it does you."

I'm not so sure about the whole souls lingering thing, but regardless, I know it will soothe *my* soul and that's enough for me to make up my mind. "I'm gonna do it. Duke is working until late tonight, so now's as good a time as any."

Ashley nods decisively. "Good. And remember, call me if you need a little boost. You got this, Mally. Love you big!"

"Love you bigger." I end our chat feeling ready to take on the world—well, maybe not the world, but at least Orchard Grove, Alabama.

———

What should only be a fifteen-minute drive takes almost double that. Nerves flutter in my belly and I ride my brakes pretty much the whole way. I'm sure if Duke were with me, he'd scold me for being an unsafe driver—I can hear him now, *'Speed limits exist for a reason, Cricket. Going under is just as dangerous as going over. Arrive alive!'*. He'd punctuate with a cocky little wink, too, God love him.

Once I finally make it to the cemetery, I shoot him a text.

ME

> Hey, handsome. I know you're busy protecting and serving, but I wanted to let you know I decided to go visit Val's grave. Stay safe…love you!

I toss my phone into the cupholder and exit the car. A singular ray of golden sunlight illuminates my sister's gravestone—fitting since she always lit up any room. Lowering myself to the ground, I read the inscribed words: *Valorie Lynn Parsons, beloved daughter gone too soon*, followed by her date of birth and her date of death.

A chill sweeps over me, turning my skin to gooseflesh as I run my pointer-finger over her name. It feels so…strange… being here, knowing that the first person to ever treat me decent, the first person to ever love me is sitting six feet beneath me in a pine box.

"I miss you," I speak aloud, hoping Ash is right and that she can hear me. "I miss you so much. I wanted to come see you sooner, but…at first I was scared to even step foot back in this place. And then…Duke happened. He's such a good man, Val." I laugh, but it's humorless. "But you know that— you know he's good and kind and honorable and selfless."

My tears fall unchecked as I lay my head against the cool marble. "I love him, you know? And he loves me—I know he does. I hope you're okay with that. Because he still loves you, too, and he always will. You're such an important part of who he is and while I wish you were here and that you two could have had your happily ever after together, I want you to know I'll always treat him right and I'll always honor your memory and your past with him.

"I don't want to replace you, Val. I don't want to diminish what y'all had. I just want to make him smile the way he does me. I just want to love him, to be there for him. I really think he and I have a chance at something special and I have to believe in my heart of hearts that you'd be okay with it because I know you loved him, too. I know it was a selfless kind of love and you'd want him to be happy."

My voice and heart break simultaneously. "I promise I'll do my best to make him happy." I stay here, with my cheek pressed into her tombstone, sobbing for what feels like an eternity in my mind, but is only mere minutes in reality.

My tears steadily flow until the sky splits open raining down tears of its own on me, the droplets of water intermingling with my own making them indiscernible. The cold rain drenches me from head-to-toe, but still, I linger. Even cold and wet, I feel a kind of peace I haven't felt in a long time.

Finally when I start to shiver, I press my lips to Val's grave, telling my sister I love her one last time before I stand, ready to make a mad dash to my car.

"It should be you in that grave," comes a voice from behind me—one that's haunted my nightmares for years. My mother. *She's here*...the thought nearly paralyzes me with dread. While most children were afraid of the monster in their closet, mine lived in the bedroom down the hall. But I'm done letting my fear of her control me.

Slowly, I turn on the spot and face her. "You really mean that?" My lower lip wobbles but I refuse to shed a single tear for Nancy Parsons.

"With every fiber of my being." She takes a step toward

me and my entire body tenses as memories of her past abuse flood me. "How dare you even come here."

"She was my sister."

My mother mocks me, cruelly parroting my words back at me. "Well, she was my daughter. My pride and joy. The best thing in my life."

Her words pierce my skin like little needles, stinging as they break the surface. "Why are you so awful?" I mutter the words to myself, but she hears them.

"You will watch your mouth, girl."

"Why? Why do you hate me? I'm. Your. Child. You should love me and want the best for me, yet my entire life you made me feel less than, like I wasn't good enough. You placed Valorie up on a pedestal and kicked me into the mud. How? Why? What kind of mother treats their own child that way? How can you stand to look at your reflection knowing how awful you were to me? It's not like I asked to be born!"

Nancy sneers. "I didn't ask for you either. All I wanted was one. One perfect child. You know, the doctor didn't even realize you were there until I was twenty-two weeks along." Her face transforms from mild disgust to full-on hate. "I would have aborted you if I could—that's how much I didn't want you."

Thunder fills the air around us as she spews her hate. "No. No!" I shake my head, desperate to dispel the wretchedness of her words. "Why?"

"I knew your sister was the baby we prayed for the moment she was born. So soft and small—precious. And then you came." Her lips curl as if even the thought of me as a newborn is enough to sicken her.

What's really sick though is my sister was born first—by mere minutes—it made her the perfect child and me cursed. A lifetime of abuse because I was born second. My heart hurts with the knowledge of Nancy's truth.

"You're demented!" I scream, tears and rain blurring my

vision. Which is why I don't see her coming. Nancy shoves me—hard—sending me down to the wet ground in a heap. I try and stand but lose my footing on the wet grass, landing on my knees. She advances toward me again and I scramble back, knocking over the flowers and knickknacks surrounding her grave as I go.

"No!" my mother howls, her words garbled with fury. I curl in on myself, covering my head with my hands, but it's no use as she drops down to her knees in front of me and grabs a chunk of my hair. "Look what you did!" She yanks my head back out of my protective embrace, forcing me to look at the mess surrounding us—framed photos lay askew and flowers lay all around us.

Nancy releases my hair with a shove, my head smacking against the marble with a sickening thud. I cradle my throbbing head in my hands as heaving sobs wrack my body. "You're worthless! It should have been you in that wreck! Not your sister! You stupid! Little! Bitch!"

I peek from between my fingers, watching as she stands and paces, her hands desperately tugging at her matted hair. Too terrified to move, I fold in on myself as she drops back to her knees and begins sifting through the mementos scattered around us, even trying to salvage the trampled flowers. "Oh, Valorie. My sweet, sweet Valorie. It's okay. Mama's here." She sounds absolutely crazed, talking to my sister's pictures as if they're a living, breathing thing.

She's completely unhinged, I realize as she turns to me with an evil glint in her eyes. "You did this!"

I RETURN to the car after dashing into Oh, Sugar to re-up mine and Nate's caffeine situation, over this day and over the rain. I want nothing more than to punch the clock and head to Mallory's. A little bit of food and a whole lot of her is exactly what I need.

"Your phone buzzed," Nate tells me as I slam the passenger door in an effort to escape the downpour.

I snatch it up from the dash, grinning when I see Mallory's name.

MALLORY

Hey, handsome. I know you're busy protecting and serving, but I wanted to let you know I decided to go visit Val's grave. Stay safe…love you!

I read and re-read her text, dread pooling in my gut. Nancy always visits Val's grave the last Sunday of the month and if she and Mallory cross paths… "Shit!"

"What?" Nate jolts at my outburst.

Without answering him, I dial Darryl. "Duke," he answers. "How are you?"

I skip right over the pleasantries. "Where's Nancy?"

"She went to visit Val."

Fuck. "When? How long ago did she leave?"

"Son, what's with all—"

"When did she leave?" I yell into the phone, garnering a weird look from Nate.

"About twenty minutes ago."

I pull the phone away from my ear and check the time-stamp on her text—twenty minutes ago. "I need you to listen to me. Mallory is at Val's grave right now."

Darryl sucks in a sharp breath. "Oh, no. No, she can't—Nancy will…Duke, she can't be there when Nancy gets there."

I mouth the word *station* to Nate, hoping like hell he understands what I'm telling him. I have to warn Mallory. I have to protect her. "Call her. Distract her. Delay her. Now!" I end the call and immediately dial Mallory. It rings and rings until her voice mail picks up. I call her again and again, my panic increasing with each unanswered call.

I hear Nate talking to someone on his phone, but my brain doesn't have the capacity to make sense of his words; the only thing I can focus on is Mallory. I don't know the extent of her mother's abuse, but I know it was enough to send her running the first chance she got and the thought of her facing her all alone eats me up inside. I should be there with her, at her side.

Nate pulls into the station lot, pulling up right next to my truck. "Xavier is coming in to cover you. Go get your girl."

Gratitude for the man next to me—my best friend, my partner—overwhelms me. "Thank you."

"Go! Update me when you can." Nate doesn't have to tell me twice; I'm out of the cruiser, in my truck, and on my way to Orchard Grove in the blink of an eye.

As a cop, there's nothing I hate more than going into a

situation blind, unfortunately it's part of the job. But with Mallory, not knowing if she's okay—it's wretched.

The pounding rain makes the drive take longer than it should and with every swish of my wiper blades, my worry intensifies. My body is rigid with tension and my grip on the wheel is so tight my fingers ache; I'm pretty sure I don't take a full breath until the cemetery gates come into view.

I pull up behind Darryl's car, my body instantly on high alert. As Valorie's plot comes into my view and the scene unfolds before me—Darryl restraining a screaming, rabid Nancy and my girl cowering on the cold, wet ground sobbing —I'm enraged and heart-stricken all at once. *How…how could anyone spew the kind of hate Nancy is at their own child? And how was I so blind to the kind of woman she really is? She's not a grieving mother; she's a monster using her loss as an excuse for behavior.*

Flying past Darryl and Nancy, I head straight for Mallory, dropping to my knees next to her. I move to wrap her in my arms but she whimpers and shoves me away. "No!" Her voice is small and shaky.

"Shh, Cricket, it's me." I try and pull her to me again; this time she allows it, clinging to me.

"D-Duke?" She presses her face into my chest and I hold her trembling body closer.

"I'm here. You're safe, baby. I've got you."

She all but melts into me with her arms around my neck and her fingers clutching the collar of my shirt as I run a soothing hand up and down her back, all the while whispering words of comfort.

A loud clap of thunder fills the air and Mallory jolts in my arms as if someone's struck her. "Hold onto me, I'm gonna stand, okay?" She gives an almost imperceptible nod and I rise to my feet, never once letting her go.

I stalk past her parents, sending a dark look their way as I pass. I place her in the passenger seat of her car, but when I try and step back, she clings to me, whimpering against my chest. The sound more heartbreaking than anything I've ever heard. "Shh, baby. I won't let anything happen to you. I've gotta let you go to start the car; you're freezing and I need to turn the heat on. Okay?"

"Oh-oh-okay," she stutters out, her teeth chattering. Ever so slowly, she releases me, allowing me to come around to the driver's side to start the car. I crank the heat, redirecting all of the vents to face her before turning on the seat heater.

"I've got a jacket in my truck. I'm gonna grab it for you, okay?"

She whispers her consent and I dash to my truck to retrieve it. I shove it under my shirt in an effort to keep it dry. After wrapping her in it, I reassure her that she's safe and that I'll protect her at all cost. "I'll be right back, okay?" She nods, but I'm not so sure she actually hears me.

I lock the doors to her car with the fob I pocketed from the cupholder, and make my way to Darryl and Nancy. She's still spewing hate like an erupting volcano, but she quiets when I approach before turning her fury on me.

"How?" she shrieks. "How could you?"

"How could I what, Nancy?" I ask, knowing damn well what she's going to say.

"How could you defile Valorie's memory by being with *her*?" She snarls the word *her* as if it's comprised of four-letters.

"By her you mean Mallory?" She's practically foaming at the mouth as she nods. I step closer to the two of them. "You listen to me right now." My tone is deadly. "Mallory is an amazing woman. She is kind and caring and so fucking good —no thanks to either of you—and I love her. Do you hear me? I. Love. Her. And I won't stand for the way you treat her. She deserves nothing but the best and you both are fucking toxic.

From here on out you will leave her alone. You will not hurt her again, not ever. Do you hear me?"

Nancy thrashes in her husband's hold like a wild animal. "You're dead to me! Dead to me if you choose that waste of space over—"

"Then consider me dead," I say calmly before I turn and walk away.

I BLINK MYSELF AWAKE, groggy and disoriented, with no memory of getting into my bed—much less falling asleep. A strong, calming presence at my back alerts me to the fact that Duke is here with me. I snuggle back into his warmth, letting the feel of his heart beating against my back soothe me. My body aches and my head pounds; but why?

"Duke," I call for him, my voice scratchy and small.

"I'm here, baby," he answers instantly, his hold on me tightening. "Are you okay?"

I wiggle in his grip, despite the pain, rolling to face him. The second my eyes meet his, I remember—visiting Val, my mom, her cruel words, my father restraining her right as she tried to attack me, Duke swooping in like my very own dark knight. "Thank you," I murmur into the space between us, a single tear cascading down my cheek.

Duke leans down, kissing the droplet away with a tenderness that astounds me. He feathers small, sweet kisses all over my face and my pain lessens with each one. *How is this huge, hulking beast of a man able to be so gentle?* He moves to pull away but I clasp my hands behind his head and draw his lips to mine. Duke hesitates a moment before slipping his tongue into my mouth, tangling it with mine.

I rake my fingers through the short hair at the nape of his neck and he groans, the sound more erotic than anything I've ever heard before—like a thread of pure lust connecting him to me as my back bows, drawing our bodies closer together.

Restlessly, I shift against him, seeking his heat and comfort and love all at once.

"Cricket, baby," Duke says between thoughtful careful kisses that light me up and make me feel completely cherished all at once. "You have no idea...the things I feel for you." He shifts back and peers down at me. My breath catches and tears threaten to fall from the way he's looking at me; with so much love and devotion. *For me.* Even without the actual words, I can *see* it so clearly. The thought would bring me to my knees if I wasn't already lying down.

"I want you." I can tell he's about to argue so I rebut before he has a chance.

"Please, Duke. Touch me, make me whole again. You're the only one who can do that."

———

DUKE

My heart is pounding, a million beats a minute, damn near coming out of my chest. Here my girl is, bent but not broken, asking me to help take away her pain. I've never seen someone more powerful...beautiful...vulnerable than Mallory is in this moment. I can't fuck this up, and even though I want to slide into her more than I want my next breath, if she isn't one-thousand percent sure, I'll back off. Besides, if I have my way, we'll have an entire lifetime together...to explore and to love and to grow.

"Are you sure?" I run my knuckles under her chin, tilting her stare to mine. "I...I don't want to hurt you."

Mallory shimmies out of my embrace and strips off the t-shirt I helped her into when we got home, tossing it carelessly to the floor. "I'm sure." Her panties quickly follow and my mouth waters at the sight of her. I take my time, devouring every square inch of exposed tanned goodness, from the rosy blush coloring her cheeks and neck down to her tight pebbled nipples. Lower still, past the alluring dip of her waist and the sweet indent of her belly button to the wetness glistening between her legs. There's no trace of the fragile woman from earlier standing before me but instead a goddess I'm all too happy to worship.

Twin flames dance in her eyes as my gaze moves over her, my mouth practically watering as I guide her back down to the mattress, taking a moment to just be—to appreciate the softness of her curves against the hard lines of my body. "You're so goddamn beautiful." I kiss her lips softly, reverently, before working my way down to her jaw, her neck and then farther south, not stopping until I reach the juncture between her thighs.

I brush my lips against her center, never lingering in any one place too long, working Mallory up into a frenzy of want and need. "Please, Duke," she begs when I graze her sweet spot, her back arching up off the bed. "Oh, God, please."

I groan, the sound coming from deep within me, content to torture and tease her. "You want more, baby? You gotta speak up—tell me what you need. Don't be shy, Cricket."

"I need..." she whimpers, her hips chasing my tongue, desperate for more.

"Tell me," I urge her as I wrap my hands around her thighs and press them farther apart, giving her a long lick from bottom to top.

Her entire body vibrates with need as I suck on her clit until she's on the brink. "I need you to make love to me."

Drawing away, I lick my lips, savoring the taste of her. "Happy to, baby." I push up from the bed, shucking off my clothes before re-situating myself between Mallory's parted thighs. Thrusting against her, I coat myself with her desire.

Mallory meets me move-for-move until we're both panting and delirious with need.

When I finally push into her, it's like I've found paradise. I feel complete in a way I never knew was possible, like I'm finally home. Being inside her is unlike anything else I've ever experienced—nirvana, pure and perfect, meant only for me. Mallory's hands rove and explore, leaving no patch of skin untouched as I move within her. My lips blaze a trail up and down her neck, licking and sucking and biting.

"You feel so good," I moan the words against her sweat-slicked skin. "You feel like…mine."

My proclamation unleashes something inside of Mallory. Her eyes clench shut and her stomach quivers as her fingers clutch at me and her ankles lock around my back. Her breathy moans turn to blissful cries as she tips over the edge and into oblivion, with my name on her lips. The sound so utterly sexy that I follow right after with a hoarse cry.

I collapse down onto her, burying my face in the space between her neck and shoulder, peppering small kisses all along her collarbone. "Mmm, Cricket, I've never felt anything as good as you." It sounds like a line, but it's the honest to God truth. Being with her—*in her*—has me feeling some kind of way. My body, my mind, my soul…they're all wrapped in a sense of rightness, of belonging, of home.

The words *I love you* sit on the tip of my tongue, but I swallow them back. Because while I mean it with every fiber of my being, I know that if I were to confess it now, Mallory would assume it was an empty post-sex platitude, and my girl deserves way, *way* more than that.

I'VE LEARNED a lot about myself over the last two weeks. For example, I love morning sex—like seriously, *love it*—but am terrified of even the thought of anal. Duke's dirty talking can get me in the mood quicker than Dale Earnhardt, Jr. can complete a lap around the track. Most surprisingly, though, is the way my body responds when he bosses me around in the bedroom—there's just something about that gravelly tone of his when he takes charge that makes me go crazy with lust.

All of that pales in comparison to what I've learned about love though. For the first time in my life, I'm experiencing limitless and unconditional love and it's…*everything*.

Sure, he hasn't come out and said those three little words, but I can feel it—down to my very marrow, I can *feel* his love for me. It's white hot and consuming, warming me from the inside out like hot chocolate on a cold day.

DUKE

When did you say that thing was?

I grin as I read his text. The *thing* he's referring to is the When I Grow Up assembly the school is putting on for the kindergarten class where various professionals come in and educate the kids about their careers. Obviously, I begged Duke to participate, which in turn means Nate will be presenting as well. Needless to say, Tatum is thrilled; especially since Alden, her dad, will be in attendance as well.

ME

It's on the last Friday of November.

ME

Also, have I thanked you lately for agreeing to help out?

DUKE

Now that I think about it, it's been a few days. Maybe you can *show* me later?

ME

Oh, however will I do that?

DUKE

Cricket, I can think of a million ways...

ME

What if I wanted to thank you on my knees?

DUKE

I'd say hell-fucking-yes.

ME

Figured you'd like that.

DUKE

Like it? Baby, I love it. The thought of you looking up at me with your pretty lips wrapped around me...damn. I've got wood while riding shotgun with Nate.

ME

HA! I'll take good care of you tonight.

DUKE

> Then let me take care of you first. How's dinner from Bayside, a movie, and me eating you for dessert sound?

ME

> Sounds like six o'clock can't come soon enough.

DUKE

> Shit! We've got a speeder. Talk later.

ME

> Love you, be safe!

I don't hear back from him again until the end of his shift when he calls to let me know he's on his way over. Thankfully the food from Bayside tastes just as good reheated as it does fresh, because the second Duke walked in the door, he was on me, ensuring I made good on my dirty little text message promises.

———

Girls' night has become a semi-regular thing for us ever since the bowling alley re-do, but it's been a while since our schedules have aligned. Duke's working tonight, which in turn means Nate is also working, so we decided tonight was as good as any to meet for margaritas. Not to mention, according to Natalie, Tatum's been begging for a daddy-daughter night—something about a recipe she found on YouTube that she wants him to help her cook. It should probably make me feel bad that a five-year-old can cook better than me, but with the parents she has, it's really no surprise.

When I arrive at El Rodeo the girls are already here waiting for me. I'll never forget the first time I ate here; I was so dang hesitant. From the outside, it looks rundown and seedy. The inside, however, is well-kept and the food is out of this world—especially their queso.

I slide my car into the only open spot in the parking lot and head inside. Jenny texted me a few minutes ago, letting me know they already have a table, so I bypass the hostess and walk straight back to where they're seated.

"So, how are things?" Jenny asks, not wasting any time.

"Things are really good."

"Like, wear his ring and have his babies good?"

Natalie laughs. "So that's where Tatum gets it from, huh? She's been on and on about you and Nate having babies after y'all get married."

Jenny grins evilly. "Well, if y'all'd just give the kid a sibling like she's been begging for…"

"Actually…we're trying," Natalie confesses.

Jenny and I squeal so loudly that several other patrons turn to stare at us. "That is amazing!" Jenny grabs her sister-in-law's hands and shakes them over their heads in a little victory dance.

"Yeah, well. We conceived Tatum on the first go, without even trying. It seems to be taking a little longer this time around." Natalie's shoulders hunch a little but Jenny's right there, doing her best to cheer her back up.

"Girl. Babe. Listen to me, it'll happen when it's supposed to." Natalie rolls her eyes and starts to interrupt, but Jenny pushes on. "I know, it sounds like such a line, but I totally mean it. Nothing about you and Alden's relationship has been a walk in the park—it's been one battle after another and you two have conquered and slayed each and every one. This won't be any different and when—that's right, *when*—he puts his bun in your oven, it'll be the best little bun ever!"

Natalie drops her head to her hands. "Oh, God, stop. I know you're trying to be encouraging, but…"—she shudders —"…just stop. You're being weird."

"You love my weird, bitch!"

Sighing dramatically, Natalie agrees. "It's true, I do. But wanna know what I love more? Chips and salsa and margs! Let's order." She signals the waiter over and we all place our order, opting to try their new margarita flight, consisting of one mango, one peach, and one strawberry along with an order of nachos all the way.

The rest of the evening is spent talking, laughing, and making memories that I'll cherish forever. I'm sure to some it seems childish of me to get so sentimental over something so small, but after spending most of my life friendless and alone, I know exactly what these moments are worth—they're absolutely priceless.

Three hours, and a few more drinks later, we decide to call it quits. I'm still laughing to myself over Jenny's antics as I pull out of the parking lot, which is probably why I don't see it coming.

The sickening sound of metal on metal fills my ears as the car spins. Lights blur as my vision swims. I seem to skid endlessly until, finally, I come to a stop in a ditch.

"Holy…shit…" I gasp out loud just before everything goes dark.

I'M COUNTING down the minutes until the end of my shift. It's girls' night out for Mallory, which means she's coming home frisky and with the way she's been eyeing my cuffs every time I'm in uniform lately, it's safe to say I've got big plans for us tonight.

"Do you ever wonder what they talk about when they all get together?" Nate asks as he signals to turn onto the highway.

"Nah, man, some things are better left unknown. I figure it's like a woman's purse—not my business."

"Even if they're talking about you?"

I grin. "Especially then. I know how Mallory feels about me. I don't mind if she talks *about* me, as long as she keeps talking *to* me."

Nate flicks his eyes over me before focusing back on the road. "Look at you; love's got you sounding wise." When I don't respond back to him, he prods. "You do love her, right?"

It feels fucked up saying something about it to him before her, but I'm at the point where I think talking it out might help. "I…yeah, I love her."

"You told her?"

I rub my hands over my face in frustration. "No. I want to. She's said it and every time I don't say it back, I feel like the biggest douche to walk the planet."

"Damn, bro. She's not mad?"

I shake my head. "Honestly, that's part of why she's so amazing. She's patient and doesn't want to rush me into anything—especially given our history. But the thing is, I *do* love her. Like, I can see myself marrying her and starting a family with her. I'm just scared. Scared I'll fuck it all up somehow."

Nate doesn't reply right away, but when he does, he kind of blows me away. "You know, at this point, I think the only way you can fuck it up is if you keep holding out. That girl has ripped her heart off of her sleeve and offered it up to you on a silver platter. Everyone can see how y'all feel about each other. Make that shit official, man. Get your girl."

Nate's pep-talk resonates with me. I'm so damn ready to get my girl; to claim her and to tell her exactly how I feel about her and then to show her, over and over again. "Damn straight. Just need this shift to end."

"Only two more hours."

"Two hours too long," I grumble under my breath just as his cell rings.

He lets it go to voice mail, but it immediately starts ringing again. "Is everything okay, GG?" he asks, skipping over any kind of greeting.

"What?" His grip on the wheel tightens. "Is she...fuck. We're on our way." I shoot him an inquisitive look as he ends the call and flips on our lights and siren.

"Everything okay?" I ask just as the radio crackles with dispatch reporting an accident, involving two vehicles at the eleven-hundred block of Main Street, unknown injuries. Dread pools in my gut—that's so close to where the girls went out and with Jenny's frantic call to Nate...I repeat my question. "Is everything okay?"

Nate radios in that we're responding to the call. "I need you to stay calm," he tells me, instantly setting me on edge. "Mallory was—"

"No!" A pained cry rips from my lips as I bring my fist down onto the dash. "No! Tell me something else. Anything!" My heart is beating so hard it feels like it might give out at any moment. I break out into a cold sweat as agony washes over me. Surely the universe isn't this cruel. "Sh-she's okay, r-right? Tell me she's okay. What did Jenny say?" I sling my questions rapid fire, one after the other, my voice sounding crazed even to my own ears.

"I don't know. Jenny says she was hit pulling onto the highway and that she spun a few times into the ditch. That's all I know, brother."

My chest heaves as I swallow down the nausea burning the back of my throat. Tears wet my eyes, threatening to spill, but I blink them back. Nate reaches over and gives my hand a firm squeeze in an attempt to comfort me. But the only thing that can calm the inferno inside of me is seeing Mallory.

Smiling.

Breathing.

Alive.

"She has to be okay," I wheeze, the effort of actually inhaling in a breath is too much for my oxygen starved lungs. The dread in my gut rolls as we pull up to the scene, the night sky lit up by a sea of red and blue flashing lights.

When I catch sight of Mallory's Rav-4 in the ditch, the driver's side smashed in and the windshield a spiderweb of cracks and fissures, I'm out of the cruiser before Nate can even put it in park.

A sick sense of déjà vu crawls over my skin as I sprint toward the wreckage, memories of Valorie's death torturing me as I pray, beg, and plead with any god who will listen for a different outcome this time around—for Mallory to be safe and whole and unharmed—for this to all have been a misunderstanding.

"Kincaid!" I barely slow as the familiar voice calls out again, this time adding three words that cause my heart to pound even harder in my chest. "Kincaid! She's over here."

"Duke?" My head snaps up at the sound of Mallory's sweet—albeit raspy—voice. My girl is wrapped in a blanket sitting in the back of the ambulance as a paramedic checks her over. "Wh-what are you doing here?"

"Cricket." I breathe her name on a sigh of relief, damn near falling to my knees as I take her in. She may not be smiling, but she's alive and breathing. "Fuck, baby!" I'm inside the box with her before the medic has a chance to say anything. Although, with the way he's eyeing me, I doubt he would even try.

My eyes rake over her body from head-to-toe, cataloging her injuries. Bruises are already forming across her chest from the seat belt and she has a small but deep cut near her left brow. "You're really okay?" Disbelief weighs heavy, like maybe this is all a dream—an illusion created by my mind to protect me from reliving the same nightmare all over again; *different twin, same outcome.*

She nods, wincing a little. The movement bringing me back to the here and now. "Yeah, yes. I'm fine. Just a little banged up." *Thank fucking God.*

I step closer to her, taking her hand in mine, needing that physical contact to prove that this is real—that she's alive and here. "You're sure?" My eyes slide over her again before flicking up to the paramedic, seeking his professional opinion.

"Heart rate and BP are slightly elevated. Aside from the laceration to her face—which should be just fine with a butterfly bandage—I suspect she may have a mild concussion. I'd suggest she gets checked over at the hospital just to be safe."

"No, I'm—"

"I'll drive her."

Mallory crosses her arms over her chest, grimaces, and immediately drops them back to her sides. "Don't I get a say?"

I kneel before her, ghosting my fingertips over her cheeks before softly clasping her chin in my hands. "Baby. Please go. For me. You're the most precious thing in my life. I fucking love you, Mallory, and I..."—my voice breaks—"...I need to *know* that you're okay."

She gasps. "You...you said..."

I lean in and press a soft kiss to her lips. "I. Love. You." Each word is decorated with a kiss. "So damn much, so let's get you to the hospital. Please, baby?"

Her throat works as she swallows. "Okay," she whispers her consent and I take what feels like my first full breath since the call came in.

I stand and help Mallory down before swooping her up into my arms and carrying her straight to the cruiser. Nate sees us as I walk past him and falls into step beside me. "You all good, Mally?"

She rolls her head to look his way. "Yeah, I am." Her voice sounds dreamy, like she's on the verge of deep sleep.

"Hey, c'mon, no sleeping, Cricket."

"I'm not," she slurs the words as her eyelids droop.

As gently as possible I pat her cheek that's not resting on my chest. "I mean it, baby. Open your eyes, look at me." She does and I find myself thanking God all over again.

At the car, Nate opens the door for me before climbing behind the wheel. I help Mallory into the back seat, sliding in after her despite the tight space; there's no way in hell I'm letting her out of my sight for the foreseeable future, not even for the five-minute drive to the hospital.

With the use of our siren, Nate makes the drive in three. He offers to wait with us, but it's late and I know if he stays

Jenny will want to be here and if she's here, Natalie and Alden will want to come. Not to mention, we're going to be here for at least a few hours. So, I send him home—with much grumbling on his part.

A CT scan and way more time than I ever imagine later, Mallory's discharged with an all-clear and we're in the back of an Uber on our way to my place, with me counting down both the miles and the minutes until I can hold her in my arms.

AT DUKE'S INSISTENCE, he carries me from the car, into his house, and straight back to his bedroom. He gently lowers me to the floor at the foot of his bed. Neither of us speak as Duke drags his eyes over me again and again. "You're really okay?" he asks, a mixture of fear and relief swimming in his green eyes.

"I am." I try not to fidget under his heavy stare. The way he's looking at me, like I'm delicate—fragile, broken—sets my soul on edge.

Duke wears his inner-turmoil on his sleeve as he brushes past me to turn down the covers. It's a battle of wills—*should he stay and comfort me or simply let me recuperate*. He moves his eyes over my body, as if checking for some hidden injury the hospital may have missed, before saying, "Rest, Cricket."

I climb into the bed and he pulls the comforter up to my chin, tucking me in like a child—strangely, it's another first for me, which makes me feel sad and cherished all at once. Still shaking from the adrenaline rush, I reach for him, desperate for his touch and the stillness it brings. "Shh, baby, it's okay," he murmurs as he turns and heads for the door. I whimper as I reach out and grab his hand, halting his retreat.

"I'll be right back. I need to make a quick phone call. Try and sleep."

"Duke," I croak, terrified at the thought of being left alone. "Please. Please don't leave me."

His eyes flash. "I swear to you, I'm not going anywhere. Not now, not ever. I just need to check in with the department. It'll only take a few minutes."

I shake my head. I can't wait a few minutes; I need him now. A lone tear slides down my cheek, dripping off my chin, splattering onto his comforter. "I was so scared. The car was spinning and spinning and all I could think was—"

He cuts me off, his own voice cracking. "God, Mallory." He falls to his knees on the floor beside the bed, his large hands cupping my cheeks. "I was so fucking scared, too, baby. When I saw your car, it almost paralyzed me. I...I thought I'd lost you." His thumbs stroke my cheeks before his lips chase away my now freely falling tears. "I can't lose you."

"Say it again," I beg and he instinctively knows exactly what I'm asking for.

"I love you, Mallory." His deep voice rumbles, the words coming straight from his heart. "I love you so fucking much. But you need to rest; to recover."

I shake my head vigorously, ignoring the slight pain. He's wrong. I don't need anything but him.

Over me.

Around me.

Filling me, making me whole again, in the way that only he can. "You love me?" I ask, nuzzling my face into his chest.

"More than anything."

I pull back and look up at him, my golden gaze pleading as my tongue darts out, wetting my lower lip. He follows the movement like a cobra coiled and ready to strike. His pupils dilate as his worry mingles with his arousal. "Then show me. Show me how much you love me."

His breathing becomes heavy as his lust takes over. He

looms over me, but I don't give him a chance to hesitate. Pushing up onto my elbow, I wrap my free hand around the back of his neck, bringing his face to mine. "Make love to me, Duke."

Gently, he lays me back onto the bed and places his hands on my hips, squeezing lightly before skimming his hands up my sides and over the dip in my waist. My belly flutters at the feel of the soft cotton sliding over my skin as Duke pushes my shirt over the swell of my breasts, before pulling it off completely.

The cool air washes over me, covering my skin in gooseflesh while Duke's hot gaze draws my nipples to pebbled points beneath the lace of my bra.

He brushes his nose over the sensitive skin of my exposed lower belly. "God, I've never been so scared in my life. I...I thought I'd lost you, too, and I...fuck, baby..."—he speaks the words against the waistband of my jeans as he undoes the button and slides down the zipper—"...I love you. So damn much. The thought of anything happening to you guts me."

"Duke." His name slips past my lips like a prayer as he slides my jeans down my legs; the combination of his heartfelt words and his calloused hands as they move over my skin has me feeling as though I may combust. I use his broad shoulders for balance as I kick my jeans away, leaving me in only my panties and bra. They don't match in the slightest, but with the way Duke licks his lips as he takes me in, it's safe to say he doesn't mind.

He stands, rising to his full height so I have to tilt my head back to see his face. He brings his hands to my cheeks and drops his forehead to mine. "I. Love. You. I've loved you since I kissed you in Alden's laundry room."

My lips tilt up. "You mean when I accused you of paying for sex?"

Duke leans down into my space and nips at my lips. "Ha-ha. Real funny."

"I thought so," I murmur, slanting my lips over his, tugging him closer to me by the front of his shirt, causing us both to topple back onto his bed. Our kiss quickly moves from sweet to scorching as Duke settles between my bent legs, shifting his hips so his hard-on rubs against the soft silk of my panties.

With great difficulty, I swallow back my moan. This man…he knows exactly how to touch me to set me off like a rocket.

"Today, tomorrow, and forever, Cricket." He says the words with a sureness and I know exactly what he means. He loves me the same way I love him—unconditionally. If ever there had been a moment of doubt over how he feels for me, that moment is long gone. In its place, there's nothing but the rightness of Duke and I.

I reach down between us, fumbling as I try and unbuckle his belt. Duke bats my hands away and I pout. "Patience, baby," he murmurs as he stands, stripping away every stitch of clothing, taking care to put away his duty belt somewhere safe.

"No time to be patient. I need to feel you now," I moan at the thought. "I need to feel us. Together. The way we're meant to be."

He climbs back onto the bed and settles between my legs. "I'm gonna love you now, Cricket, real good." With a thrust of his hips, he pushes inside me; stretching and filling me in the best way. *How is it that every time between us is better than the last?*

A strangled curse falls from his lips as he rocks his hips, my own lifting to meet him stroke for stroke. Any lingering soreness from my accident falls to the wayside, pure bliss replacing it as he continues driving into me.

Duke Kincaid is one-thousand percent the man I'm meant to be with, and as he licks at the hollow of my throat, his body trembling, I know that I'm the woman he's meant to be with as well.

"Fuck, you feel so good, baby," he groans into my neck.

Words fail me, my body steadily cresting the peak toward the orgasm I'm so desperately in need of.

"I'm close," he grunts, quickening his pace. I answer his punishing tempo, matching him thrust for thrust until we're both crying out our release, falling over the edge and into oblivion at the same time.

Once we both come back down to earth, Duke rolls off of me and onto his back. Chest still heaving he says, "Love you."

I roll to my side, laying my head on his chest and tangling my legs with his. As horrible and as terrifying as the wreck was, here with him, I only feel happiness. "Love you, too," I sigh contentedly as I trace my finger up and down Duke's strong, muscled chest.

"Marry me, Cricket?"

My heart lurches in my chest. "Th-that's your orgasm talking." I laugh lightly, trying to mask the cyclone of emotions bearing down on me—a dizzying mixture of hope, joy, and disbelief.

"Nah, I mean it. I'm gonna marry you one day. Just wait, baby, you'll see." He tugs me closer and kisses the top of my head. "But until then stay here. With me."

"I am here with you."

"No, baby. That's not what I mean. I want—need—more than the occasional sleepover. I want your toothbrush next to mine, your clothes in my closet, your hair ties scattered all over the house. I want my sheets to smell like you—like us, because they're ours."

I blink my tired eyes, wondering if I heard him right. "You…you want me to move in?"

"Yeah, baby, I do. Let's make this house a home."

His words hit me right in the feels. *A home.* I've never truly had a home before; the closest I've ever come is with Ashley in college. But this—this is different. It's more. I want all of the things he does. I want to fuss at him for leaving the seat up, I want to fall asleep with him each night and wake up to him every morning. I want all of these things and more. Because Duke, he is *my home*. He's my safety, my comfort, my heart, my soul. Duke Kincaid is my everything. "I'll do it," I whisper, shifting up to press a kiss to his chest right over his heart.

"Do what?" Now he's the one asking for clarification.

"Move in with you, but I have conditions."

He snorts out a single laugh, the sound warming me from the inside out. "Of course, you do. Let's hear 'em."

"First, you have to promise to make me your special breakfast at least twice a week."

"You got a thing for the way I make eggs and bacon, baby?"

"And toast. Don't forget the toast."

His body shakes with silent laughter. "Consider it done. What's your second condition?"

I grin even though from our cuddled position he can't see it. "Well, someone's gotta tell my landlord I'm breaking my lease."

"Okay, Cricket. I think I have an in there; that's a deal I can make." He kisses my temple before skimming his nose along my hairline. "Sweet dreams, Mallory."

I snuggle deeper into him, letting the feeling of his heartbeat and strong arms soothe me. "Love you, too," I mumble, the words almost unintelligible, through my exhaustion.

My grin never fades, even as sleep overtakes me, knowing that with my morning alarm, I'll be waking up to the first day of our forever.

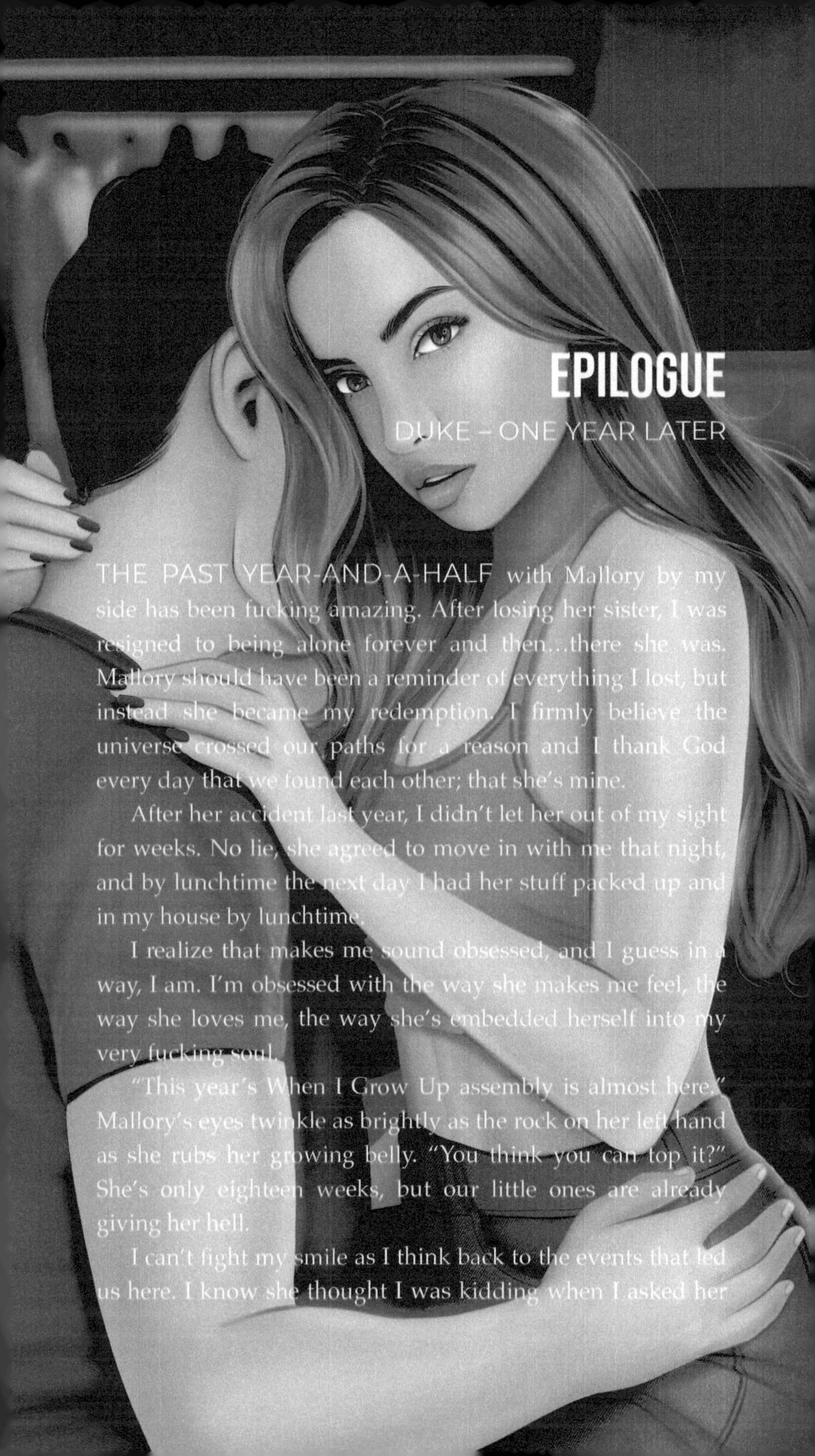

THE PAST YEAR-AND-A-HALF with Mallory by my side has been fucking amazing. After losing her sister, I was resigned to being alone forever and then...there she was. Mallory should have been a reminder of everything I lost, but instead she became my redemption. I firmly believe the universe crossed our paths for a reason and I thank God every day that we found each other; that she's mine.

After her accident last year, I didn't let her out of my sight for weeks. No lie, she agreed to move in with me that night, and by lunchtime the next day I had her stuff packed up and in my house by lunchtime.

I realize that makes me sound obsessed, and I guess in a way, I am. I'm obsessed with the way she makes me feel, the way she loves me, the way she's embedded herself into my very fucking soul.

"This year's When I Grow Up assembly is almost here." Mallory's eyes twinkle as brightly as the rock on her left hand as she rubs her growing belly. "You think you can top it?" She's only eighteen weeks, but our little ones are already giving her hell.

I can't fight my smile as I think back to the events that led us here. I know she thought I was kidding when I asked her to marry me the night of her wreck, but I was dead-ass serious. For as long as I live, I'll never forget the look on her face when I surprised her at last year's assembly.

The way her eyes clouded with confusion as Nate and I called her class down to help us. Or the way she gasped when "For Her" by Chris Lane started pumping out of the sound system as her kids held up signs reading *Ms. Cricket, please say yes!* and I dropped to one knee. Truly, it was epic.

"Baby, I already beat it when I put those twins in your belly."

"You're so cocky." She shakes her head at me, but she's smiling; she loves it.

"Mallory Kincaid," the nurse calls and we both stand. She greets us with a warm smile. "Right this way, you two." She leads us down a short hallway and into a dimly lit room. "Okay, Dad, you can take a seat over there and, Mom," she passes Mallory an ugly-as-sin robe, "I'll need you to change into this and take a seat on the exam table."

Mallory accepts the robe with a smile and heads into the bathroom while the nurse fiddles around on the ultrasound machine. "Alright, the technician will be in in just a minute."

Mallory returns just as she exits, climbing up onto the table. Her hands fidget and her legs kick as we wait. I reach over and grab her hand, knowing my touch will help soothe her—and vice versa. "Nervous?" I ask.

"No, more like excited. You?"

"Definitely excited." I stroke my thumb over her knuckles. "How far along is Natalie now?"

"She's almost thirty weeks." Her lips turn down in a pout. "And I'm more than twice her size. How is that fair?"

I stand from my chair, coming around to stand in front of her. Clasping her cheeks in my palms, I press my forehead to hers. "First of all, you're carrying two babies, she only has one. Secondly, you're a ten all day every day, but knowing that my babies are growing in your belly, makes you a full-blown twenty, Cricket."

Her cheeks take on that rosy hue I love so much. "Sweet talker."

"Only for you, baby."

"Speaking of babies," the ultrasound tech says in lieu of a greeting as she enters the room, "are you two ready to check on your little ones?"

Mallory and I exchange loaded looks before simultaneously answering, "Yes!"

"Great." She fiddles around on the machine before snapping on a pair of gloves. "Go ahead and lie back; this may be cold." She squirts a glob of jelly onto Mallory's rounded stomach and begins pushing it around with the wand. My heart beats a mile a minute as she moves through the standard routine, taking various measurements and checking their heart rates.

I'm about ready to come out of my skin when she finally says, "Do y'all want to know the genders?"

Once again, we both reply in sync. "Yes!"

"Great." She begins moving the wand again, pushing it around until she gets the view she wants. "It looks like baby one is a...boy!"

I look from the screen to Mallory. Her big honey eyes are brimming with tears. "A boy..." she whispers, her voice nothing more than a rasp.

The technician moves the wand, repeating the process all over again. "And baby two is a...girl! Congrats, Mom and Dad; one of each!" Mallory and I wear matching expressions of wonder and joy as the technician prints off a few images and hands them to me.

I stare down at the grainy photos with watery eyes, so completely enraptured that I barely hear the tech giving Mallory instructions to redress before she leaves us alone.

I stand and help her up from the table. "A boy and a girl,

Cricket." I sweep my wife into my arms and seal my lips to hers. "You got any names?" I ask, breaking our kiss.

She beams. "I was thinking Callum Alexander for our son. Callum after Cal and Alexander after—."

"After me. I really like that. What about our daughter?"

"I...I, um, I was thinking I wanted to honor my sister and your grandma. H-how you do you feel about Abigail Valorie?"

Tears fill my eyes. How in the hell did I wind up with this amazing, strong, and beautiful—inside and out—woman? "I think it's fucking perfect. You're perfect." I kiss her again, completely uncaring that we're in an exam room at her OB-GYN's office. I kiss her like my life depends on it; like her breathy little moans are my oxygen and her lips are my sustenance.

When Valorie died, I thought I'd never be happy again; that she took every good part of me to the grave right along with her. But now, here in this moment with Mallory in my arms and our children growing in her belly, I know good and well that the best of me is right here in this room and even though getting here was a hard—and at times painful—journey, I wouldn't change a thing.

THE END.

KEEP READING FOR A SNEAK PEEK OF SWEET LITTLE NOTHING

PROLOGUE

EMMY

There isn't a single cell of my body that doesn't ache.

It's the kind of hurt that pierces your skin and sinks into your veins, your bones, your fucking soul. It's the kind of pain that eats away at you like poison, consuming all of the good within you until all that's left is a shell.

I stumble, tripping over my own feet as I cross my bedroom. "Stupid, so stupid," I mutter, righting myself. I flip on the lights as I enter my bathroom, recoiling at the bright light. God, even my eyes hurt.

I guess days upon days of crying will do that, huh?

My fingers tangle in my limp, dirty hair, and I wince as I tug on the ends, my past and my present colliding in my mind, morphing into a single mangled nightmare.

"It's okay, Em. When you love someone, this is okay," my step-brother croons in my ear, his soft tone a stark difference to his rough touch. I wanted to tell him I didn't love him. I wanted to yell and shout and scream for help, but my fear of him far outweighed my self-preservation. The last time I called for help, he backhanded me; when my mother asked what happened, Rob said I tripped and hit the dresser.

She believed him, too—didn't even ask me.

My heart beats raggedly, like someone ripped the already damaged organ from my chest, shredded what was left of it, stomped on the pieces, and then hastily shoved the tattered remains back beneath my ribs.

"You like that puppy my daddy brought you?" Rob asks, and I nod. *"Then you better do what I say or he might just disappear."*

"Stop, stop, stop!" I plea, the words a garbled cry to the universe. I want it all to go away, for the memories of then and the horrors of now to all stop. But I learned long ago there's no one out there listening. Not to the likes of me, anyway. My own mother didn't even hear my cries as I begged and pleaded for her to take my side.

"Not enough." I pivot in a wide circle, clipping my hip on the vanity. "Never enough. Stupid!"

Tears cloud my vision as I struggle to breathe. I want... *I need* the pain to stop. For my past to stop haunting me. For the taunts and leers to go away.

I'm a top spinning out of control, desperate for someone —*anyone*—to save me from the path my own self-loathing is shoving me down. If I'd have been stronger—smarter—none of this would've happened to me.

I thought a fresh start would be the cure, but like a dark cloud, my secrets and scars followed me. And now, this place, what should have been a safe haven, is as tainted as the home I fled.

All because of Sterling Abbot—Rob's best friend. With a torch in one hand and a pitchfork in the other, Sterling's on a mission to make me pay for my alleged transgressions against my stepbrother.

"You thought you'd get off scot-free? That you'd run away and hide your sins? Not on my watch. You ruined him, his entire life, and now I'm going to ruin you. I'm going to dismantle everything you've ever loved. I'm going to dissect you, take you apart, and scatter the pieces. You think you regret spreading your legs for him? You're going to regret spreading those lies even more. Take a seat, Emmalyn. Class is about to start."

My breaths heave in and out of my lungs as a humorless laugh slips past my trembling lips. God knows, there's not a single person on this planet who cares enough to try and pull me from the murky depths of my misery. *If anything, they'd press their boots to the back of my head and hold me under.*

My hands shake as I press down on the lid, pushing to the right.

"Dammit," I cry as the orange bottle slips, and my blessed relief falls to the floor. The tablets scatter and roll around my feet as I fall to my knees in a desperate attempt to gather them.

With one hand clutching pills, I grip the edge of the vanity and pull myself back to standing with the other. The reflection staring back at me is the face of a stranger. She looks like me, but different, too. The face in the mirror is how I feel inside—worthless… empty… hollow.

Already gone.

I watch as she raises her hand and jams the pills into her mouth. The plasticky outer-coating quickly gives way to a bitter taste. Her face puckers, and so does mine.

She is me, but she's more than me. She's all of my hurt and bitterness and suffering personified. She's the part of me that's broken beyond repair—used up and dirty, unwanted and unloved. She's the voice urging me to end it all. I've fought her for so long, but now… my fight is gone.

With a flick of my wrist, water pours from the faucet. I lean down and suck the liquid into my mouth, my throat working overtime as I swallow it all down.

With the bottle empty, I collapse back down to the floor, the water still running.

I sit slumped against the tub for God knows how long, waiting—praying—for death. For relief. Time has no meaning here.

A fine sheen of sweat covers me as my vision blurs. My head feels heavy, and my stomach churns as unwanted visions plague me behind my heavy, drooping lids.

"If you loved me you, wouldn't do this," I sob as Rob smiles cruelly down at me.

His lips curl into an ugly sneer. "If you really loved me, you'd give freely. Then I wouldn't have to take."

But I don't… I don't love him.

And because of him, no one will ever love me. Not that it matters. Nothing matters. Nothing about me matters to anyone. I'm a waste of space, wasting away.

I try to laugh at my own morbidity, but no sound comes out. My body sways and I slump sideways, banging my head on the side of the tub.

I struggle against his hold, but it's no use. "Love is kind," I whisper brokenly. "And you're a monster; you're incapable of love."

His gaze darkens as his hand around my throat tightens, crushing my windpipe. "And you're a little bitch. Always walking around here, teasing me." Rob skims his index finger over the apple of my cheek and I flinch. "You're pure, but don't worry, Em. I'm going to dirty you up real good."

The phone rings again… or maybe it's my ears.

Who would even call me? Not even Stella, my one and only friend on campus, would care now—Sterling made sure of that.

My heart thunders in my chest.

Someone knocks on the front door.

He's never taken things this far before. "Rob, please. Please don't." Tears stain my cheeks as my pleas for him to stop pour out of me.

I vomit into my lap as the sound of my name reverberates through the house. *No, that's not right. There's no one—I'm hearing things.*

Even though my eyes are closed, I'm weeping. Sobbing for my stolen innocence.

"You're mine, Em." He fists my hair with the hand that isn't wrapped around my throat. "Mine."

A sob breaks free as he destroys my virtue with just one thrust.

Countless tears paint my cheeks as I force my mind to drift away to somewhere better... somewhere safe.

"Emmalyn!" someone—*no one*—yells as tremors overtake my body.

Only one person calls me that, but he wants me gone, too. I wonder if he'll smile when he hears the news? It might be the first time I make someone happy.

Someone bangs on the door. "Emmalyn!" His voice sounds crazed, worried even. *I must be dreaming, because Sterling Abbot doesn't give a shit about me.*

The door splinters open, and everything goes dark.

READ SWEET LITTLE NOTHING FREE WITH KU

ALSO BY LK FARLOW

All of LK's titles can be read as standalones & most are available with Kindle Unlimited.

An * beside a title denotes it is also available in audio.

A 🖤 denotes it is available with KU.

His to Save (a stepbrother/heroine on the run romance suspense) 🖤

His to Keep (an enemies to lover/forced proximity romantic suspense)

Sweet Little Nothing * (an enemies-to-lovers/bully romance)

Dirty Little Secret * (an older brother's best friend/second chance romance)

Pretty Little Thing * (a single mom/forced proximity/mistaken identity romance)

Best Laid Plans * (an older brother's best friend/secret baby romance) 🖤

Best of Intentions * (a friends-to-lovers/little sister's best friend romance) 🖤

Rebel Heart (an enemies-to-lovers jock/tutor rom-com) 🖤

Rebel Soul (an arranged baby/friends-to-lovers rom-com) 🖤

Rebel Desire (an unrequited soulmates/surprise single dad rom-com) 🖤

Coming Up Roses * (a small-town/single mom romance) 🖤

An Uphill Battle * (a frenemies-to-lovers romance) 🖤

Weather the Storm (a second chance at love romantic suspense) 🖤

Come What May (an age gap/single dad romance) 🖤

ABOUT THE AUTHOR

Known by Kate to most, LK Farlow is an Amazon Top 40 bestselling author of more than a dozen romances, ranging from sweet, to sexy, to rip your heart out, and everything in-between.

She has a heart built for happily-ever-afters, which is lucky since she found hers at the young age of nineteen. Now, at thirty-something, she is the wife to one hunky man and the mother to four semi-feral humans, three lizards, a chameleon, a tortoise, and a handful of stray cats.

Kate often jokes that her life is all out chaos on most days, but she wouldn't trade it for the world.

www.authorlkfarlow.com